NINETEENTH CENTURY CANADIAN STORIES

Selected by
David Arnason

Macmillan of Canada

ISBN 0-7705-1345-X Cloth
      0-7705-1346-8 Paper

Printed and bound in Canada for
The Macmillan Company of Canada Limited
70 Bond Street, Toronto
M5B 1X3

Contents

Acknowledgements

For permission to reprint copyright material grateful acknowledgment is made to the following:

Lady Joan Roberts for "Do Seek Their Meat from God".

The work of Duncan Campbell Scott is reprinted with the permission of John G. Aylen, Ottawa.

From *Literary Lapses* by Stephen Leacock reprinted by permission of The Canadian Publishers, McClelland and Stewart Limited, Toronto.

Introduction

The nineteenth century in Canada was a far more vital and lively period than we have been led to believe. Dry-as-dust history texts have created the impression of a time characterized chiefly by an infinity of dated events and documents too numerous for anyone to remember. On the contrary—this was the true age of settlement in Canada, an age filled with excitement and human drama. Our forebears were not too busy struggling to survive to create a literature which captured the drama, the humour, the dreams, the expectations, and even the defeats of people of high enterprise in an exciting and challenging new land. The stories, the poetry, and even the newspapers of nineteenth-century Canada give a far better picture of life as it was actually lived than most histories.

The colonies were not raw, barbaric places, devoid of culture, as is often assumed. Books existed, and they were treasured; there were even some substantial libraries. Books were not, however, as generally available as they were in England or even in the more developed American Colonies. The result was that newspapers and periodicals became the intellectual and cultural centre of community life. Such early newspapers as the *Acadian Recorder* and the *Nova Scotian* met the strong demand not only for news but also for literature. Though the short story as we know it today had not developed by the early part of the nineteenth century, short fiction nevertheless dominated the front pages of newspapers; excerpts from novels alternated with fables and romantic tales, loosely constructed pieces that were often written in contrived and artificial "literary" language.

One solution to the problem of providing brief and readable short fiction was the development of the letter to the editor as a specialized literary form. Editors seeking to boost the circulation of their newspapers found it a particularly satisfying solution. The letter was brief, pointed, self-contained, and complete. It spoke directly to the audience in informal and easy language so that it had a wider appeal than more consciously literary pieces, but it could, and did, reach a high level of sophistication. A series of letters could serve the same purpose as a serialized piece of fiction, with the added advantage that it could be extended or shortened in relation to audience response. It was a flexible genre so that stories, fables, satires, or political criticism could constitute the subject matter. Best of all, it was a form that was natural to the newspaper.

The first six stories in this anthology all appeared as letters to the *Acadian Recorder*, the *Nova Scotian Magazine*, and the *Quebec Mercury*. "The False Accuser: A Tale" is typical of much of the reading fare of the period. It is essentially a secularized sermon, a moral fable written in elevated and contrived language. It stands in stark contrast to the vitality of the equally anonymous "Letters of Patty Pry" and the vital vernacular satire of McCulloch and Haliburton.

Early literary magazines which offered competition to the newspapers were often published by ministers who obviously felt that they were performing cultural missionary work. Such journals as the *Halifax Monthly Magazine* (1830 – 32), *The Colonial Pearl* (1837 – 40), and *The New Brunswick Religious and Literary Repository* (1829 – 32) published reprints of stories from England or, occasionally, stories by Canadians, provided that these stories were conspicuously pious and elegantly written. The stories and poems by Canadians that appeared in these early literary magazines are not a fair indication of the literary life of early Canada. They are conscious and contrived imitations of what their writers took to be "real literature", which was, of course, English literature. The best early writing in Canada appeared in newspapers.

By the 1830s and 40s a new wave of immigration into the Canadas had provided a larger reading public, and more sophisticated kinds of literary magazines were coming into existence. The most important of these was the *Literary Garland*, published by John Lovell and his brother-in-law John Gibson. The *Garland* represented a remarkable breakthrough for Canadian magazines: it paid its contributors and, as a result, attracted the best work that was being written in Canada at that time.

The short story evolved from shorter prose pieces during the

1820s and 30s, though the stories that appeared in the *Literary Garland* are by no means perfect examples of the form. Many of them are called "tales", "legends", or "sketches" and are better described by those words than they would be by the term short story. Few of these stories have the immediacy of action and language that characterized the earlier newspaper stories, and few have the dramatic intensity that was to become the distinguishing mark of the true short story. In their loose form, their elevated, consciously elegant language, and their romantic vision, they reflect the sensibility of their writers and their audience. The language, in particular, points to a distinct difference in social class between the readers of the literary periodicals and the readers of newspapers.

The stories that the *Garland* published were, nevertheless, of sufficiently high quality to stand comparison with the stories appearing in comparable journals in England and the United States. The fierce competition of foreign journals guaranteed that a Canadian journal had to offer equal quality in order to survive.

Some of the *Garland*'s stories were romantic escapes set in exotic lands, detailing the loves of an exquisite aristocracy, and few of these will bear rereading. The best stories, though, still have a literary value. They succeed on their own merit, at the same time reflecting Canadian experience, hopes, and aspirations. Writers like Susanna Moodie and her sister Catherine Parr Traill provided highly competent sketches of Canadian life. The *Garland* published six of Susanna Moodie's sketches as a series called "Canadian Sketches". These were later revised and collected in her *Roughing it in the Bush*, 1852. "Brian, the Still Hunter" appears here in its original form. As well, John Richardson published "Jeremiah Desborough; or, The Kentuckian", the first chapter of what was to have been a sequel to his enormously successful novel *Wacousta*, though there is no evidence that any more than the initial chapter was ever printed. Like *Wacousta*, it shows the violent energy of Richardson's imagination. It also demonstrates a fierce anti-Americanism which, though it appears in a number of stories of that day, is taken into little account by historians.

Other stories played on what were obviously important fantasies: the lost estate in England suddenly regained or, in some other way, fortune restored; the exiled sinner repentant on his own or at his lover's deathbed; the orphaned child raised because of her humility, her Christian devotion, and her cheerfulness to the "best society" of the village. Most of the stories with Canadian settings reflect a sense of lost class and a profound distrust of "American" levelling democracy.

Many stories are historical looks at Quebec, which, in retrospect, becomes a feudal, fairy kingdom. A noble aristocracy and a colourful peasantry provide the background for tales of high adventure and intrigue. A dual attitude is displayed towards Indians: sometimes they are savage beasts with tawdry tastes; at other times they are noble examples of the unfettered freedom and goodness of the wilderness. Beautiful Indian princesses who are also devout Christians are often the heroines of such tales.

One of the best of the *Garland*'s regular writers was Mrs. Rosanna Leprohon who, while still in her teens, published a number of stories under the initials R.E.M. "Alice Sydenham's First Ball" employs clean and simple language and creates a kind of dramatic tension not often encountered in stories of that period. Like Maupassant's later story "The Necklace", it tells of lost jewellery, but in this case, true to the sensibility of the period, a wealthy uncle intervenes to save the situation.

The *Literary Garland* collapsed in 1851, partly as a result of strong competition from American magazines and partly as the result of a major recession in Canada. The *Garland*'s audience was composed of middle-class readers, largely in Montreal and Toronto, who were severely affected by the economic recession. One result was a decline in support for such "frills" as literary magazines, and, though the number of writers apparently did not decline, the potential for publication certainly did for the next twenty years.

Confederation channelled Canadian energies into, among other things, an explosion of literary production and publishing. By that time new magazines had been established. The generation of writers which had flourished during the age of the *Garland* had disappeared, and a new generation of writers which was intensely Canadian had arisen. The stories that appeared during the last third of the nineteenth century revealed a recognizable form, its most frequent pattern being the story of local colour.

In the United States, Bret Harte, Mark Twain, and others were writing stories in which dialect, setting, and local character types provided the chief focus of interest. Kipling in England and Chekhov in Russia were also writing stories of local colour. In Canada, the chief *types* for the story of local colour were the French-Canadian habitant, the Métis, and the Westerner. E. W. Thompson's "Old Man Savarin" is a classic example. The plot of the story is trivial; it gains its chief interest through the French-Canadian dialect and its development of the type of the habitant. French-Canadian culture, of course, had been the subject of stories in earlier periods, but there is a marked difference in approach in these later stories.

The democratization of Canadian society is reflected in the democratization of the short story. Older stories had dealt with aristocratic heroes in a feudal setting; new stories were making the lower-class types the central interest and revealing class conflict from a different viewpoint. Language, too, was affected by democratization, and not only in the use of dialect. The narrative voice of Canadian writers was beginning to lose its piety, its self-conscious elegance, and its elevated tone, and to sound more and more Canadian. In the best stories of the new period are echoes of Sam Slick's voice.

Other types are in evidence: the half-breed, or Métis, figured in many stories, as did the farmer, the seaman, and the Westerner. They all reflect a new nationalism that was the result of Confederation. The emergence of Canada as a country intensified the search for a Canadian identity and each of the regional stories is an examination of some facet of the Canadian character. For instance, the "well-made story" (the story so deliberately constructed as to engage interest, however trivial its subject) became popular. The best example of the form is to be found in the stories of O. Henry and in women's magazine stories of the twentieth century. Robert Barr specialized in this kind of story and became very popular both here and abroad. His story "My Stowaway" is an excellent example of the type.

A more important and certainly more artistic form was the realistic or psychological story. Henry James and W. D. Howells in the United States gave a particularly North American form to ideas that were rooted in the work of Flaubert and Zola. They demonstrated that action can rise out of character and that examination of that action from the point of view of realistically drawn characters can provide a vital experience. Their work created a type of story that repays serious study, and they gained for the short story a respectability that it had not previously possessed. The form developed later in Canada and is chiefly a product of the twentieth century: writers like Morley Callaghan and Raymond Knister are its chief Canadian examples. Some of Duncan Campbell Scott's stories, however, go beyond the superficial aspects of local colour and type to become serious and powerfully realistic studies. "Labrie's Wife", for instance, though it has all the paraphernalia of the story of local colour, succeeds because of the character development of the narrator and the irony of his obtuse and selfish refusal to see the obvious.

There developed, as well, a form that achieved special sophistication in Canada, and that is the animal story. Some of the more romantic and anthropomorphic stories, such as those by Margaret Marshall Saunders, were widely popular, and her novel *Beautiful Joe* in particular has become a classic that is still in print. The best Canadian writers of animal stories, however, did not write for children, and their stories are free from cuteness and excessive anthropomorphizing. Charles G. D. Roberts's "Do Seek their Meat from God" brings together the human and animal worlds, but it does so in a way that reveals both man's similarity to that world and his profound differences from it. Roberts's restraint and objectivity make a powerful and chilling story out of what may, in other hands, have become a simple romantic tale.

Stephen Leacock is not, strictly speaking, a writer of the nineteenth century. His best work, *Sunshine Sketches of a Little Town*, was not published until 1912. His sensibility, nevertheless, is nineteenth-century, and his satire, sometimes gentle, sometimes biting, is directed at a Canada that is just emerging from the nineteenth century, thereby justifying his inclusion here. "A, B, and C" is a good example of the Leacock humour. It appeared originally in *Grip* magazine in 1894.

Canadians are prone to the danger of forgetting the past and its influence on the present. A Canadian who reads the lead editorials in Canadian literary magazines over the past one hundred and fifty years will be struck by an amazing and somewhat horrifying similarity. Nearly every editorial insists that there has been no literature of consequence in the past, but that a new age is dawning and Canadian literature is just coming into its own. We live on the edge of tomorrow, denying the past but brimful of hope for the future. Modern Canadian writing is far more rooted in the past than we usually care to admit. The themes, the trends, and the concerns that characterize nineteenth-century Canadian literature are manifest, mutated somewhat by time, in the literature of the twentieth century. Canadian literature is naturally affected by world literature, but it has a character that is distinct and different from any other literature, and a reading of nineteenth-century stories can help to identify and define that character.

David Arnason

Early Beginnings: The Story as Letter

The False Accuser: A Tale

Anonymous

Mr. Editor:

The following tale is founded for the most part on truth. I have sketched the detail in moments of relaxation from other occupations; if you should deem it worthy a place in your paper please insert it, though I have but feebly imagined forth a single instance from out the many where slanders deal destruction. I may yet hope it will, in some measure, answer its purpose with you. If it should be the means of correcting any, or deferring one, from breaking up the repose of another by recklessly detracting from his or her good name, we may both be satisfied with the result.

> Be thou as chaste as ice, as pure as snow, thou shall not escape calumny.

Never was this beautiful apothegm of the great Master Poet of nature more fully exemplified in any real instance which ever came within the narrow precinct of a country circle acquaintance than the following. Caroline B*** was the only daughter of a respectable merchant who died in the full vigour of his manhood, leaving no other inheritance to his bereaved and sorrowing family than that of a good man's name: his humble prayer through life had been that he might be allowed to receive, as the benediction of an indulgent providence, immunity from woe; and when dying he repeated it, that the favour might be extended to those dear relics of his name whom he should leave behind, that they too might at least escape the keen blights of worldly chill, if it was not their happier boon to taste the luxury of worldly sweets: and he went to sleep with his Fathers in that long, bright home "where the wicked cease from troubling, and the weary are at rest," with a last hope that this meek petition might be granted to them.

His wife, thus widowed and bereft of nearly all that earth contained of interest or happiness for her, was left to struggle against the many ills which crowd upon all in every situation, and, as it often seems, with increased violence upon those whom misfortune and weakness have rendered less adequate to repulse them; she, however, succeeded in spite of all her cares and sufferings, with the feeble assistance which Caroline could render for herself, to instill into the latter the seeds and principles of a substantial and beneficial education, combining, in part, the lighter with the more solid branches — giving a delicate polish to the useful substance, adding to the "flash of the gem its solidity too". She who is the subject of this simple history removed at the age of fourteen from the home of her childhood with her maternal guardian into the interior of Vermont, to subsist in part upon the generosity of friends who had kindly offered to both an asylum from their troubles and a home for the remainder of their years. Here, under the able and careful instruction of a kind and prudent mother, she grew up an ornament and a praise to all connected with her, free from the ostentation and vanity thought often inseparable from her sex — she was learned without display, accomplished with show, and sought only to become virtuous and to be beloved in the obscure circle in which it was her uncomplaining destiny to move. Self-satisfied with her own endowments and the happy consciousness of perfect innocence, she had no ambition but to please her benefactors and companions, no hopes but to live unmolested and undisturbed in contented seclusion, blessing heaven, loving all about her, doing every good her limited circumstances would admit.

It is not my purpose to draw a deeply tinted picture of the beauties and appearance of Caroline, nor to throw about her an ideal colouring of brightest hues, making her all light and loveliness and radiance—a creature of the frenzied poet's fine imagination, embodying in her some dazzling Houri of an oriental vision —without mingling with the richness and gilding of the sumptuous portrait some darkening shades for the jaundiced eye to lust upon and feast its viler appetites. She was human, and therefore could not be faultless.

> There's not that thing on earth so bright,
> But has its shadows too —

Her beauty had about it lines of detraction, and her figure, though strikingly impressive, was not of that perfect contour and symmetry that ravishes the fancy rather than soothes the senses, which fascinates with a passing rapture rather than fastens itself to the remembrance as something pleasingly attractive. She appeared to gain upon her acquaintance without exertion, artlessly winning upon their favour by all those amiable and pleasing attractions which seek only for esteem as the guerdon, and are the meed of goodness and unsophisticated and unpretending virtue. Her graces were of that unassuming class which, from their want of splendour, are felt much more often, and that deeply too, than properly delineated. It was not in the outward mien alone that we could discover the excellence of Caroline B***; it was only by looking upon her heart, that worthier criterion, that we could wisely discern how superior she was to very many who shone with a brighter but a falser light. It was pure as the unsunned, undiscovered pearl, cave-locked in some deep recess of its native sea, and soft, and sensible to every inch of sympathy and love, as the trembling forest flower which shrinks intuitively from before the breath that nourishes it, and withers at the approach of every rude assailant — she was truly a creature of deep and fervent feelings. Schooled in the vicissitudes of a stormy world, she had been early taught gratitude and pity, without having stifled one native impulse of tenderness. Too susceptible, her commiseration for the sufferings and scorns and neglects of others remained unbroken, and as her own innocence and simplicity had taught her to live without even a thought of inventing or doing harm to any, she unfortunately judged that all were as sanguine as herself — "to the pure all things are pure". This is a sweet delusion, but when the change comes, as come it will, every fondly nourished dream flies before it. It brings with it ruin and distress. The glittering chain of life is crushed in every link and widely severed. Nothing will remain but the wreck of prospects floating helmless in the dark and gloomy sea of reality. The bosom becomes filled with bitterest emotions and sinks in despondency.

Caroline, having arrived at an age somewhat matured, and

feeling anxious to relieve her mother of some portion of her burthen and to secure for herself an easy and respectable subsistence, was, for a time, the successful preceptress of a small number of scholars of her own sex, who derived much advantage from her exemplary instruction. She maintained herself in this situation with credit, and exchanged it after much solicitation to become the private tutoress of the only son, an interesting boy, then only eight years of age, of Col. I***, an eminent and respectable gentleman, in whose family she was to reside. The lad did not fail to receive much improvement from the direction and instruction of his teacher, whose conciliating manners were peculiarly adapted for this task. Her little charge soon became much attached to his monitress, and sought by steady exertion to repay her mild attentions. The father, whose every hope was placed upon this darling son, when he thus at a tender age saw him rapidly advancing in his scholastic exercises, could not but feel much for that person to whose exertions he considered himself principally indebted for the flattering promise his sole offspring now held out to him. With the partial eye of an indulgent parent, he already began to view him climbing with successful and hasty steps the rugged steep where "Fame's proud temple shines afar". Through a flattering vista of years, he perceived he would be full of comfort in the glory of that child, who, when he should be stricken by the sure hand of time, was to pillow his dotage, and "rock his cradle of declining age" with all the gratefulness of filial affection. It is not therefore matter of wonder he should highly prize the worth and companionable qualities of the person from whom he was receiving so many collateral favours. Experience had manifested that few, if any, in this situation could please in all respects so well as Caroline, and, being a man of discernment, he was not tardy in discovering the innate merit his friend possessed, for she now had received from the generosity and best feelings of a kind family the benefits and the thousand little kindnesses and favours which should ever attend this appellation.

Col. I***, whose situation and circumstances in life were considered affluent, having thus early begun to indulge in high expectations, resolved to spare no pains to establish a good basis on which to build up the education of his child, who had already acquired the rudiments of several important branches of learning and seemed well qualified to commence a course of classical studies, preparatory to which, in order to perfect his advances, it was considered advisable to remove him to a neighbouring province, that he might acquire a correct knowledge of the French language. This being decided upon, the next inquiry was who should have the charge of this juvenile favorite, as he was yet too young to be without a guardian among strangers in a strange land. There were but few who would consent to undertake the task, and they were not properly adequate to it. Almost as a matter of course Caroline was looked upon to proceed to Canada to continue her watch over her pupil, the more as it was probable the opportunity by this means afforded her to acquire the language for herself would be eagerly sought after.

This, as the sequel will show, was unfortunately the case. The proposition was made, and after some little deliberation accepted. The innocent girl saw nothing in this step that could excite envy or suspicion, or so improper as to waken malice. Perfectly conscious in heart, she little thought seeming friends were seeking with avidity to prowl upon the little remnant she held of this world's blessings—a spotless reputation; it was her only dower. How often, how very often, do we attach to the most harmless intentions of others the vilest of motives. We are all too prone to detract and accuse, as if humanity was not bad enough in its fraility without bringing upon it baseness and crime, and corruption wholly engendered in the defamer's mind; while the defamed, far more spotless, has not ever erred in thought. How often when I have heard such mockers with counterfeit grace accused has the thought rushed upon me that the reproach was from the bad tongue of a bad character, striving to prop its own weakness by the ruins it makes of another. Virtue, noble in its nature, screens vice that it may correct it. Vice, ever mean in its conception, traduces virtue to its own level, not having magnanimity enough of spirit to rise above its degraded self-abasement. I do not like, nay, more, cannot endure that person who continually thinks he discovers some evil design in every shift, move or word of another. Such an one betrays at least a total want of generosity, if not much depravity.

Col. I*** and son, accompanied by Caroline, after necessary preparation proceeded to the City of M. where the two latter remained to accomplish the purpose of their journey. Here, unforeseen circumstances rendered it indispensable that they should separate. It was found that the most advantageous situation for the pupil was in a public seminary where his guardian might visit, but could not remain with him. Col. I***, however, generously offered if Caroline would remain for a time to have an occasional direction over her former charge, and reconcile him to his change, that he would afford her an opportunity of studying the French, as she had previously anticipated. This offer, after much persuasion, was accepted with reluctance.

On adopting this conclusion, Caroline evinced a discretion which one might well suppose would have silenced clamour. On being left, she selected for her abode a boarding school attached to one of the seminaries in that place, as being there most respectable and respected, immured by its high and sombre walls from the stir and vices of the city, and secluded also by rigid custom from all but the most chaste society. By selecting such a residence it would seem that suspicion should be completely hushed. It could not be that in this sanctified cloister a young female would be guilty of crime, or seek it as a hiding place for its consequences. It would be a thing as ill judged as it is impossible, and besides a violation of all religion and custom and rules. There is no place, let the prejudiced and ignorant say what they will, where there is so much purity of life and manners as in a nunnery.

Here Caroline remained a stranger to society, seldom leaving her school unless to meet with her young friend to soothe his loneliness and encourage him in his studies. Consequently, study was the only business left to sweeten the bitterness of separation from other friends. Shut out from all communion with the gay, and noise, and stir of the busy hum about her, she was left to brood in less occupied hours, if not in contentment, at least without complaint, over the misfortunes and ills of the past with a hope that they lived only in memory, and were passing away to a returnless distance to trouble the mind no more, while anticipation served to gild the dreams of the future with many a hue of blissfulness and joyfulness. It buoyed her spirits up through the gloom and solitariness of her sequestered situation, and pointed, after a short procrastination, to a home of rest, and almost of perfect happiness. She had but little else to relieve the continued austerity of her cloistered life save the letters occasionally received from friends she had left, and from one who had become, by his many virtures and the nameless charm that unconsciously weaves a spell around the kindred heart, life, health, and comfort to her. She loved, and was beloved. There was a perfect unison of sentiment and blending of sympathy between Caroline and her betrothed, Mr. A.

In saying this I have said all. Love is woman's happiness. The only uncontaminated spring of joy left as a token of primeval blessedness to the daughters of earth, it gathers bliss from every resource of human affection, drawing all the golden cords of hope towards the centre of her heart, and ties them around its very core, fully completing their uttermost promise. It animates and kindles all those precious feelings none can ever buy. Love, in her imagination, is embosomed in a paradise of sweets, luxuriant in delicious blessings, free and unsullied by care, as the air-rocked cherubim of Eden in its cradle of Lotus flowers. It is her business and her purpose, and mingled with the faith of her religion; alike constant in every change, neither forgotten in the temple-worship of her Creator or omitted in the less important occurrences of life. Such was the love of Caroline — rich, deep, fervent, and passionate even to idolatry; but when the spider comes with crippled wing and pestilent breathing, angered and venomous, crushing with a touch and poisoning with a breath, all her enchantments vanish to nothingness, and the illusive ray that seemed a beaconlight to direct the wanderer to the goal proves a meteor gleam of vanity, false and worthless. Oh then, how the young enthusiast in passion mourns in unbroken anguish over the ruin of her dream. The sweet promise melts into "thin air" and mocks the sickened spirit with all that thus could cheat. Even recollection is a pain that opens afresh the half-cicatrized wound.

> There is no balm by memory brought
> To hopes betray'd and hearts forsaken.

The time having arrived when Caroline was to return to the open arms of her greeting friends, Col. I*** came and conveyed her with his son to their separate homes where those most remote received her with the fondest cordiality and welcome. All elated, the schemes for happiness she had long been planning and treasuring in her absence rushed upon her mind like the sudden breaking of sunshine. They seemed fast approaching to reality. No obstacles appeared to oppose them. Relieved from the lonesomeness of her sometime school, and basking in the smiles of a few dearly loved and kind friends, for a while her cup of delight was filled to the brim; but it was doomed a change should come over this vision. There were dregs in the cup, and she was destined to drain them. For a while friends endeavoured to deceive her, and convey the belief that all viewed her with the same partial eye as before she had left, but it was idle. She soon discovered something was wrong. Some of her only familiar friends were quite estranged from her, and she seemed in a manner forgotten by many who had previously felt a pride in her acknowledgement of them, while others, triumphing in the victory of malicious envy, assumed an affected air of cold disdain towards her; and the elasticity of her spirits caused them to droop and fall from the height to which they had been elevated. Uneasy and disturbed, she sought most importantly for the cause. It was in vain to attempt a repulse. She was unceasing in enquiry, and unsatisfied with reply. It was impossible to baffle her solitude, or gainsay her uneasiness; and at length it was thought best to break the melancholy truth to her at once—that slander had plundered without remorse from her her good name—and support her by increased attentions through the trial of conflicting emotions, and perhaps she might forget that evil tongues had been busy with her. The person selected for this most unpleasing task was her best friend, he who was expected to become her husband,

and who wholly engrossed every warm affection of her heart: as it was most probable, if he should be the commentator, she would not bear the loss of his esteem, which she prized above any that earth, can enumerate of its favours, and would console herself with the thought that if deserted by all the world else, she would still be happy in the security of his remaining attached and sincere. But here character was of a higher mood, and when the fatal tale was revealed, when she knew she had been accused and was suspected of having wandered willingly from the path of rectitude, the startling truth flashed dreadfully upon her mind. Helpless, fatherless, and cruelly plundered of her reputation, she felt herself hopelessly abandoned, and told him who had her soul's devotion and conflicting feelings of pride, regret, and duty that she rendered from that hour every claim to his hand and affections; but her fortitude was divided between her heart and lips, for with this sacrifice she almost rendered life. It was only left to linger with her for a while, a burden and a regret. To his solicitation to love him and wed him still, she was inexorable: her only reply was, I am innocent, I am innocent, but I am unworthy of you. I am suspected, and it may be that when it will be too late you may repent your haste, and we both should continue wretched forever. Persisting in her rash determination, deaf to argument and persuasion and the powerful advocate of love existing in her own breast, she refused to listen to the importunities of friends. She returned to Mr. A. every token she had received from his kindness, and begged as a last request that he would consent to her retaining his letters, which would remain the records of their attachment, and the mementos of the fallaciousness of every hope for happiness. This he felt no inclination to deny, and after an interview most afflicting to the feelings of both, they separated "with a long and breathless clasp" and wild, vacant look of agony: one to brood over her heart's deep excess of passion and cruel wrongs; the other dispirited and discouraged, to lose his affection if possible in the busy toils and fame of the world; and though fortune afterwards prospered him, wealth brought not contentment. Busy meddling memory still renewed the visions of the past to his "mind's eye", and threw a dark, unmoving cloud over every future scheme his shattered feelings planned for the fruition of any delight; his attachment stood resolute and firm; his affections would remain unalterable. Too principled to engage the thoughts and inclinations of another where he could not give his own in exchange, he remained unmarried through life, always manifesting the fondest respect for Caroline, and ever deeply regretted her misfortunes and the resolution which forced her to separate their destiny and widow both their hearts in bitter joylessness.

The world to Caroline now wore a different aspect. It had undergone a total change. She felt herself isolated and exiled, an unprotected female, young, helpless, homeless, and almost friendless. The only rich page in her book of life rent from it, torn and scattered to the four winds of Heaven, and reputation, that purest treasure of earth without which woman is viler than the putrid weed that rottens in corruption, marred and blasted by perjury and falsehood. She attempted to seek out the cause. She reviewed the past, reflected and pondered, turned over in her mind every change, looked through the record of past events, and found not any thing she could reproach or accuse herself with, save the venial fruits, inseparable from all: "she knew not the doctrine of ill doing, no, nor dreamed that any did." She had been accused of incontinency when anxiously striving to do good. She was condemned by the voice of the calumniator for a crime, when, at most, she had only been guilty of an imprudence. She had been placed in a situation where guilt might have followed and remained without transgression, was where temptation might have been, but did not fall; but the accusers, less virtuous or less conscious, supposed the impulse of crime inherent and irresistible. It is not always thus; many pass through the furnace uninjured, yea, it may be, unassailed. There are men, too, who have virtue enough to revolt at seduction, and who value peace of conscience too highly to fling it from them in an offering to lust and rapine.

Sickened and disgusted, Caroline became melancholy and dejected. Her eyes no longer laughed with wonted radiancy. The sunshine of her brow became a lurid light of despair, and concealment, day by day, drop by drop, in protracted sorrow sapped away the foundation of life and hope. Her spirit was now sullied

by the rust of care, and a wearied mind, diseased, was the carking
canker that carelessly corroded in the heart. Shunning society,
her abiding place was her lonely chamber where she secluded
herself and remained the greater portion of her time, leaving that
occasionally to wander in lonely abstraction to a neighbouring
copice, pleasantly though gloomily situated on the margin of a
pleasant river which wound its way in silence from the distant
hills, presenting to the sorrowing eye a landscape of picturesque
but lugubrious beauty. Here she would ceaselessly mourn that
stern and unrelenting fate which had separated her for some
unconscious wrong from the hopes she had so fondly cherished.
In these retirements, when her thoughts would admit of it, she
occasionally sought solace in books, and by indulging her genius
in sketching her desultory thoughts with the pencil and pen. She
was, however, wholly without pretension, and but seldom gave
loose to inclinations that only portrayed more plainly the heavi-
ness of her grief. One of the productions of these moments I
have. Her "harp was given to sorrow's wail", but she had once
touched it with notes of gaiety and lightness that would have
been a credit to any. Now it remained stringless to any other
effort than that which told a tale of sadness and complaint. The
following, though by no means one of her best, paints something
of the anguish of her bosom!

> Oh earth, — I could have clung to thee,
> With nerve and pulse in passion's trance,
> But fate has rudely wrung from me,
> Each bright avid dream of youth's romance.
>
> I can't but weep, — for smiles of mine,
> And faded hopes of other days;
> When free I stroll'd in pleasure's shine,
> And only knew truth, love, and praise.
>
> A cloud is fix'd upon my fate,
> An altar to the thrill of joy;
> I now am lone and desolate: —
> No bliss is left — hate can destroy.

Forsaken and oppress'd, I mourn
'A stricken deer from out the herd,'
With spirits crushed and sorrow-worn,
My hopes are riven, not deterr'd.

I have not err'd, tho' I am blam'd;
I feel that Heav'n will yield me rest,
That holy one, indulgent there,
Will kindly take me to his breast.

Oh God! my only refuge now,
From falsehood's bright and slander's chill;
To thee I gave my warmest vows,
And bid this trembling heart be still.

It was in vain to think of Caroline that her withered prospects would revive: "that falsest of false things, a mask of smiles" was worn in vain. She was too far gone in wretchedness, and wearied, to seek or hear any thing of comfort as she should. She deemed herself a worthless "waif upon the world's wide common", and wholly gave herself up to despondency. I will not judge her for being too susceptible, perhaps too weak, in suffering abuse to take such deep hold of her feelings. Some other natures would have defied the storm and buffeted its approach with pride and self exultation; and it may be, by such means, have overpowered its force, and quelled and shamed the attack, but Caroline was too delicately, too exquisitely moulded in her mind, as many others are, to endure or repulse what was so wrongfully flung upon her fair frame. Soon, too soon, her wan, emaciated cheek and livid lip betrayed that grief was preying too strongly upon her vitals. The sorrow-drop stood ever in her eye, now lustreless with a dim funereal hue, and her young, bleeding heart lay seared and broken in her breast. She calmly put her trust in Heaven-ward hopes, and died the innocent victim of slander.

If beneficence is ever a duty, if charity is ever a virtue and becomes the human heart, if the tear of pity is ever crystalized to deck an angel's diadem, or flows to wash away an earthly stain, if Christian forgiveness is ever spiritualized on earth, a meet offering for the throne of redeeming grace, it is when they are exerted and spring for the helpless and crimeless sufferings of a defenceless and offenceless female.

How odiously detestable is that person, male or female, who deliberately or incautiously trifles away with the life-long happiness of another, who by the slow poison of his viciousness places a gangrene in the core of existence to embitter it forever. Even open crime is less to be condemned. The slanderer by sly innuendoes and all the "kind mendacity of hints", with a deadening, damning influence, preys by a slow but steady fang upon his victim. Secured by the seeming vagueness of his purpose and the fatal impurity of human sentiment, he passes with a little affectation, cautiously shrinking from imputation, unharmed and unassauged, while his cruelty is perniciously working its way. Yes, I had rather meet the highwayman and give the hand of fellowship to him, while his eyes flashed wickedness and he bared his weapon to plunge it in my bosom, than grasp the hand of the slanderer, extended with a treacherous smile upon his lip, from which he pours forth words of kindness upon me, while he inwardly plots my ruin: the first is the safer the better man, and will (forgive me for judging) find more grace in eternity.

Let all beware how they accuse; we know not always the motives and interests of another. We cannot judge of mind before it is developed, not does it follow because a person does different from what our reason would dictate that he is culpable; different situations and circumstances give different impulses. And that person who perverts every action of his neighbour to some end should be aware that the discerning eye may judge him also; the continually suspicious are, for that reason alone, often suspected. The divine exhortation of the mote and beam rises to the fancy and aids the doubt. The incautious whisper should ever be avoided. It goes from a friend's friend to a friend's friend, and the mischief, before we are aware, is too fully accomplished, and the burthen of sin returns to our shoulders. We who engendered the doubt, and set the false suspicion agog, are accountable for the consequences, and must be made to answer for them.

Letters of Mephibosheth Stepsure
To the Editors of the Acadian Recorder

Thomas McCulloch

LETTER 1

GENTLEMEN: Happening one day to call upon Parson Drone, the clergyman of our town, I found him administering his old, standard consolation to my neighbour Solomon Gosling. The parson has been long among us, and is a very good sort of man; but, I believe, he has fared very hardly: for though my townsmen all respect him, and are the most active people in the world at selling watches and swapping horses, they have never made themselves richer and, therefore, have little to give but good wishes. But the parson, except when he is angry, is very good-natured and disposed to bear with a great deal; and, having acquired a large fund of patience himself, he has become a quack at comforting, and prescribes it indiscriminately for all sorts of ills. His own life has been spent between starving and preaching; and having no resources himself, it never occurred to him that, for the wants and troubles of others, there can be any remedy but patience.

My neighbour Gosling is completely an every-day character. His exact likeness may be found at any time, in any part of the Province. About thirty years ago, his father David left him very well to do; and Solomon, who at that time was a brisk young man, had the prospect, by using a little industry, of living as comfortably as any in the town. Soon after the death of old David, he was married and a likelier couple were not often to be seen. But unluckily for them both, when Solomon went to Halifax in the winter, Polly went along with him to sell her turkeys and see the fashions; and from that day the Goslings had never a day to do well. Solomon was never very fond of hard work. At the same time he could not be accused of idleness. He was always a very good neighbour; and at every burial or barn raising, Solomon was set down as one who would be sure to be there. By these means he gradually contracted the habit of running about; which left his own premises in an unpromising plight. Polly, too, by seeing the fashions, had learnt to be genteel; and for the sake of a little show, both lessened the thrift of the family, and added to the outlay; so that, between one thing and other, Solomon began to be hampered, and had more calls than comforters.

When the troubles of life arise out of idleness, a return to industry is usually the last shift. The habits which my neighbour had been gradually contracting, left him little stomach for the patient and persevering toils of a farming life; nor would urgent necessity permit him to wait for the sure but slow returns of agricultural exertion. But necessity is the mother of invention; and though the family of Goslings were never much noted for profundity of intellect, Solomon, by pure dint of scheming, contrived both to relieve himself from his immediate embarrassments and to avoid hard labour. Though Goose Hill farm, from want of industry, had not been productive, it was still a property of considerable value: and it occurred to Solomon, that, converted into goods, it would yield more prompt and lucrative returns than by any mode of agriculture. Full of the idea, accordingly, my neighbour went to town; and by mortgaging his property to Calibogus, the West India merchant, he returned with a general assortment of merchandise suited to the wants of the town. When I say a general assortment, it is necessary to be a little more explicit. It did not contain any of those articles which are employed in subduing the forest, or in cultivating the soil. These he knew to be not very saleable. He was aware that though old Tubal Thump supplies the whole town with iron work, he is so miserably poor, that he can scarcely keep himself in materials. The only article of the iron kind which he brought was a hogshead of horse shoes, which a blacksmith in Aberdeen, who knew something of America, had sent out upon speculation. From the number of horses and young people in the township, Solomon knew that horse shoes would meet with a ready sale.

When a merchant lays in his goods he naturally consults the taste of his customers. Solomon's, accordingly, consisted chiefly of West India produce, gin, brandy, tobacco, and a few chests of tea. For the youngsters, he had provided an assortment of superfine broad cloths and fancy muslins, ready-made boots, whips, spurs, and a great variety of gumflowers and other articles which come under the general denomination of notions. In addition to all these, and what Solomon considered as not the least valuable part of his stock, he had bought from Pendulum & Co. a whole box of old watches elegantly ornamented with lacquered brass chains and glass seals; little inferior in appearance to gold and Cairngorms.

When all these things were arranged, they had a very pretty appearance. For a number of weeks, little was talked of but Mr. Gosling's Store; for such he had now become by becoming a merchant. Little was to be seen but my neighbours riding thither to buy, and returning with bargains. During the course of the day, long lines of horses, fastened to every accessible post of the fences, rendered an entrance to his house almost impracticable. By these means, the general appearance of the town soon underwent a complete revolution. Homespun and homely fare were to be found only with a few hard-fisted old folks, whose ideas could never rise above labour and saving. The rest appeared so neat and genteel upon Sundays, that even the Reverend Mr. Drone, though I did not see that his flock had enabled him to exchange his own habiliments for Mr. Gosling's superfine, expressed his satisfaction by his complacent looks.

Mr. Gosling, too, had in reality considerably improved his circumstances. The greater part of my neighbours being already in debt to old Ledger and other traders about; and considering that if they took their money to these, it would only go to their credit, carried it to Mr. Gosling's Store; so that by these means he was soon able to clear off a number of his old encumbrances, and to carry to market as much cash as established his credit.

Among traders punctuality of payment begets confidence in the seller; and the credit which this affords to the purchaser, is generally followed by an enlargement of orders. My neighbour returned with a much greater supply; and here his reverses commenced. Credit could not be refused to good customers who had brought their money to the store. Those, also, who formerly showed their good will by bringing their cash, proved their present cordiality by taking large credits. But when the time for returning to the market for supplies arrived, Mr. Gosling had nothing to take thither but his books. These, it is true, had an imposing appearance. They contained debts to a large amount, and my neighbour assured his creditors that, when they were collected, he would be able to pay them all honourably, and have a large reversion to himself. But, when his accounts were made out, many young men who owed him large sums, had gone to Passamaquoddy. Of those who remained, the greater part had mortgaged their farms to Mr. Ledger and the other old traders, and now carried their ready money to Jerry Gawpus, who had just commenced trader by selling his farm. In short, nothing remained for Mr. Gosling but the bodies or labours of his debtors, and these last they all declared themselves very willing to give.

About this time it happened that vessels were giving a great price; and it naturally occurred to my neighbour that, by the labour which he could command, he might build a couple. These, accordingly, were put upon the stocks. But labour in payment of debt goes on heavily; and besides, when vessels were giving two prices, nobody would work without double wages; so that the vessels, like the ark, saw many summers and winters. In the meantime peace came, and those who owned vessels were glad to get rid of them at any price. By dint of perseverance, however, Mr. Gosling's were finished: but they had scarcely touched the water, when they were attached by Mr. Hemp, who at the same time declared that, when they were sold, he would lose fifty per cent upon his account for the rigging. Such was my neighbour's case when, happening, as I have already mentioned, to step into Parson Drone's, I found that Mr. Gosling had been telling his ailments, and was receiving the reverend old gentleman's ordinary, clerical consolation: "What can't be cured, must be endured: let us have patience."

"I'll tell you what it is, parson," replied my neighbour; "patience may do well enough for those who have plenty, but it won't do for me. Calibogus has foreclosed the mortgage; my vessels are attached; and my books are of no more value than a rotten pumpkin. After struggling hard to supply the country with goods, and to bring up a family so as to be a credit to the town, the country has brought us to ruin. I won't submit to it. I won't see my son Rehoboam, poor fellow, working like a slave upon the roads, with his coat turned into a jacket and the elbows clouted with the tails. My girls were not sent to Mrs. M'Cackle's boarding school to learn to scrub floors. The truth is, parson, the country does not deserve to be lived in. There is neither trade nor money in it, and produce gives nothing. It is fit only for Indians, and emigrants from Scotland, who were starving at home. It is time for me to go elsewhere, and carry my family to a place that presents better prospects to young folks."

In reply, the parson was beginning to exhort Mr. Gosling to beware of the murmurings of the wicked; when Jack Catchpole, the constable, stepped in to say that the sheriff would be glad to speak with Mr. Gosling at the door. Our sheriff is a very hospitable gentleman; and, when any of his neighbours are in hardship, he will call upon them, and even insist upon their making his house their home. Nor did I ever know any shy folks getting off with an excuse. As it occurred to me, therefore, that Mr. Gosling might not come back for the parson's admonition, I returned home; and soon learned that my neighbour had really gone elsewhere, and made a settlement in the very place where Sampson turned miller. This event has not added much to the respectability of the Goslings; nor is it calculated to brighten their prospects. My neighbour's children are as fine a young family as any in the town; but it unavoidably happened, that the apparent prosperity of their father introduced among them habits, not very friendly to regular industry and saving. Hob Gosling, the oldest son, is really a smart young fellow; and in haying time or harvest, he can do more work in a day than any three labourers. But hard work requires recreation; and when a young man does any thing uncommon, he wishes to receive credit for it among his neighbours. Accordingly, it would sometimes happen, that it would take Hob a week to tell about the exertions of a day. He would also occasionally recreate himself by riding races, or playing a game at cards when he was drinking a glass of grog with other youngsters over Mr. Tipple's counter; and by these means, though Hob is not a quarrelsome young man, his name was frequently called over in court in assault and battery cases. This, it is true, was not without its advantages. Hob acquired a great knowledge of the law, and the character of being a 'cute young man. But I am inclined to think that the gain ended here; for I remember that after one or two of these cases were tried, a few acres of Mr. Gosling's best marsh passed into the hands of Saunders Scantocreesh, a hard-faced, hard-working Scotchman, who, a few years ago, came among us with his stockings and shoes suspended from a stick over his shoulder, but now possesses one of the best farms in the town.

My neighbour's daughters, too, are very agreeable young ladies. Everybody allows that Mrs. M'Cackle has done justice to their education. For painting flowers and playing upon the pianoforte, they have few equals. Some of my neighbours, indeed, used to complain that, when Mr. Gosling asked them to dinner, the meat was always ill-cooked, and the puddings and pies mere dough; but the reason was that neither Mrs. Gosling nor the young ladies could get the black wench to do as she was bidden, unless they were always at her heels.

But this was not the only hardship which my neighbour suffered by the elegant accomplishments of the young ladies. To be genteel in the country, is attended with difficulties and losses of which you townsfolks can have no conception. Morning visits in the afternoon, dressings and other things, interrupted so frequently with rural industry, that great show and sad accidents are usually combined. I recollect when Jacob Ribs married his fourth wife, Mr. and Mrs. Gosling were invited to the wedding; and as it happened to be on churning day, the young ladies were left to look after the butter-making. But, when the chaise which carried the old folks to the marriage returned, it occurred to the young ladies, that, before proceeding to domestic toil, they would have plenty of time to return Miss Trotabout's last morning visit; and off they set, leaving directions with the black girl to have the churn before the fire by the time they returned. During their absence, it unfortunately happened that the wench descried one of her black cronies passing; and, running down the lane to enjoy a little talk, left the kitchen door open, when Mr. Gosling's boar pig Mammoth, who was always a mischievous brute, finding a clear passage, entered without ceremony and upset the churn. My neighbour's kitchen was immediately converted into the country of the Gadarenes. To guzzle up the contents was but the work of a moment. The succeeding scarcity also aroused that inquisitive disposition for which swine, as well as ladies, are noted; when one of the vile animals, perceiving something in the churn as it lay upon its side, thrust in its snout to examine. In this state of things, the black wench, having descried the young ladies at a distance, returned to her post. Vengeance succeeded amazement; and the first object of it, and apparently the most guilty, was the individual whose fore-quarters had already passed from observation. Now, it so happens that no way has yet been invented to drive a pig straight forward, but to pull it by the tail. As soon, therefore, as it found itself assaulted behind, the unclean beast made a fair entrance into the wooden tabernacle; and, when the young ladies returned to make butter, it was rolling round the floor, to the utter dismay of the girl, and complete discomfiture of the whole herd of swine. From such trials as these, you townsfolks, who have nothing else to do but be genteel, are altogether exempted.

After Mr. Gosling's unfortunate confinement, I went to call upon his family, imagining that the countenance of an acquaintance would help to soothe and keep up their spirits. Parson Drone, too, had prepared a long discourse upon patience, and was come to deliver it. But we found them all very cheerful; and the parson, unwilling to lose his labour, made his visit short, and carried his discourse to old Caleb Staggers, whose mare had just died of the botts. Mr. Gosling's confinement they considered merely as a temporary inconvenience, arising from the spite of his creditors. But when his debts were called in, he would pay everybody; and the whole family agreed that, then, with the rest of his property, they would go to a country better worth the living in. I found among them, however, a diversity of opinion about where this should be. Mrs. Gosling spoke of the Ohio; but Mr. Rehoboam declared that it was a new country, without roads, where a young man could not lay a leg over a saddle from the one year's end to the other. Miss Dinah preferred the Cape of Good

Hope, but she was afraid of the Caffres, who sometimes carry off white women. To elope with a lord or a duke, she observed, would be a very pretty incident, but should any person ever write a novel about the Goslings, to be carried off by a Hottentot would appear so droll. Upon the whole, they seemed to think the opinion of Miss Fanny most feasible: that it would be best to go to Botany Bay, where every genteel family like the Goslings, receives so many white niggers, sent out every year from Britain by Government for the supply of the colony.

As your warriors for the winter have not yet opened their campaign, I hope you will find room in your paper for the preceding account of my neighbour and his family. It will not, I know, be very interesting to your readers in general; for they have all seen the like, and heard the like a hundred times before; and as it is no fable but a true story they will not be able to deduce from it any sage moral for their own direction in life. Yet its insertion will oblige a great many of your readers. By looking over the list of your subscribers, you will see that the Gosling family have extensive connexions in every part of the province and in every kind of occupation; and I am sure it will gratify them all to hear how their relation Mr. Solomon is getting on. Should you oblige them and myself thus far, I may be induced to send you, at some future period, the sequel of my neighbour's trading career.

LETTER 14

GENTLEMEN: I formerly stated that in this country there are many public duties and private necessities which call a farmer from home. I showed you also that from a number of the first I was relieved, by being neither a constable nor juryman, Justice of the Peace nor captain of Militia. I shall now explain to you how I managed those private necessities which lead so many of our young people astray.

It has often occurred to me that our townspeople and Snout's pigs resemble each other very much. Whether pigs derive any instruction or amusement from their mutual gruntings, I do not know; but, though they are often quarrelling, and fighting, and tormenting each other, they always keep in company. Exactly in the same way, though our townsmen are needed at home, and might, with good management, be very comfortable there, they would rather meet at Tipple's, the court, or any other place of general resort; and though, on this account, they suffer many domestic privations, and occasionally, when abroad, get themselves beat and abused like pigs, they return again to the same place and company with as much eagerness as if nothing had happened. On mentioning to Parson Drone this feature of the character of our people, he observed that the causes of it are simple, and the cure very easy, if they were only willing to be cured of a disease which had destroyed the industry, domestic comfort, and religion of the town.

"Man," said the parson, "is, by the principles of his nature, attached to society. He cannot live alone, without a perversion of mind or a deprivation of those social enjoyments for which he was formed. But the most of our townsmen, though married, have no *home*. The link which attached them to the wife of their choice has been broken; and, hence, the society which they cannot find in their own houses they expect in Tipple's, or in other places of public resort.

"Besides, in the human constitution, a principle of curiosity or a desire of knowledge, as philosophers term it, is an ingredient of powerful operation. When the mind is not adding to its stock of information, it becomes dissatisfied. But our people in general have not acquired the intelligence which can enable them, by reflection and reasoning, to deduce from the stores of their own minds additional knowledge; and they have no disposition, by a perusal of books, to acquire the valuable information which these would afford them. Still, their desire to know something continues in operation; and to allay the uneasiness which always attends ungratified desire, they will neglect their business and travel about the town, to learn what their neighbours are doing; and when a few of them meet, a conversation about Snout's pigs, or any other trifle, as it fixes their attention and removes the uneasiness of the mind, becomes, in the meantime, a sufficient gratification.

"But that is not the worst of it. Repeated absence from home ingrafts upon the mind habits which are stronger and more pernicious than the perversion of original desire. Many of our people are often abroad when they have really no cause. They can no more stay upon their farms, than their dogs can stay at home upon Sundays; and along with this wandering disposition, some of them, you know, have contracted a habit of drinking which now forces them abroad, in the face of reason and religion, and at the expense of true enjoyment in time and happiness forever.

"Married persons, who would avoid such terrible evils, have only to unite in making their house a *home* to them both; and whoever does so will find society there which reduces, within reasonable bounds, all inclination for other kinds of social intercourse. With respect to the desire of knowledge, no man who gives it a rational direction finds it necessary to quiet his uneasiness by running about the town. When he cannot enjoy useful conversation with his neighbours, by the perusal of books he will converse with both the living and the dead; and, from the stores of his own mind, he will derive topics of reflection which will leave him no taste for the company and gratifications that draw other persons to Tipple's."

How far the parson was right, I shall leave your readers to judge. For myself I can only say, that, having found a home and society there, I had no wish to wander. I gradually furnished myself, also, with a good collection of books and a newspaper; and, though no man enjoys a rational conversation with more relish then myself, I have never felt the least inclination either to go to Tipple's, or to talk about Snout's pigs. By these means, my necessities to go from home were considerably abridged.

In the course of my life I have frequently observed that, as a domestic disposition delights in *home*, it has fewer causes to be abroad. Every person endeavours to be near those things upon which he imagines his happiness to depend; and, in proceeding upon this principle, a farmer of domestic habits who manages well easily relieves himself from a great deal of wandering. Some of the straggling of our town arises from domestic wants. Whatever necessaries a farmer does not derive from his own land, he must collect from a different quarter. Now, among us, there have been always a great many articles which our townsmen have judged it cheaper to buy than to raise. To provide themselves, therefore, with what a family needs, much time and running about are unavoidably expended. You are aware also, I presume, that, in this country, purchasing and paying belong to different sides of a book. A man in our town would sooner think of asking Parson Drone to preach one of his longest sermons upon a week-day, than he would think of buying an article without three, six, or twelve months' credit. On this account, after a great deal of running about and lost time, a necessary article is purchased at a high rate (for all townsmen stand out for great prices), and then it makes a fair entry upon the one side of the book. But, before it finds its way to the other, much additional lost time and running about, I assure you, are indispensable; and, after all, the high price must be paid.

But, though my legs are pretty long, as I stated to you before, I was never any great hand at the running; and, indeed, I have rarely tried it, except when I was going *home*. Besides, I did not like to be from home. I have always had a notion, too, that time is money. I therefore concluded that it would be best for me to raise upon my own farm the provisions which others collected from the different parts of the town. By these means, no time was lost. Labour, also, was expended as it ought to be; and, upon my fields and crops, this had a wonderful effect. But, after all, I must give our townsmen the praise of being, to an industrious farmer, a very useful and accommodating sort of folks; they find it cheapest to buy provisions, and I sell them. Thus, by the produce of my farm, my travelling necessities were further reduced.

But a number of our people raise considerable produce upon their farms, and, of course, sell occasionally; and when this happens, I do assure you, it costs them no little labour and travelling. As they are often going about, they cannot be expected to have a great deal to spare. On this account, it is requisite to dispose of what they have to the best advantage; that is, to sell it for the promise of a great price, and the payment as soon after as possible. But, in our town, those who have money in their pockets, are very shy about promises; and when they do make them, they are rarely of a size sufficient to please persons who need and expect great prices. The people of our town, therefore, generally deal with such as Moses Slack, who is poor from thoughtless, ill management; or with the like of Trot's sons, who, when the day of payment arrives, are not easily found. By proceeding upon this plan, some of them become rich in promises and notes of hand, which, by the by, are amongst us a staple article of trade. But though they expend much time and travel looking after the promises of great prices, they usually continue still rich in promises; and as for the notes of hand, they are at last sold for what they will bring, to Truck and other chaps, who put them into some lawyer's hands, just to keep him out of mischief and prevent him from ruining the country.

From all this labour, and loss of time and trucking, I relieved myself by very simple means. As I owed no man anything myself, I was not willing to keep a register of other people's debts; and, therefore, though I was as forward as any of the neighbours to help a poor settler beginning the world, the hope of a great price could never induce me to sell to idle folks or to ill-doing vagabonds. My dealings have uniformly been with those whose payment gave me no trouble. But, as some of your farming readers may not believe that I could always meet with good and ready pay, I shall show them how I managed.

Some farmers go to market with a bad article, and, perhaps, meeting with an ignorant purchaser, obtain a price which they do not deserve. By and by, they carry him a better; but the good article brings rogue along with it. Other farmers again are uniformly noted for the inferior quality of their produce. In both cases they must hawk about for a customer, receive a low price, and then return home, complaining of dull markets and poor pay. I, on the other hand, considering that the world generally treats men as it finds them, was careful in the first place to establish a character. Whatever I sold, I sold it as it was, and at a reasonable rate, for good payers always expect to buy reasonably. During the whole course of my life, also, quality as well as quantity has occupied my attention. On this account, my produce of every kind was generally good; and this, you may depend upon it, is a great help to me in these dull times, for now it is bespoke. All your readers will now be satisfied, I hope, that a farmer, by much running about, does not always arrive at the best market at last.

But beside the preceding causes of absence from home, the store, the mill, and the blacksmith's shop are serious items among the travelling necessities of our town. As for the church, it scarcely deserves to be mentioned. Though our people generally go there, I never knew it gave any of them a habit of travelling. On the contrary, were they obliged to hear a sermon from our parson every time they go abroad, I do think they would become a very domestic sort of folks; for Mr. Drone has scarcely finished upon Sunday, when they all hurry homeward with as much haste as Snout's pigs when the dogs are at their heels. But, if any of them go to the other places which I have mentioned, the case is altogether different. Then, nobody can tell when they will be home. When they leave their own houses, it is true, they are in a great hurry, as our people going from home usually are. But, as they get over the road they get over their hurry too; for, except my cousin Harrow, Saunders, and a few others, I never, at those places, found our townsmen in haste. On the contrary, they will very contentedly hang about them the whole day, discussing the news, and a number of half-pints which they fetch from Tipple's; and then, toward evening, instead of sending for any more, they find it most convenient to adjourn to his house and stay all night.

But neither the store, the mill, nor the blacksmith's shop ever cost me much travel or lost time. The produce of my farm saved me many a journey to Mr. Ledger's. My spouse and I were a homespun couple, so that neither silks nor superfine produced travelling from home; and when I did go to the store, I must say that I always found Mr. Ledger a very considerate gentleman. To the neighbours who were crowding about his counter, he would say that, as they were in no hurry, he would serve Mephibosheth first. To the mill, my journeyings were comparatively few. I did not, like many of the neighbours, for the purpose of being often there, carry my grain thither by a bushel at a time; and, as for old Tubal, when he saw me enter his shop, he knew that my pocket contained the money to pay him for the job; and, if even Puff's horse was there, he was put out till Mephibosheth's was shod.

As yet, I have said nothing about borrowing and lending, which, in our town, are both the cause of no small travel. With respect to borrowing, this, in ordinary cases, was with me out of the question. Without the necessary tools, a farmer can no more work to advantage than a tradesman. My first care, therefore, has always been to provide myself with every farming article, which I keep in good order, and each in its own place. By these means, when I proceed to do anything, I save myself the trouble of running about to borrow bad articles; for borrowed articles are generally in bad order, and need a great deal of repairing before they can be used; and my own tools, carefully kept, enable me to go to work at once. Thus, my job is always well done; and, in the same time, I can do much more than any of the neighbours.

With respect to lending my farming articles, I confess I have ever been very shy. I consider them as part of my farm; and, except to a poor settler beginning the world, I have never been willing to let them out of my possession. At first, this procured for me the name of a particular kind of man; but it saved me a great deal of travel (for no man in our town, except Saunders and a few others, carries home a borrowed article); and as I am, in other things, as obliging as any of the neighbours, they are now used with my way, and do not take it ill, and my farming tools keep at home pretty well. Upon this subject, and indeed upon farming in general, I derived much useful instruction from the experience of my neighbour Moses Slack.

Mosey, as we usually call him, is a good-natured, easy man. Unlike most of our townsmen, who, as I said before, are pretty long-legged, Mosey, from his youth, was a squab little fellow. Nature had given him a good broad face, and a quantity of nose which equalled old Trot's; but somehow or other she put her foot upon this last member after it was made; and ever since, its breadth has been much more remarkable than its length. Mosey, of course, cared nothing for news; nor, indeed, did he care a great deal for anything else. My neighbour Saunders frequently says that nature never intended him to be his own master, and that if he had only got his face blackballed when he was young, and been put into the hands of some decent master who would have provided for him and made him work, he would have been a very good Negro. Certain it is, that Slack has never managed well for himself. But still Saunders may be mistaken; for he says exactly the same thing of many of our people who have as long legs and sharp noses as any in the town.

Though Mosey could work very well in company, he would just as well let it alone. Yet he cannot be called lazy, for he has spent a very busy life and wrought a great deal. About the time that my spouse and I were married, Mosey was joined in wedlock to one of Mrs. Drab's daughters; and, as he settled upon a lot not far from mine, I had frequent opportunities of observing his progress. Before his marriage I helped him to put up a little log hut, which, he said, would do very well for a sheep house when he raised his new frame. Into this the young couple entered, and there they continued till it came down about their ears. Both he and his wife were fond of fine clothes, which, like all the Drab family, they were better at having on than taking care of. Like most young folks, too, they liked to live pretty well; so that, by the beginning of next summer, Mosey, instead of labouring upon his farm, was obliged to work the most of his time to Mr. Ledger, and the neighbours who had supplied him with provisions. His own crop, therefore, was small, and ill taken care of. Now, a life of this kind is much more easily begun than altered. He who spends his wages before they are due is always behind with his payments. He is, of course, the servant of his creditors; and, when he happens to work for himself, everything which he does he does to a disadvantage. What should have provided Mosey with the necessary articles for getting on with his farm had found its way to the back and belly of the young couple; and even those things which he had, as he was often from home working for other people, were always out of order. When he needed a little firewood, a horse was to be sought among the neighbours. After finding the horse, perhaps, finding the collar cost him a great deal of running. Then his own traces or the dog was lost; and when these were found, and Mosey had got to the woods, probably the first stroke separated the axe from the handle, which had been split before. Mosey never thought of going to the mill till there was no flour in the house. Then in a great hurry a bushel was threshed, carried thither, and brought home at the expense of a day's waiting and a half pint or two. In this manner he managed the whole of his business.

When farming is so conducted, little can be raised. Mosey had, therefore, a great deal of travelling about the town in search of provisions; and as may be supposed, he traded with those who expect great prices, so that at last he became very poor. With this kind of life, however, he dragged on, till he owned a few fields, which, partly from want of thought and partly from necessity, received from him a miserable kind of cultivation. Mosey, in the management of his land, was a rigid adherent of the old system of farming. This, some of your readers may not understand. I shall therefore explain it.

During winter, every farmer, by means of his cattle makes, about his barn, so much manure, which, when he can find sufficient leisure in the spring, he lays on his land. I say, when he can find sufficient leisure, for the manure is not always used. A number of years ago, I recollect, our parson advised old Stot to lay lime upon his field; but the old man very justly observed that to toil himself burning lime would be folly, when he could never find time to carry out the dung of his cattle. If a farmer's hurry, however, permit him to lay his manure upon his fields, they first yield him potatoes; and then wheat, as long as it will grow. When the wheat fails him, the ground is fit for oats; and after the oats refuse to grow any longer, it is in good state for laying down in grass. But it somehow happens that, though our people who follow this rotation, sow very good grass, it turns always into sorrel. A few years after, the land is again broken up, and yields a special good crop of weeds, which, as our townsmen never sowed them, produce a great deal of wondering how they happened to get there. This is the system of farming which Mosey followed; and, indeed, I may say, it is the general system of the town. How it may fare with the rest, I cannot exactly tell; but Mr. Ledger, after long forbearance, has been forced to sell out Mosey, and be satisfied with partial payment, for to put him in jail was of no use; and now he is jobbing about among the neighbours, till he can get away to the Ohio, Upper Canada, or to some other country better worth the living in.

From the experience of Mosey, as I formerly observed, I derived much useful instruction. Though he laboured his little fields so mightily, as rarely to give him rest, his crops were miserable. The principal part of them was weeds, and even these were not like the stout healthy fellows which I occasionally pick out of my own ground. All Mosey's ploughing and harrowing could not bring even weeds to perfection. I could therefore easily see that fields, like cattle, unless they be well fed and well taken care of, have a beggarly appearance, and are very little worth; and, during the course of my life, I have uniformly treated them in a similar way. For my cattle, I provide abundance of fodder; and for my ground, as much manure as possible; and, as I expect from my cattle only reasonable work, from my fields I never seek more frequent nor more abundant crops than nature and good heart enable them to afford. By pursuing this plan, I have always plentiful returns; and, as I labour for profit, I take care to raise only what is saleable. Though our townsmen purchase a great many useless articles, nobody buys weeds, for they have all plenty of their own, and therefore I never raise them.

The experience of Mosey, and also of my neighbour Pumpkin, showed me that neither labour nor large fields are sufficient to make a farmer wealthy. No man in our town ploughs so much, nor, in haying time, goes over so much ground, as Pumpkin; yet he is obliged to purchase flour for his pies, and his cattle are half-starved in winter. I therefore resolved to try how a smaller farm, kept in good heart, would do. This diminished the toil of fencing, and indeed labour of every kind; but strange as it may appear to some of your farmer readers, it increased the produce of my land wonderfully; and now, beside maintaining my own family well, I supply Pumpkin and many of the neighbours.

Thus, by getting on in my own way, I own a snug farm. I have also bought a good property for Abner; and I can tell you a pretty long and feasible story about where the cash has been going to in these hard times. Let no person, however, suppose that I am one of the great folks in our town. On the contrary, neither Mr. Cribbage nor any of the Sippit family would demean themselves so far as to ask the like of me to visit them. Still, among our folks, I pass for a remarkable kind of man: *I have a pair of lame legs—I stay at home—I mind my own affairs—I wear homespun, and I have become wealthy by farming.* In short, as I have been all along telling you, I am

MEPHIBOSHETH STEPSURE.

The Letters of Patty Pry

Anonymous

My Dear G——

My Aunt Tabitha and I were sitting last Saturday afternoon, very busily employed, as nineteen-twentieths of the ladies are in every Christian country, preparing for the decorations of the Sunday, when Aunt desired me to lay aside my work, and see if there was any thing pretty in the poetical corner of the *Recorder*. Poor, good soul! although she is now blind with the labours of the single sisterhood, and has to wear spectacles old enough for a grandmother, she has not yet lost her early prepossession for the scraps of poetry, which are found in the newspapers; and as it is a kind of reading which is not particularly disagreeable to my own feelings, I frequently oblige her by reading them aloud — especially, if they are upon love!

Turning to the paper, or rather making the paper turn to me, I glanced my eyes down the columns and found three scraps of poetry standing in order, but with titles not very attractive to the lovelorn eye. First — "Stepsure in Town" — a kind of would-be funny, serio-comic ditty according to my mind; but the point of which, although it has reached a thirteenth canto, is quite too deep for me—silly simpleton as I am, being but a young lady and in my teens. Next, a scrap upon "Misery"—Some old-fashioned prig of a fellow, thought I, writing to his dissipated comrades about the gout, and preaching patience and water gruel. I was ready to exclaim with Sangrade, "It cometh not within my practice, therefore let it pass." Now pray, don't think me pedantic—for this allusion comes from my french lesson in Gil Blas. — And third "An address to Caledonia" — a country and its race for which I cherish a mortal abhorrence, ever since I knew they feed children upon oatmeal to give them a complexion, dance to the tune of the bagpipes, and suffer Gentlemen to go to a drawing room with kilts—as memo the King's levee at Holyrood House. However, in running my eye down the second time, a couplet of the first order purporting to be an effusion from an "Acadian Bard", caught my attention,

> Oh youth do not an idiot be
> And live for love in slavery.

My eye balls were stretched; as this is the article in which we deal and by which we hope to make our bread, to my infinite horror and indignation, I read over the whole piece, written "to warn a young friend, from that kind of delusion" yclept love, which, as the author very pathetically observes, "often leads to neglect of business, and not unfrequently deadens the energy of exertion, enervates the power of genius, and ultimately terminates in ruin" — a concatenation of events which is truly horrible.

"Come, Liby, dear, why don't you begin," said Aunt Tabitha, in her very kindest manner.

And without preface, I commenced this philosophic effusion upon misery, determining to watch the effect it would have upon mine good old Aunt. I knew as well how it would affect her, as if any one would tread upon her corny toe. And in the thoughtless gaiety of a giddy girl, I determined to look on and to laugh—not in my sleeve, but behind the unfurled sheet of Holland's *Recorder*.

She tired, fidgetted on her chair, and then plied her needle with a redoubled speed, to the no small injury of her thimble finger, as I more than once witnessed with ineffable satisfaction. But when I had reached the paragraph

> Love is a chain that idiots wear,
> At first it is so light to bear.

Tabby (as Papa calls her for shortness), while she turned her head to the window, took off her spectacles; and I could scarce believe my own eyes, when I saw that one of the glasses was bedimmed with a large swollen tear. 'Tis of no use denying it—I know I did curl up my nose, and looked with queer astonishment at her puckered lips, and at the lank locks which were swagging on her shrivelled cheek. The side of Aunt's cheek is just like the coating of a shrivelled winter apple in June. A pretty puss, thought I, to cry at a love story. But as I proceeded with one eye on the paper and t'other off, a sigh and a palpable quivering at the lip cut me to the heart, and yielding to the better and, I am sure, the more amiable and becoming sympathies of our hearts, I threw my arm round Aunt's neck and kissed her as fervently as I would ... ah! but that's a secret.

"What ails you, Aunty love?" I said, in my most tender and coaxing way.

For a little she was silent, and then answered, "Nothing, my dear Elizabeth, it is past. Come, have you nothing else to read?" And looking up, her countenance seemed perfectly calm, and she commenced her work with an air of dignity and even grace.

Hang it, thought I, a pretty termination to a real romance; for I was thinking at the moment about the story of Malvina in the *Spectator*.

Aunt Tabitha maintained her rigidity during the afternoon; but contrary to her usual custom, she retired to her own room, immediately after tea; Papa shortly after inquired for the paper—it was not to be found.

A sudden thought flashed across my mind. I went softly up stairs, stole into my own room, and peeped through a small hole in the partition, which separated Aunt's chamber from mine; when, behold! I saw her sitting with the paper in one hand, and a small miniature in the other, looking the very image of wretchedness.

Aunt Tabby have a miniature and I not know it. Beshrew me! as Shakespeare's heroines very often exclaim. I shall be at the bottom of this mystery, before I am a week older, else

... curiosity liveth not in woman

I have discovered the whole secret; and if you, my dear G——, for the sake of filling up an odd corner will print it in your paper, it is very much at your service; and it will oblige me, for you know it is a proverb and a true one that a "lady cannot keep a secret".

I am just going to my French lesson; and if Monsieur Perro is in good humour and does not scold, I will write out Aunt Tabby's story for you this very night, so adieu.

Yours very truly,
PATTY PRY

Monday evening. June 19

My Dear G ——

I told you in my last that I had discovered the secret of Aunt Tab's miniature, and promised to write it out as soon as possible, but what with dress, dancing, and parties in the evenings — the blues, music, and household concerns during the day, I have not been able to snatch a favourable opportunity till this very moment.

On Sunday afternoon Papa was enjoying himself after dinner by lolling on his easy chair — Mama and Aunt had gone to hear the rector, and I thinking it a favourable time drew near to Papa, in the hope of getting at the bottom of the secret — if he know it! — by a little coaxing and cunning cross-questioning. Ladies, you know, are the very d ... for curiosity.

I sat down upon Pa's knee, and threw my arm round his neck. Papa, I know, loves me like the apple of his eye, and this was a sure way, as I knew well before of making him good natured. So after he called me a good girl and began playing with my curls, I ventured to ask him if he had noticed how melancholy Aunt Tabby had been on the evening previous.

"I did, my dear Patty; I should have been glad to interfere, but sister Tabby you know is older than I am and she knows me too well not to be aware that, had she conceived it proper to confide in me, I should have given her my sympathy and best advice."

"Papa, I think I know the cause of Aunt's melancholy."

"You do, — pray what is it? No quarrel I hope with your mother. Patty, you surely have not hurt her feelings. I have always thought you a girl of a better and kinder heart than to irritate and annoy those feelings of disappointment, which are naturally engendered by a life of celibacy — and the more particularly in her case."

He said all this with so tender and endearing a manner, that I felt the tear rise in my eye and trickle on my cheek.

"No, Papa, I am proud of your good opinion, but my mother and I were neither the cause of Aunt's dejection — it was something different."

"You know if you say — come — tell it me then. I may be able to remove it, for I remarked at dinner to-day, that the cloud still hung on her brow."

"I became acquainted with it, Sir, in a way, I am inclined to think enforces upon me secrecy."

"My dear child, I respect your scruples, but you can know nothing about your Aunt, which is not fitting for me to hear."

After he had said this, I related the whole circumstance to my reading the poetry &c. as it was detailed to you in my letter in your paper, but when I came to the incident connected with the miniature, my father passed his hand across his brow and hastily interrupted me.

"Stop, Patty, stop. I do not wish to hear further. Is it possible that that remembrance can still be cherished — is it possible that that miniature can still excite such feelings?"

"O then, Papa, you know about the miniature?"

"Yes, my dearest Patty, and since also you have become aware of its existence, I shall relate the circumstances connected with it. It affords a good lesson to the young and inexperienced. It shows that much of the happiness of life depends upon one single step and ought to teach us to be doubly careful and prudent in all our conduct." Father here set himself erect in his chair and thus began: —

"'You are aware, my dear Patty, that my parents were respectably descended and that my father was a provision merchant of good credit and fair character, in that beautiful city called Cork. The whole family consisted of only three children — your uncle John (who inherited my father's business and his wealth and who resides now in the same house in which we were all born) — your Aunt Tabby, and myself. John and I both received a good school education to fit us for pushing up in the world, and as for Tabby, it wasn't a little her *larning* cost her father—God rest his bones in peace! After being a due time at the reading and writing and sewing school she was brought home by her mother to be instructed as was usual in those days in the mysteries of housekeeping. No girls, bating those of the nobility, were, at that time, instructed in drawing or music or French, which are now so common a part of female education; and they only learned enough of dancing to trip off a reel on the green on a summer's afternoon, and to the tune of the pipes."

"And were there no quadrilles then, Pa — no parties in the evenings?"

My father's brow seemed to gather to a frown and he shrugged his shoulders. "Quadrilles or parties—any? No, no, Patty, folks had other fish to fry. They passed their time like reasonable beings, went to bed in proper hours, rose early, attended to their business, and as to being happy believe me, child, that is not to be found in balls or quadrille parties. But to proceed: —

"I recollect those days well, and often look back to them with regret. It is truly said that the days of youth are the season of enjoyment. There was in the neighbourhood of the city, only about three miles distant, a farmer of good character & very respectable in his way of life. He rented a farm about 200 acres, which his forefathers to the tenth generation had occupied before him, and was generally accounted a man of good circumstances, although not affluent. He and his family consisting of three sons were in the habit, whenever they came to the city, of making your grandfather's house their home, and in return he was frequently invited to pay them a visit too, and remain with them for a week or two in the country. Their place of residence was a very beautiful one. It stood upon a hill, the house was surrounded with trees, and the wide view of cultivated land, that spread around like an arm of the sea, was only terminated by the ocean and the sky. Even in those days, young and thoughtless as I was, I used to delight in the prospect, but as it presents itself now to my memory it seems something like the prospects of Paradise. Oh! it is many the pleasant hour I wore out my sight in looking at it. But this life, my child, is a changeable one. Our sources of pleasure wither away like the blossoms on the 'tatoe stalks. That same view which was connected in my memory with so many agreeable associations, I never can think of now without a sore heart and a troubled mind.

"I had well nigh reached my eighteenth year before any thing had occurred either to alter my opinion of, or my warmth of friendship toward, the family of Mister Terrence O'Donnelly. We had lived till then in the most perfect harmony, and felt no happiness equal to that of receiving from or paying a visit to the inhabitants of Ballynog Cottage.

"About this time sister Tabby was one of the most beautiful girls that I had ever put eyes upon and moreover just as good as she was pretty."

"What, Papa, do you mean Aunt Tabby?" — for I had never recollected her but as a dark, withered, skinny old maid. And as I thought upon her dark elf locks, and her dry puckered lips I said again — "Was Aunt Tabby really so pretty as you say?"

"Patty, my dear, if you ever number as many years, which God grant you may, as Aunt Tabby, and suffer as much sorrow, which God grant you may not, no one will be able to discover in your appearance, then, any rememberance of those lively blue eyes, and bright cheeks, which you now pride yourself so much on. Grief and old age together furrow the smoothest brow, and break down the strongest and most shapely form. Yes, Patty, Tabitha was then, as I said to you before, a girl as much handsomer then, as you are handsomer than her now. She was always the queen of the company. The young men used to crowd round her at all times, and to think themselves honoured even by a smile — but he who was fortunate enough to secure her hand as a partner in the strathspey was envied by every one. And after all she is single; but this did not happen for the want of offers, and good ones too. She might have been a rich man's lady, had she liked— but there is a fate which rules all these things—Tabby was never meant to be a bride!"

"And for what reasons did she refuse those who offered her? Did her parents thwart her, or did she act from her own foolish whims?"

"You are impatient, Patty. Hear! your mother and Aunt have just returned — go to the door and meet them. Come to my sitting-room to-night, after your Aunt retires, as she usually does on Sunday evening to her devotions—and I will explain to you the cause of her refusals."

I need not tell you, my dear G——, that I waited upon Papa at the appointed hour and place—but it is now near one o'clock in the morning and I hear Papa walking in his own room. If he should come down stairs and find my candle burning, I should get a pretty scold. So for the present I kiss my hand and say adieu.

Yours

PATTY PRY

Friday Night —
My Dear G ——

On entering the Library I found Father casting his eye over a manuscript, which he had unpacked from an old-fashioned trunk which stood in a corner of the room, and which I knew was filled with family relics, for I had more than once taken out my Grandad's coat from it, and laughed at its queer cut, deep-waisted pockets, and buttons as large as the full Moon. Papa nevertheless had a very great reverence, like the rest of his countrymen, for this auld surtie, and used to honour St. Patrick —God's blessing to his memory!—by getting drunk in it once a year, by the way of glorifying entirely at one and the same time the Saint and the *grane* sod. And well he might—for there was "Erin go Bragh" each letter as large as a pewter spoon, twisting round the rim of every button on it.

Well, when I entered the apartment this said auld coat, with a hoop petticoat above it were airing themselves on the floor, and Father was reading away at the durty manuscript, with a candle which had a snuff to it as long and as red as a turkey-cock's bill. My father, think I, like Sir Corny in Castle Rackrent, is just reading a bit of the ancients to pleasure himself like, and without speaking a word I sat down on a chair right forenent him.

"Are you sure sister Tabby has gone to her own room, Patty, my dear?" said Papa, now looking up.

"Yes, and I believe by this time is in bed."

"Turn the key in the door then, for I do not wish to be disturbed, and I shall proceed with the history I was telling you in the afternoon. Fifty years is a long time to look back, and I was just looking over this manuscript to refresh my memory with some circumstances which had escaped it. This is a family manuscript kept by my father, which was found in his desk at his decease, and was sent me out by John three or four years ago,— Father was a very methodical, but a very eccentric man. His journal is just like himself. Here Patty, look how he notes down my birth.

"July 26th, 1758. Born to me this morning, at one o' the clock, bating a quarter, a thumping boy, who shall be called Bat, by the blessing of God, in honour of his Grate grand fader, who was killed, by a ball no less, at the battle of the Boyne. He came into the world crying; it is to be hoped, he won't go out of it the same way. He makes the promise of a powerful man, and because he kapes his hand clenched, it is I thinks, he'll be a soldier" — a prediction which you see, Patty, is not verified, for here I am a simple dealer in clothes, cottons, and haberdashery," and saying this Papa turned down the manuscript and thus begged my attention to Tab's memoirs: —

"I mentioned to you before my dear that Mr. O'Donnelly had three sons. The elder named after himself Terry. He wished to be the farmer, and nature seemed also to have backed the father's wish; for he was a strong, powerful, well-made lad, able to work and willing to put his hand to it, and hadn't his match at pitching a bar, jumping a ditch, or giving a thump with his fist in all the County of Cork. Nevertheless, it was only on fair days and holidays and Saint-days, which in Ireland was then only six months in the year, that he ever tried his skill or prowess in such fetes; at other times he was a plain steady-going lad, and worked early & late when the sun and rain would let him. Jerry, the second son, was totally different. He was feeble in his strength, with a weak constitution, and fond of solitude and books. His father gave him a good education, sent him to college, and by dint of perseverence and good luck he entered into the priesthood, and is now Father O'Donnelly to a thriving congregation in the District of Munster."

But here as Father paused a minute I couldn't help thinking to myself — Now what has all this to do with Aunt Tabby, and for the life of me I could not help yawning right in Pa's face.

"I see, Patty, your patience is beginning to fail, but recollect my darling, it isn't the easiest way always to rise a hill to go straight up."

I assured Papa I was not the least fatigued, but I was given to yawn on Sunday night, which is quite true for me, as you know, Mr. G——. I begged him to proceed.

"But the third son, Dick," continued Father, "was a lively, rattling lad as ever walked a bog or footed it on the Corry Kildare. He was extremely well made, being tall and gracefully proportioned in his figure—had a complexion as rosy as a red apple, and an eye so black and fiery that samed to spake for itself. Dick and I were great companions, and he was so funny and frolicksome and kind withal, that I loved him as well as a brother, and it wasn't a little he liked me. At first his father thought to keep him at home and make a farmer of him like Terry; but Dick would never give his mind to the work. He had a spirit far above it, and as his father saw in his *bould* and determined character the indication of something above the common, he determined to give him some education and send him to the army under the patronage of his Landlord and noble, Lord Daldgyle. So Dick went to school, and learned faster than any of them, though he never seemed to study a bit; and his Master was so pleased with him, that he often said to his father, "Yere boy, Mister O'Donnelly, is a mighty *grate genus* surely, and bad luck to the day that he'd go to the wars to be kilt and murthered; kape him at home, Mister O'Donnelly, and give him the law for a breadwinner, and if he beant a 'Torney or Counsellor of a shining degree, it isn't I that knows P from a pig"; and so it was determined. The notion of Dick's going to the Army was abandoned, and behold him at the age of sixteen after he knew enough of Horace and a power of grammar, as his dad used to say, apprenticed to John Maloney, Esq. Attorney at Law and Notary Public, by the king's high commission. But Mr. Maloney chiefly made his bread by the agency of a large estate, which he managed well for nobody at all, saving himself. Master and tenant were both kept as poor as a horse tied to a stall without having fodder—while Mr. Maloney fattened in his pockets and carcase, like a jackass in a clover field. But it was this that spoil poor Dick entirely. He never could bring his mind to read dusty manuscripts or moth-eaten books, and what with the *distastsome-ness* of the law and the disgust he felt at Maloney's roguery and screwing of the tenants, he took such an aversion to the office and its *concarns* that it was a thousand times oftener he was to be found in the hills with his fowling piece than in his office with his pen in his fingers. A nate shot he was and a good dancer to boot, and a likely lad to please the girls, and he had a clever turn at that too, as I could tell you. For there was one Kitty O'Leary, the daughter of Tim O'Leary, game keeper no less to the Earl of Kilmore," —

Now I knew that Father was going to tell me some long-winded story, so I thought I would just interrupt him, and put him in mind of his first purpose, — "Papa, you promised to tell me you know first about Aunt Tabby, and now it is getting so late."

"Well, well, Patty, my dear, I'se tell yees of Kitty O'Leary another time, God willing! but about Dick as I was saying afore he was a likely lad, and a great dancer to boot; and if he set his heart to pleasing the girls there was not one from Bantry Bay to Bally Castle that he couldn't charm and win the heart right out of her.

"In the middle of the summer, after Dick had begun to *clark* it to Mr. Maloney, sister Tabby and I went down to-gether to pay a visit to Ballynog. Dick and I — fond of the same frolics, sporting and fishing with the likes of them — were soon as thick as two yolks in a duck egg; and it was neither the day nor the night that parted us, for we walked from morning to evening on the hills and at night slept on the same feather-bed. Tabby too was fond of a frolic as either us, and with a little coaxing used often to lend us her company to the hills and the lake; and it seemed a mightly pleasure to Dick to help her over a ditch or to carry her from the boat without letting her foot even so much as touch the water. He did it all in so kind and attentive manner that one couldn't help being pleased with it. Tab at least seemed to be so, and she expressed her thanks in so winning a way that Dick told me at night afore we went to slape that he would carry Tab from Ballynog to Cork just to get a kind word and a smile at the end of the journey. At the first I never had a thought what all this was to come to. But I began to suspect something, when one afternoon I saw Dick very loving with Tabby under the great oak trees that were aback of the house, and when I came fornent Tab she blushed like a milkmaid that had been travelling of a frosty morning in the teeth of the last wind, and as for Dick he looked like a gassoon caught in an orchard stealing.''

At this moment the clock struck ten. —Father told me it was a good hour to go to bed, and promising me to relate the rest of the history at his first leisure, bade me good night. And here for the present I stop and bid your Editor's mightiness

A third—but not a long adieu.

PATTY PRY

Monday Morning.

N.B. I know some critics will be saying that I have altered my style in this letter—but there is an old proverb, ''suit your song to your supper, and your words to your company,'' which in the above I have tried to do. Father is a clever spoken man as ye'd ever wish to hear, and has not a bit of the brogue on his tongue, unless he begins to speak about his dear ould Ireland, and then it comes as thick as *buttermilk*. If I have been successful in imitating him — the more to my credit — ant it?

My Dear G ——

I waited very impatiently for several days to hear from Papa the continuation of Aunt's history; but a press of shop business, society meetings, and card parties occupied his time so much day and night that I could never find him during a full week with any leisure at his hands. However, one afternoon last week after he had cracked a bottle of the best Madeira, and seemed as happy as if he had been primed with the real potsheen, and was just falling back to take an afternoon's nap, I drew near and begged him to go on with Tab's story; for I had ever since been dying with curiosity to get to the end of it.

''Yere a botherment to your dad entirely, Pat, but it is I that will give ye the rights of it; so be after sitting down anent me, my sweet darling, and there's my foot to hold till I be done''; and stretching out his leg across my lap, and balancing himself upon his chair, he thus commences: —

"I *tould* ye I believe how I catched them, walking and talking under the oak trees as softly as two nightingales singing in the twilight. Oh, they were loving and coaxing like and seemed as if saying to each other, "sweet is your hand in a pitcher of honey, my darling." I didn't break in upon them as a constable would, bad luck to him! into a cotter's pig-sty; but came creeping on slyly enough, till Dick began to kiss Tab; and this was too much for me, for I didn't like it.

"So I walked bouldly forward, and Tab blushed and Dick hung down his head as I tould you afore. And putting on a stern look; Dick, says I, it isn't what I expected from you. Is this all yere friendship for me and mine, that you would be practising a beguilement on Sister Tabby and blarneying her up with yere nunsinse. It isn't what I expected, Dick — it isn't acting like a friend — no, nor a man."

"I shall never forget the scene that followed. Tabby's breast hove and fell like a rolling sea, in a moment after she watered her pretty cheeks with a shower of tears. Dick looked at her for an instance, and then walking straight up to me, in his own determined manly way, while, poor fellow! the tear was in his eye. 'Tim,' says he, 'don't be after saying again what ye were saying now, unless ye want to break my heart entirely! By all the saints, I love your Sister Tabby as I love the mother that bore me. And after ye have known me as ye have done—is it you that suspects me for beguilement to ruin a simple innocent girl. God forgive you, Tim, you have done me a great wrong.' His heart now seemed fairly to close his throat; he bit his lip to prevent the tear from falling that was brimming in his eye; and I, no longer able to contain myself, put my hands into his—'Forgive me, dear Dick, it was I that was the worst of the two, for suspecting the wrong. Yere the same to me Dick as ever ye was; and if you win you are welcome to her for me; and whenever you can, shall carry a brother's blessing with her portion.'

" 'Thank you for the kind word, Tim. It is the pleasantest I have heard this month back, and since you have made the promise it has given me some heart both to win and be worthy of her.'

"After this explanation it became quite an understood thing between Dick and myself that he was the lover and of course the intended husband of sister Tab, and I was fairly bothered with his nonsense about it, for I couldn't be walking with him for five minutes at a time, but he'd be after telling me what a jewel she was.

"Notwithstanding my great regard for Dick, I began to bethink myself that I wasn't acting altogether the fair thing to Father and Mother to let their love be gathering like a rolling snow-ball without letting them know never a word at all, at all about it — 'So' one evening to Sister Tabby, says I, 'Tab, my sweet, since Dick has taken himself to court yees, it is your duty no less to let yere mother know of it. And I determined, if yees wont, to do it myself, to clear my own conscience, and let her know all about it from the beginning, to the end.'

"Tab answered never a word, but began crying, as if she had a notion to make a river with her tears. However, after a while, I pressed the matter and showed her both the necessity and the right of it. And she consented to let me write a note about it. And strange to say, Patty, the very identical note is transcribed word for word into my father's manuscript; and as I was reading it a day or two ago I chanced to pitch on it itself. Go up stairs to the Library, Patty, and ye'll find it in the drawer of my escrutoire, bring it down and I'll read you the identical same."

After returning with the paper Father fumbled over it a bit, & then read as follows; —

"MY DEAR MOTHER,

This comes to let yees know I am stout and hearty as a pig in a paratoe field, hoping with the blessing of God ye're the same. It is plenty of shooting and fishing I have had ever since I came to the country, and this together with a plenty of milk night and morning and pork and peas as sweet as nuts, has made me grow so fat, that if I didn't put on my jacket with all civility, it would soon be laughing on my back. And it is the same with Tab, the Lord be praised, only she be bothered a bit in her mind which makes her a little paler than she would be without it, and it is I thinks ye should know the reason because yere her own mother, and because it wouldn't be dutiful or properer to be kaping it from ye. So ye must know that Dick O'Donnelly and she have been after making love to one another;

and I never knew or suspected a word about it, till I catched him one afternoon kissing Tab very loving-like: and after speaking mighty angry to him, thinking he did not mean the *nate* thing, he confessed it was all in honour. And well he's worthy of her, my dearest mother. There is not a kinder heart in the County Cork than Dick's own, nor a cleverer lad, and although he be neither kith nor kin to me, I couldn't love my own brother better. Tab too, I think, loves him well, and as they have set alonging upon each other, I hope yees wont be saying No, and make sorrow grow out of young hearts — always remembering that they must wait, till Dick has got comfortable, and he able to keep the wife and the childer after her."

The part relating to Aunt Tab's courtship concluded here, and as I suppose neither you nor your readers would feel much interest in the rest of it — here I stop.

"Early the very morning after the letter was dispatched, Father came down from the city in a great hurry and told Tab and I that we must come instantly home. I saw the reason of this just as clear as I could see a hole through a ladder; and I saw Tab suspected the truth too for she looked mighty sorrowful and down-hearted; and as for poor Dick bould and manly as he was, the tear was in his eye, for the thought of losing Tabby was like a rusty darning needle run into his heart, — and indeed he was certain sure this was to happen, for Father, when he arrived, in place of shaking hands with him as he did formerly, wouldn't give him the tip of his little finger, and looked as huffy as a Lord would on his Tenant who hadn't voted just as he directed him.

"Ah, Patty, my darling [continued Father] Ireland, dear Ireland, is the only place for warm hearts and true lovers. It isn't till the day I'll die, that I shall ever forget the looks that passed between Tab and Richard, on the morning we left the cottage of Ballynog; God bless me, it was the morning of sorrow, and it was followed by a day that was gloomy and dismal enough."

At this moment the servant announced a gentleman who called upon Father on business; and the story of course was here interrupted till a more seasonable opportunity.

Yours, &c.
PATTY PRY

Monday, July 19th.

My Dear G——

My father's narrative has lately been so broken, and has winded into the mazes of such long and trivial detail, that I feel quite unable to communicate it to you at full length, or in his own words; and I have therefore determined to sketch the remainder of Aunt Tab's history, and to relate a plain, unvarnished tale.

Reverting then to the conclusion of my last, I now proceed:—

Immediately after Aunt Tab had returned home, the illness, brought on by anxiety of mind, at the cottage of Ballynog, returned with an encrease; and my mother soon remarked, with regret, that the pretty and happy girl she had sent from her had returned, in a few weeks, with a load of sorrow at the heart, which was weighing down and chilling her spirit. It availed not that she knew the cause, for my father was inexorable to all entreaty and swore stoutly that he had shown some disposition to an industrious life, to gain a livelihood, and do well in the world.

Tab's departure from Ballynog had a similar effect upon her lover. Mr. Maloney's law office, with his musty folios upon title-deeds, mortgages &c. &c. became even more distasteful to Dick than they were before—even the hills and lakes lost their attraction to him; and he was oftener seen moping under the shaded walk, formed by the oak-trees, at the back of the cottage, than away scouring hill and dale, bearing his gun or rod, and giving elasticity to his own step, by the liveliness of a troll or whistle.

He endured this kind of life for six months, during which time he had managed to make a dozen or more stolen visits to the city; and my father, as his accomplice and confidant, contrived to afford him opportunities of seeing his darling. These secret meetings did little good to either, and Father, when he informed me of them, and that on this account, he had always regarded himself in part implicated in the sin of destroying his sister's happiness.

At last, however, one of these visits was *blown*. Dick's bed was found one of those nights, in which he was plodding his weary way to Cork, tenantless; and as a trap was laid by his parents for discovery, his visit, and its object, by circumstances too clear to be denied, was fully exposed. Dick's father was a man of great spirit.

He had seen latterly some change—a coolness in his old friend's (my grandfather's) manner, and he did not well know what to ascribe to it. It never crossed his mind that the Cork merchant would refuse his daughter to a son of his—provided he was able to marry and wanted a wife. But the truth was forced upon him at length. Dick confessed that he dared not darken Mr. O'Donnelly's door — *becase,* for the love of Tabby. "And yees has the *maneness* to go after her nevertheless, unworthy son of the ould sod—by the powers yere a bastard and have no blood of mine in ye at all, at all," said his father, and raising his arm, he struck Dick a blow which laid him at his feet. A convulsive twitching played across his features, and he immediately left the room. Dick shed no tear, but he formed his resolution; that night with a bundle of clothes tied in a silk handkerchief, he turned his back upon his father's door, with the determination never to return to it again, unless good fortune and a fair name should be gained by him through after life.

It was a dark night in the month of September. The winds howled with an autumnal fury, and as they drove the clouds over the sky, the stars and the moon occasionally broke through a deep dark opening, which served only to impart a wildering dreariness to the solitary road. Some minds would have taken the dreariness of the night as a manifestation of divine wrath for an undutiful resentment; but Dick did not view in it this light, and being one of those who rather buckled the firmer, when opposed, than yielded to difficulties, he hastened forward with a quicker step; and with a more resolute, if not a more cheerful spirit.

After reaching the city he paced the streets for the remaining part of the night, and on the following morning sent a message for my father, requesting to see him immediately. On arriving at the appointed place of meeting, Dick related every circumstance as it had occurred, and the plan which he had formed for his future career.

He had an uncle, who was a major in one of the regiments which were despatched under General Burgoyne—for the subjucation of the American rebels. At that time his detachment was lying in the Cove of Cork, waiting a fair breeze to sail for North America; and Dick had determined, if my father could only furnish him with a fitout, to proceed immediately to the cove, throw himself upon his uncle's protection, and accompany him on his distant enterprise. My father, having the command of some small funds, readily yielded to the solicitations of his friend, promised both to get a *suit* prepared for him during the course of the day and to allow him to see Tab that evening—perhaps, as he then said, for the last time.

The meeting took place between the Lovers as agreed upon. My father was present, and he represented it, although upon such a subject, of course, he would not speak to me very fully, as tender and affecting. The parting was dreadful. Tab wept like a child and as Dick tore himself from an embrace, during which he swore solemnly before God never to love or marry any other but herself, and in which she reciprocated his pledged vow, Tab uttered a scream, which alarmed the household, brought my grandfather hastily downstairs; and Dick had just time to make his escape out of doors, and Tab, to make good her retreat to her room, before he burst into the Lobby to enquire the cause of this unexpected cry. By the invention of an artful tale, my father succeeded in deceiving, and of course in quieting, Grandpa, but as he followed him to their separate chambers, he was oppressed with a guilty conscience and a heavy heart, for he knew he had done EVIL, and out of this GOOD could not come.

Dick reached the cove on the following morning just as the vessel, in which his uncle had taken passage, was under sail. He succeeded in getting on board, before the ship had left the harbour; and by pretending that he came, at the express request of his father, who was, as he said, fully convinced he was totally unfit for the law, his uncle yielded an unwilling consent to his entreaties.

Thus far my father has brought down his narrative, and he has promised again and again to communicate to me a full relation of Dick's adventures upon this side of the water; but he has been so frequently prevented that I have given up all hope, at all events for the present, of being able to communicate them to you.

I have learned however that Dick, shortly after he reached America, by the influence of Lord Dalgyle, was presented with a commission, and that he distinguished himself for a brave officer and was much beloved and esteemed both by his companions and his men. He was present at the battle where General Burgoyne was taken prisoner and escaped himself into Canada by a lucky chance of war, having immediately after their disgrace, been sent with an account of their defeat to Quebec. For 3 years after, while he remained in Canada he regularly wrote through my father, to Tab—but before the end of that time, there existed no longer any necessity of concealing the receipt of his letters, for Grandfather had began to think that Dick would be a very creditable connection. The last packet received from him, contained his own miniature enclosed to my Aunt, & was dated in the spring of 1780. He was just then going to the back country with a body of troops to quiet some disturbances among the Indians — what befell him there, whether he was murdered or died a natural death, has never been ascertained till this hour.

Aunt lived in the widowhood of love for many years, always hoping that her Dick, or as he ought more properly to be called, Capt. O'Donnelly would return. But he came not, and she has since persisted in the resolution of honouring his memory by continuing single. Poor soul! it is not likely any one will tempt her to break her generous resolve—but I shall die, before I ever again pry into her secret hours, or laugh at the misgivings of her heart to the olden times.

My father emigrated here in 1806 — I was then a chick. My grandfather and grandmother had been dead then many years— God rest their bones in peace! Dick's father departed about six months after the report of his son's sudden disappearance had reached Ireland, and on his death bed, he expressed his sincere sorrow for the manner in which he had treated the runaway. Terry succeeded him in the possession of Ballynog, and as for Jerry he is at present, as I have mentioned afore, a reverend father to a parish in Munster. And so, with never a word more

I remain,

Yours &c. &c.

PATTY PRY

The Clockmaker

Thomas Haliburton

I had heard of Yankee clock peddlars, tin peddlars, and Bible peddlars, especially of him who sold Polyglot Bibles (*all in English*) to the amount of sixteen thousand pounds. The house of every substantial farmer had three substantial ornaments: a wooden clock, a tin reflector, and a Polyglot Bible. How is it that an American can sell his wares, at whatever price he pleases, where a Bluenose would fail to make a sale at all? I will inquire of the Clockmaker the secret of his success.

"What a pity it is, Mr. Slick,"—for such was his name,—"what a pity it is," said I, "that you, who are so successful in teaching these people the value of clocks, could not teach them also the value of time."

"I guess," said he, "they have got that ring to grow on their horns yet, which every four-year-old has in our country. We reckon hours and minutes to be dollars and cents. They do nothing in these parts by eat, drink, smoke, sleep, ride about, lounge at taverns, make speeches at temperance meetings, and talk about 'House of Assembly'. If a man don't hoe his corn and he don't get a crop, he says it is owing to the bank; and, if he runs into debt and is sued, why, he says the lawyers are a curse to the country. They are a most idle set of folks, I tell you."

"But how is it," said I, "that you manage to sell such an immense number of clocks, which certainly cannot be called necessary articles, among a people with whom there seems to be so great a scarcity of money?" Mr. Slick paused, as if considering the propriety of answering the question, and looking me in the face, said in a confidential tone, —

"Why, I don't care if I do tell you, for the market is glutted, and I shall quit this circuit. It is done by a knowledge of *soft sawder* and *human natur'*. But here is Deacon Flint's," said he; "I have but one clock left, and I guess I will sell it to him."

At the gate of a most comfortable-looking farm-house stood

Deacon Flint, a respectable old man, who had understood the value of time better than most of his neighbours, if one might judge from the appearance of everything about him. After the usual salutation, an invitation to 'alight' was accepted by Mr. Slick, who said he wished to take leave of Mrs. Flint before he left Colchester.

We had hardly entered the house before the Clockmaker pointed to the view from the window, and, addressing himself to me, said, "If I was to tell them in Connecticut there was such a farm as this away down East here in Nova Scotia, they wouldn't believe me. Why, there ain't such a location in all New England. The deacon has a hundred acres of dyke — "

"Seventy," said the Deacon, "only seventy."

"Well, seventy; but then there is your fine deep bottom, why I could run a ramrod into it — "

"Interval, we call it," said the Deacon, who, though evidently pleased at this eulogium, seemed to wish the experiment of the ramrod to be tried in the right place.

"Well, interval, if you please — though Professor Eleazer Cumstick, in his work on Ohio, calls them bottoms — is just as good as dyke. Then there is that water privilege, worth three or four thousand dollars, twice as good as what Governor Cass paid fifteen thousand dollars for. I wonder, Deacon, you don't put up a carding-mill on it; the same works would carry a turning-lathe, a shingle machine, a circular saw, a grind bark, and — "

"Too old," said the Deacon, "too old for all those speculations — "

"Old!" repeated the Clockmaker, "not you; why, you are worth half a dozen of the young men we see nowadays; you are young enough to have"—here he said something in a lower tone of voice, which I did not distinctly hear; but whatever it was, the Deacon was pleased; he smiled, and said he did not think of such things now.

"But your beasts, dear me, your beasts must be put in and have a feed"; saying which, he went out to order them to be taken to the stable.

As the old gentleman closed the door after him, Mr. Slick drew near to me, and said in an undertone, "That is what I call *soft sawder*. An Englishman would pass that man as a sheep passes a hog in a pasture, without looking at him; or," said he, looking rather archly, "if he was mounted on a pretty smart horse, I guess he'd trot away, if he could. Now I find —" Here his lecture on "soft sawder" was cut short by the entrance of Mrs. Flint.

"Jist come to say good-bye, Mrs. Flint."

"What, have you sold all your clocks?"

"Yes, and very low too, for money is scarce, and I wish to close the consarn; no, I am wrong in saying all, for I have just one left. Neighbour Steel's wife asked to have the refusal of it, but I guess I won't sell it; I had but two of them, this one and the feller of it, that I sold Governor Lincoln. General Green, the Secretary of State for Maine, said he'd give me fifty dollars for this here one— it has composition wheels and patent axles, is a beautiful article, a real first chop, no mistake, genuine superfine — but I guess I'll take it back; and besides, Squire Hawk might think kinder hard that I did not give him the offer."

"Dear me!" said Mrs. Flint, "I should like to see it; where is it?"

"It is in a chest of mine over the way, at Tom Tape's store. I guess he can ship it on to Eastport."

"That's a good man," said Mrs. Flint, "jist let's look at it."

Mr. Slick, willing to oblige, yielded to these entreaties, and soon produced the clock, — a gaudy, highly-varnished, trumpery-looking affair. He placed it on the chimney-piece, where its beauties were pointed out and duly appreciated by Mrs. Flint, whose admiration was about ending in a proposal, when Mr. Flint returned from giving his directions about the care of the horses. The Deacon praised the clock; he too thought it a handsome one; but the Deacon was a prudent man; he had a watch; he was sorry, but he had no occasion for a clock.

"I guess you're in the wrong furrow this time, Deacon; it ain't for sale," said Mr. Slick; "and if it was, I reckon neighbour Steel's wife would have it, for she gave me no peace about it." Mrs. Flint said that Mr. Steel had enough to do, poor man, to pay his interest, without buying clocks for his wife."

"It is no consarn of mine," said Mr. Slick, "as long as he pays me, what he has to do; but I guess I don't want to sell it, and besides, it comes too high; that clock can't be made at Rhode Island under forty dollars. Why, it ain't possible," said the clockmaker, in apparent surprise, looking at his watch, "why as I'm alive it's four o'clock, and if I haven't been two hours here. How on airth shall I reach River Philip to-night? I'll tell you what, Mrs. Flint, I'll leave the clock in your care till I return, on my way to the States. I'll set it a-going, and put it to the right time."

As soon as this operation was performed, he delivered the key to the Deacon with a sort of serio-comic injunction to wind up the clock every Saturday night, which Mrs. Flint said she would take care should be done, and promised to remind her husband of it, in case he should chance to forget it.

"That," said the Clockmaker, as soon as we were mounted, "that I call 'human natur'!' Now that clock is sold for forty dollars; it cost me just six dollars and fifty cents. Mrs. Flint will never let Mrs. Steel have the refusal, nor will the Deacon learn until I call for the clock that, having once indulged in the use of a superfluity, how difficult it is to give it up. We can do without any article of luxury we have never had, but when once obtained, it is not in 'human natur'' to surrender it voluntarily. Of fifteen thousand sold by myself and partners in this Province, twelve thousand were left in this manner, and only ten clocks were ever returned; when we called for them they invariably bought them. We trust to 'soft sawder' to get them into the house, and to 'human natur'' that they never come out of it."

Cumberland Oysters Produce Melancholy Forebodings

The soft sawder of the Clockmaker had operated effectually on the beauty of Amherst, our lovely hostess of Pugwash's inn; indeed, I am inclined to think with Mr. Slick that "The road to a woman's heart lies through her child", from the effect produced upon her by the praises bestowed on her infant boy.

I was musing on this feminine susceptibility to flattery, when the door opened, and Mrs. Pugwash entered, dressed in her sweetest smiles and her best cap, an auxiliary by no means required by her charms, which, like an Italian sky, when unclouded, are unrivalled in splendour. Approaching me, she said, with an irresistible smile, "Would you like, Mr. —?" Here there was a pause, a hiatus, evidently intended for me to fill up with my name; but that no person knows, nor do I intend they shall; at Medley's Hotel, in Halifax, I was known as the Stranger in No. 1. The attention that incognito procured for me, the importance it gave me in the eyes of the master of the house, its lodgers and servants, is indescribable. "Would you like, Mr. —?"

"Indeed, I would," said I, "Mrs. Pugwash; pray be seated, and tell me what it is."

"Would you like a dish of superior Shittyacks for supper?"

"Indeed I would," said I, again laughing; "but pray tell me what it is?"

"Laws me!" said she with a stare, "where have you been all your days, that you never heard of our Shittyack oysters? I thought everybody had heard of them."

"I beg pardon," said I, "but I understood at Halifax that the only oysters in this part of the world were found on the shores of Prince Edward Island."

"Oh! dear, no," said our hostess, "they are found all long the coast from Shittyack, through the Bay of Vartes, away to Ramshag. The latter we seldom get, though the best; there is no regular conveyance, and when they do come, they are generally shelled and in kegs, and never in good order. I have not had a real good Ramshag in my house these two years, since Governor Maitland was here; he was amazing fond of them, and lawyer Talkemdeaf sent his carriage there on purpose to procure them fresh for him. Now we can't get them, but we have the Shittyacks in perfection; say the word, and they shall be served up immediately."

A good dish and an unexpected dish is most acceptable, and certainly my American friend and myself did ample justice to the oysters, which, if they have not so classical a name, have quite as good a flavour as their far-famed brethren of Milton. Mr. Slick ate so heartily that when he resumed his conversation he indulged in the most melancholy forebodings.

"Did you see that 'ere nigger," said he, "that removed the oyster shells! well, he's one of our Chesapickers, one of General Cuffy's slaves." I wish Admiral Cockburn had a taken them all off our hands at the same rate.

"You have heard tell of cotton rags dipped in turpentine, haven't you, how they produce combustion? Well, I guess we have the elements of spontaneous combustion among us in abundance; when it does break out, if you don't see an eruption of human gore worse than Etna lava, then I'm mistaken. There'll be the very devil to pay, that's a fact. I expect the blacks will butcher the Southern whites, and the Northerners will have to turn out and butcher them again; and all this shoot, hang, cut, stab, and burn business will sweeten our folks' temper, as raw meat does that of a dog; it fairly makes me sick to think on it. The explosion may clear the air again, and all be tranquil once more, but it's an even chance if it don't leave us the three steam-boat options, — to be blown sky-high, to be scalded to death, or drowned."

"If this sad picture you have drawn be indeed true to nature, how does your country," said I, "appear so attractive as to draw to it so large a portion of the population?"

"It ain't its attraction," said the Clockmaker; "it's nothin' but it's power of suction; it is a great whirlpool — a great vortex; it drags all the straw and chips, and floating sticks, drift-wood, and trash into it. The small crafts are sucked in, and whirl round and round like a squirrel in the cage — they'll never come out. Bigger ones pass through at certain times of tide, and can come in and out with good pilotage, as they do at Hell Gate up the Sound."

"You astonish me," said I, "beyond measure; both your previous conversations with me, and the concurrent testimony of all my friends who have visited the States, gave a different view of it.

"*Your friends!*" said the Clockmaker, with such a tone of ineffable contempt that I felt a strong inclination to knock him down for his insolence, — "your friends! Ensigns and leftenants, I guess, from the British marchin' regiments in the Colonies, that run over five thousand miles of country in five weeks on leave of absence, and then return, looking as wise as the monkey that had seen the world. When they get back they are so chock full of knowledge of the Yankees that it runs over of itself; like a hogshead of molasses rolled about in hot weather, a white froth and scum bubbles out of the bung, — wishy-washy trash they call tours, sketches, travels, letters, and what not; vapid stuff jist sweet enough to catch flies, cockroaches, and half-fledged gals. It puts me in mind of my French. I larnt French at night school, one winter, of our minister, Joshua Hopewell (he was the most larned man of the age, for he taught himself e'enamost every language in Europe); well, next spring, when I went to Boston, I met a Frenchman, and I began to jabber away French to him: 'Polly woes a french shay,' says I. 'I don't understand Yankee yet,' says he. 'You don't understand?' says I, 'why, it's French. I guess you didn't expect to hear such good French, did you, away down East here? But we speak it real well, and it's generally allowed we speak English, too, better than the British.' 'O,' says he, 'you one very droll Yankee; dat very good joke, sare: you talk Indian, and call it French.' 'But,' says I, 'Mister Mountshear, it is French, I vow, real merchantable, without wainy edge or shakes — all clear stuff; it will pass survey in any market; it's ready stuck and seasoned.' 'O, very like,' says he, bowin' as polite as a black waiter at New *Orleens*, 'very like, only I never heerd it afore; O, very good French dat—*clear stuff*, no doubt, but I no understand; it's all my fault, I dare say, sare.'

"Thinks I to myself, a nod is as good as a wink to a blind horse. I see how the cat jumps: minister knows so many languages that he hain't been particular enough to keep 'em in separate parcels, and mark 'em on the back, and they've got mixed; and sure enough, I found my French was so overrun with other sorts that it was better to lose the whole crop than go to weedin', for as fast as I pulled up any strange seedlin' it would grow right up ag'in as quick as wink, if there was the least bit of root in the world left in the ground; so I left it all to rot on the field.

"There is no way so good to larn French as to live among 'em, and *if you want to understand us, you must live among us, too;* your Halls, Hamiltons, and De Rouses, and such critters, what can they know of us? Can a chap catch a likeness flying along the railroad? Can he even see the featurs? Old Admiral Anson once axed one of our folks afore our glorious Revolution (if the British had a known us a little grain better at that time, they wouldn't have got whipped like a sack as they did then) where he came from? 'From the Chesaperke,' said he. 'Ay, ay,' said the Admiral, 'from the West Indies?' 'I guess,' said the Southerner, 'you may have been clean round the world, Admiral, but you have been plaguy little in it not to know better than that.'

"I shot a wild goose at River Philip last year, with the rice of Varginny fresh in his crop; he must have cracked on near about as fast as them other geese, the British travellers. Which knowed the most of the country they passed over, do you suppose? I guess it was much of a muchness—near about six of one, and a half dozen of t'other; two eyes ain't much better than one, if they are both blind.

"No, if you want to know the ins and the outs of the Yankees— I've wintered them and summered them; I know all their points, shape, make, and breed; I've tried 'em alongside of other folks, and I know where they fall short, where they mate 'em, and where they have the advantage, about as well as some who think they know a plaguy sight more. It ain't them that stare the most that see the best always, I guess. Our folks have their faults, and I know them (I warn't born blind, I reckon), but your friends, the tour writers, are a little grain too hard on us. Our old nigger wench had several dirty, ugly lookin' children, and was proper cross to 'em. Mother used to say, *'Juno, it's better never to wipe a child's nose at all I guess than to wring it off.'* "

The Age of the Garland

Jeremiah Desborough; or, The Kentuckian

John Richardson

Our Canadian readers doubtless bear in mind the spot called Elliott's Point, at the western extremity of Lake Erie. Some considerable distance beyond that again, (its intermediate shores washed by the silver waves of the Erie,) stretches a second, called also from the name of its proprietor, Hartley's Point. Between these two necks, rise three or four farms; one of which, and adjoining Hartley's, was, at the period of which we treat, occupied by an individual of which, unfortunately for the interests of Canada, too many of the species had been suffered to take root within her soil. For many years previous to the war, adventurers from the United States, chiefly men of desperate fortunes, and even more desperate characters, had, through a mistaken policy, been suffered to occupy the more valuable portion of the country, to the exclusion of the natives themselves. Upper Canada, in particular, was infested by these people, all of whom, even while taking the customary oath of allegiance to the British crown, brought with them, and openly professed, all the partialities of American subjects. By the Canadians and their descendants, French and English, they were evidently looked upon with an eye of distrust, for, independently of the fact of their having been suffered to appropriate, during pleasure, many valuable tracts of land, they had experienced no inconsiderable partiality on the part of the government. Those who believe in the possibility, not merely of attaching a renegade to the soil of his adoption, but in converting him into a servicable defender of that soil in a moment of need, commit a great error in politics. The shrewd Canadians knew them better. They maintained, with bitterness, that at the first appearance of a war they would hold their oaths of fealty as naught, or that if they did remain it would only be with a view to embarrass the province with their presence, and secretly to serve the cause of their own countrymen. The event proved they knew their men. Scarcely had the American Delcaration of War gone forth, when numbers of these unprincipled wretches, availing themselves of their near contiguity, abandoned their homes, and embarking all their disposable property in boats, easily succeeded in gaining the opposite coast, under cover of the night. Not satisfied, however, with their double treason, they, in the true spirit of the dog in the manger, seemed resolved others should not enjoy that which was no longer available to themselves, and the dawn that succeeded the night of their departure, more than once broke on scenes of spoliation of their several possessions, that it required one to know these desperate people well, to credit as being the work of their own hands. Melancholy as it was, however, to reflect that the spirit of conciliation had been thus repaid, the country had reason to rejoice in their flight; for, having thus declared themselves, there was nothing now, beyond their open hostility, to apprehend. Not so with the few who remained. Alike distrusted with those who had taken a more decided part, it was impossible to bring any charge home to them, on which to found a plea for compelling them to quit the country, in imitation of the example of their fellows. They had taken the oaths of allegiance to England — and, although ninety-nine had deliberately violated these, there was no legal cause for driving forth the hundredth, who still kept the "sound of promise to the ear", however he might break it to the hope. Not that, on this account, the hundredth was held to be one whit more honourable or loyal. It was felt and known, as though it had been written in characters of fire upon his brow, that if he did not follow in the steps of his predecessors, it was because his interests, not his inclination, induced his pursuing an apparently opposite course. It is true those who remained were few in number; but scattered, as they were, in various isolated parts of the country, this only rendered them greater objects of suspicion. If the enemy became appraised of any of our movements, for the successful termination of which it was necessary they should be kept in ignorance, it was at once taken for granted their information had been derived from the traitors Canada had so long nourished in her bosom; and as several of them were in the habit of absenting themselves for days in their boats, under the pretence of duck-shooting, or some other equally plausible, nothing was more easy of accomplishment. Under these circumstances of doubt, the general succession of the Yankees, as they were termed, which had first been regarded as a calamity, was now looked upon as a blessing; and if regret eventually lingered in the minds even of those who had been most forward to promote their introduction into the country, it arose, not because the many had departed, but because the few remained. That they were traitors, all believed; but, although narrowly watched, in no one instance could their treason be ever traced, much less brought home in accusation. In the course of time, however, they committed themselves in some one way or other, and then, of necessity, their only resource was to flee, as their companions had fled before them, until, ultimately, very few indeed were left of their number. If Canada has reason to feel happy in the late war, inasmuch as that war offered a means of proving the devotedness of her attachment to the mother country, she has no less reason to rejoice in it as being the indirect means of purging her unrepublican soil of a set of ruffians who were a disgrace to any age and any country. Should she, failing to profit by the experience of the past, again tolerate the introduction of subjects of the United States into her flourishing provinces when there are so many deserving families anxious to emigrate to her from the mother country, then will she merit all the evils which can attach, in a state of warfare, to a people diametrically opposed to their interests, their principles, their habits, and their attachments. But we think the cloven foot has been too openly displayed to afford much chance to the Americans on that score.

An individual of this description had his residence near Hartley's Point. Unlike those, however, whose dwellings rose at a distance, few and far between, hemmed in by the fruits of prosperous agriculture, he appeared to have paid but little attention to the cultivation of a soil, which, in every part, was of exceeding luxuriance. A rude log hut, situated in a clearing of the forest, which had been the imperfect work of lazy labour, was his only habitation, and here he had for years resided without its being known how he contrived to procure the necessary means of subsistence; and yet, in defiance of the apparent absence of all resources, it was subject of general remark, that he not only never wanted money, but had been enabled to bestow something like an education on a son who had been absent from him upwards of five years. From his frequent voyages, and the direction his canoe was seen to take, it was inferred by his immediate neighbours that he dealt in contraband, procuring various articles on the American coast, which he subsequently disposed of in the town of Amherstburgh—one of the principal English posts—to advantage, among certain subjects domiciliated there, who were suspected of no desire to benefit the revenue of the country they called their own. So well and so wisely, however, did he cover his operations, that he always contrived to elude detection — and, though suspicion attached to all he did, in no instance had he openly committed himself. The man himself, a tall, stout, forbidding-looking ruffian, was of a fearless and resolute character, and if he resorted to cunning, it was because cunning alone could serve his purpose in a country the laws of which were not openly to be defied.

For a series of years after his arrival, he had contrived to evade taking the customary oath of allegiance; but this, eventually, awakening the suspicions of the magistracy brought him more immediately under their surveillance, when, year after year, he was compelled to a renewal of the oath, for the infliction of which, it was thought, he owed more than one of those magistrates a grudge. On the breaking out of the war, he still remained in undisturbed possession of his rude dwelling, watched as well as circumstances would permit, it is true, but not so narrowly as to be traced in his various nocturnal excursions by water. Nothing could be conceived more uncouth in manner and appearance than this man — nothing more villainous than the expression of his eye. No one knew from what particular point of the United States he had come, and whether Yankee or Kentuckian, it would have puzzled one of that race of beings, so proverbially notorious for acumen—a Philadephia lawyer—to have determined; for so completely did he unite the boasting language of the latter with the wary caution and sly cunning of the former, that he appeared a compound of both. The balance of opinion, however, seemed rather, if at all, to incline in favour of the presumption that he was more Kentuckian than Yankee.

The morning was just beginning to dawn, as two individuals appeared on the skirt of the rude clearing in which the hut of the man we have just described had been erected. The persons of both these, wrapt in blue military cloaks, reposed upon the dark foliage in a manner to enable them to observe, without being themselves seen, all that passed within the clearing, from the log hut to the sands of the lake shore. There had been an indication on the part of one of these to step forth from his concealment into the clearing, and advance boldly towards the house; but this had been checked by his companion, who, laying his hand upon his shoulder, arrested the movement, indicating, at the same time, the leisurely but cautious advance of two men from the hut towards the shore, on which lay a canoe half drawn up on the sands. Each, on issuing from the hut, had deposited a rifle against the rude exterior of the dwelling, the better to enable them to convey a light mast, sail, paddles, several blankets, and a common corn-bag, apparently containing provisions, with which they proceeded towards the canoe.

"So," said the taller of the first party, in a whisper, "there is that d —— d rascal Desborough setting out on one of his contraband excursions. He seems to have a long absence in view, if we may judge from the contents of his provision sack."

"Hist," rejoined his companion, "there is more here than meets the eye. In the first instance remove the pistols from the case, and be prepared to afford me assistance, should I require it."

"What the devil are you going to do, and what do you mean?" asked the first speaker, following however the hint that had been given him, and removing a pair of duelling pistols from their mahogany case.

While he was in the act of doing this, his companion had, without replying, quitted his side, and cautiously and noiselessly advanced to the hut. In the course of a few minutes he again appeared at the point whence he had started, grasping in either hand the rifles so recently deposited there.

"Well, what is the meaning of this feat? you do not intend, Yankee fashion, to exchange a long shot with poor Molineux, I hope — if so, my dear fellow, I cry off, for, upon my honour, I cannot engage in any thing of the sort that is not strictly orthodox.

He, thus addressed, could scarcely restrain a laugh at the serious tone in which his companion expressed himself, as if he verily believed he had that object in view.

"Would you not like," he asked, "to be in some degree instrumental in banishing wholly from the country, a man whom we all suspect of treason, but are compelled to tolerate from want of proof of his guilt — this same notorious Desborough?"

"Now that you no longer speak and act in parables, I can understand you. Of course I should, but what proof of his treason are we to discover in the mere fact of his departing on what he may choose to call a hunting excursion? Even admitting he is speculating in the contraband, *that* cannot banish him; and *if* it could, we could never descend to become informers."

"Nothing of the kind is required of us — his treason will soon unfold itself, and that in a manner to demand, as an imperative duty, that we secure the traitor. For this have I removed weapons which may, in a moment of desperation, be turned at backwoodsman's odds against our pistols. Let us steal gently towards the beach, and then you shall satisfy yourself; but I had nearly forgotten — suppose the other party should arrive!"

"Then they must in their turn wait for us. They have already exceeded their time ten minutes."

"Look," exclaimed his companion, as he slightly grasped the shoulder on which his hand rested, "he is returning for the rifles."

Only one of the two men now retrod his steps from the beach towards the hut, but with a more hurried action than before. As he passed where the friends still lingered, he gave a start of surprise, apparently produced by the absence of the rifles. A moment's reflection seeming to satisfy him it was possible his memory had failed him, and that they had been left within the building, he hurried forward to assure himself. After a few moments of apparently ineffectual search, he again made his appearance, making the circuit of the hut to discover his lost weapons, but in vain; when, in the fierceness of his anger, he cried aloud, with a bitterness that gave earnest of his sincerity.

"By Gosh, I wish I had the curst British rascal who played me this trick, on t'other shore — if I wouldn't tuck my knife into his b——y gizzard, then is my name not Jeremiah Desborough. What the h——l's to be done now."

Taking advantage of his entrance into the hut, the two individuals first described had stolen cautiously under cover of the forest, until they arrived at its termination within about twenty yards of the shore, where, however, there was no outward or visible sign of the individual who had been Desborough's companion. In the bows of the canoe were piled the blankets, and in the centre was deposited the provision bag that had formed a portion of their mutual load. The mast had not been hoisted, but lay extended along the hull, its sail loosened, and partially covering the before-mentioned article of freightage. The bow half of the canoe pressed the beach, the other lay sunk in the water, apparently in the manner in which it had first approached the land.

Still uttering curses, but in a more subdued tone, against "the fellor who had stolen his small bores," the angry Desborough retraced his steps to the canoe. More than once he looked back to see if he could discover any traces of the purloiner, until at length his countenance seemed to assume an expression of deeper cause for concern than even the loss of his weapons.

"Ha, I expect some d——d spy has been on the look-out — if so, I must cut and run I calculate purty soon."

This apprehension was expressed as he arrived opposite the point where the forest terminated. A slight rustling among the underwood reduced that apprehension to certainty. He grasped the handle of the huge knife that was thrust into the girdle around his loins, and, rivetting his sinister eye on the point whence the sound had proceeded, retreated in that attitude.

Another and more distinct crush of underwood, and he stood still with surprise on finding himself face to face with two officers of the garrison.

"We have alarmed you, Desborough," said the younger, as they both advanced leisurely to the beach. "Do you apprehend danger from our presence?"

A keen searching glance flashed from the ferocious eye of the Kentuckian. It was but momentary. Quitting his firm grasp of the knife, he suffered his limbs to relax their tension, and aiming at carelessness, observed, with a smile, that was tenfold more hideous from its being forced:

"Well now, I guess, who would have expected to see two officers so far away from the fort at this early hour of the mornin'."

"Ah," said the taller of the two, availing himself of the first opening to a pun — (he was a sad punster) — which had been afforded — "We are merely out on a *shooting* excursion."

Desborough gazed doubtingly on the speaker — "Strange sort of dress that for shootin', I guess — them cloaks must be a great tanglement in the bushes."

"They serve to keep our *arms* warm," continued Middlemore, perpetrating another of his execrables.

"To keep your arms warm! well sure-ly, if that arn't droll. It may be some use to keep the primius dry, I reckon; but I can't see the good of keepin' the fowlin' pieces warm. Have you met any game yet, officers. I expect as how I can pint you out a purty spry place for pattridges and sich like."

"Thank you, my good fellow; but we have appointed to meet our *game* here."

The dry manner in which this was observed had a visible effect on the settler. He glanced an eye of suspicion around, to see if others than the two officers were in view, and it was not without effort he assumed an air of unconcern, as he replied:

"Well, I expect I have been many a long year a hunter, as well as other things, and yet, dang me if I ever calculated the game would come to meet me. It always costs me a purty good chase in the woods."

"How the fellow *beats* about the *bush*, to find what *game* we are driving at," observed Middlemore, in an under tone, to his companion.

"Let the Yankee alone for that," exclaimed his friend—" I will match his cunning against your punning any day."

"The truth is, he is *fishing* to discover our motive for being here, and to find out if we are in any way connected with the disappearance of his rifles."

During this conversation *apart*, the Yankee had carelessly approached his canoe, and was affecting to make some arrangements in the disposition of the sail. The officers, the younger especially, keeping a sharp look out upon his movements, followed at some little distance, until they, at length, stood on the extreme verge of the sands. Their near approach seemed to render Desborough impatient:

"I expect, officers," he said, with a hastiness that, at any other moment, would have called immediate reproof, if not chastisement, "you will only be losin' time here for nothin'—about a mile beyond Hartley's, there'll be plenty of pattridges at this hour, and I am jist goin' to start myself for a little shootin' in the Sandusky River."

"Then, I presume," said the younger officer, with a smile, "you are well provided with silver bullets, Desborough—for, in the hurry of departure, you seem likely to forget the only medium through which leaden ones can be made available: not a rifle or a shot-gun do I see."

The Yankee fixed his eye for a moment, with a penetrating expression, on the youth, as if he would have traced a meaning deeper than the words implied. His reading seemed to satisfy him that all was right.

"What," he observed, with a leer, half cunning, half insolent, "if I have hid my rifle near the Sandusky swamp, the last time I hunted there."

"In that case," observed the laughing Middlemore, to whom the opportunity was irresistible, "you are going out on a *wild goose chase*, indeed. Your prospects of a good hunt, as you call it, cannot be said to *be sure as a gun*, for in regard to the latter, you may depend some one has discovered and *rifled* it before this."

"'You seem to have laid in a store of provisions for this trip, Desborough," remarked the younger officer; "How long do you purpose being absent?"

"I guess three or four days," was the sullen reply.

"Three or four days! why your bag contains," and the officer partly raised a corner of the sail, "provisions for a week, or, at least, for *two* for half that period."

The manner in which the *two* was emphasised did not escape the attention of the settler. He was visibly disconcerted, nor was he all reassured when the younger officer, whom we shall call Grantham, proceeded:

"By the bye, Desborough, we saw you leave the hut with a companion — what has become of him?"

The Yankee, who had now recovered his self-possession, met the question without the slightest show of hesitation:

"I expect you mean, young man," he said, with insufferable insolence, "a help as I had from Hartley's farm, to assist gittin' down the things. He took home along shore when I went back to the hut for the small bores."

"Oh ho, sir! the rifles are not then concealed near the Sandusky swamp, I find."

For once, the wily settler felt his cunning had over-reached itself. In the first fury of his subdued rage, he muttered something amounting to a desire that he could produce then at that moment, as he would well know where to lodge the bullets—but, recovering himself, he said aloud:

"The rale fact is, I've a long gun hid, as I said, near the swamps, but my small bore I always carry with me — only think, jist as I and Hartley's help left the hut, I pit my rifle against the outside wall, not being able to carry it down with the other things, and when I went back a minute or two ater, drot me if some tarnation rascal hadn't stole it.

"And if you had the British rascal on t'other shore, you wouldn't be long in tucking a knife into his gizzard, would you?" asked Middlemore, in a nearly verbatim repetition of the horrid oath originally uttered by Desborough, "I see nothin' to warrant our interfering with him," he continued in an under tone to his companion.

Not a little surprised to hear his words repeated, the Yankee lost somewhat of his confidence as he replied, "Well now surely, you officers didn't think nothing o' that — I expect I was in a mighty rage to find my small bore gone, and I did curse a little hearty to be sure."

"The small bore multiplied in your absence," observed Grantham; "when I looked at the hut there was two."

"Then maybe you can tell who was the particular d——d rascal that stole them," said the settler eagerly.

Middlemore laughed heartily at his companion, who observed:

"The particular d—— d rascal who removed, not stole, them thence stands before you."

Again the Yankee looked disconcerned. After a moment's hesitation, he continued, with a forced grin, that gave an atrocious expression to his whole countenance:

"Well now, you officers are playing a purty considerable spry trick—it's a good lark I calculate—but you know, as the saying is, enough's as good as a feast. Do tell me, Mr. Grantham," and his discordant voice became more offensive in its effort at a tone of entreaty, "do tell where you've hid my small bore — you little think," he concluded, with an emphasis then unnoticed by the officers, but subsequently remembered to have been perfectly ferocious, "what reason I have to vally it."

"We never descend to larks of the kind," coolly observed the youth, "but as you say you value your rifle, it shall be restored to you on one condition."

"And what may that be?" asked the settler, somewhat startled at the serious manner of the officer.

"That you show us what your canoe is freighted with. Here in the bows I mean."

"Why," rejoined the Yankee quickly, but as if without design, intercepting the officers' nearer approach, "that bag, I calculate, contains my provisons, and these here blankets that you see, peepin' like from under the sail, are what I makes my bed of while out huntin'."

"And are you quite certain there is nothing under those blankets? — nay do not protest — you cannot answer for what may have occurred while your back was turned, on your way to the hut for the rifles."

"By Gosh," exclaimed the settler, blusteringly, "were any man to tell me, Jeremiah Desborough, there was any thin' beside them blankets in the canoe, I would lick him into a jelly, even though he could whip his own weight in wild cats."

"So is it? Now then, Jeremiah Desborough, although I have never yet tried to whip my own weight in wild cats, I tell you there is something more than those blankets; and what is more, I insist upon seeing what that something is."

The settler stood confounded. His eye rolled rapidly from one to the other of the officers at the boldness and determination of this language. Singly, he could have crushed Harry Grantham in his grip, even as one of the bears of the forest, near the outskirt of which they stood; but there were two, and while attacking the one, he was sure of being assailed by the other; nay, what was worse, the neighbourhood might be alarmed. Moreover, although they had kept their cloaks carefully wrapped around their persons, there could be little doubt that both officers were armed, not, as they had originally given him to understand, with fowling pieces, but with (at present close quarters at least) far more efficient pistols. He was relieved from his embarrassment by Middlemore exclaiming:

"Nay, do not press the poor devil, Grantham, I dare say the story of his hunting is all a hum, and that the fact is, he is merely going to earn an honest penny in one of his free commercial speculations—a little contraband," pointing with his finger to the bows, "is it not, Desborough?"

"Why now, officer," said the Yankee, rapidly assuming a dogged air, as if ashamed of the discovery that had been so acutely made, "I expect you won't hurt a poor fellor for doin' a little in this way. Drot me, these are hard times, and this here war jist beginnin', quite pits one to one's shifts."

"This might do, Desborough, were your present freight an arrival instead of departure, but we all know that contraband is imported, not exported."

"Mighty cute you are, I guess," replied the settler, warily, with something like the savage grin of the wild cat, to which he had so recently alluded, "'but I expect it would be none so strange to have packed up a few dried hog skins to stow away the goods I am goin' for."

"I should like to try the effect of a bullet among the skins," said Grantham, leisurely drawing forth and cocking a pistol, after having whispered something in the ear of his companion.

"Nay, officer," said Desborough, now for the first time manifesting serious alarm — "you sure*ly* don't mean to bore a hole through them innocent skins?"

"True," said Middlemore, imitating, "if he fires, the hole will be something more than *skin* deep I reckon—these pistols, to my knowledge, send a bullet through a two inch board at twenty paces."

As Middlemore thus expressed himself, both he and Grantham saw, or fancied they saw, the blanket slightly agitated.

"Good place for a *hide* that," said the former, addressing his pun to the Yankee, on whom however it was totally lost, "show us those said skins, my good fellow, and if we find they are not filled with any thing it would be treason in a professed British subject to export thus clandestinely, we promise that you shall depart without further hindrance."

"Indeed, officer," muttered the settler, sullenly and doggedly, "I shan't do no sich thing. You don't belong to the custom-house I reckon, and so I wish you a good day, for I have a considerable long course to run, and must be movin'." Then, seizing the paddles that were lying on the sand, he prepared to shove the canoe from the beach.

"Not at least before I have sent a bullet, to ascertain the true quality of your skins," said Grantham, levelling his pistol.

"Sure*ly*," said Desborough, as he turned and drew himself to the full height of his bony and muscular figure, while his eye measured the officer from head to foot, with a look of concentrated but suppressed fury, "you wouldn't *dare* to do this — you wouldn't dare to fire into my canoe—besides, consider," he said, in a more supplicating tone, "your bullet may go through her, and you would hardly do a fellor the injury to make him lose the chance of a good cargo."

"Then why provoke such a disaster, by refusing to show us what is beneath those blankets?"

"Because it's my pleasure to do so," fiercely retorted the other, "and I won't show them to no man."

"Then it is my pleasure to fire," said Grantham. "The injury be on your own head, Desborough — one — two — "

At that moment the sail was violently agitated — something struggling for freedom, cast the blankets on one side, and presently the figure of a man stood upright in the bows of the canoe, and gazed around him with an air of stupid astonishment.

"What!" exclaimed Middlemore, retreating back a pace or two in unfeigned surprise; "has that pistol started up, like the ghost in *Hamlet*, Ensign Paul Emilius Theophilus Arnoldi, of the United States Michigan Militia? a prisoner on his parole of honour! and yet attempting a clandestine departure from the country—how is this?"

"Not this merely," exclaimed Grantham, "but a traitor to his country, and a deserter from our service. This fellow," he pursued, in answer to an inquiring look of his companion, "is a scoundrel, who deserted three years since from the regiment you relieved — I recognized him yesterday on his landing. Let us secure both, Middlemore, for, thank Heaven, we have been enabled to detect the traitor at last, in that which will cause his final expulsion from the soil, even if no worse befall him. I have only tampered with him thus long to render his conviction more complete."

"Secure me! secure Jeremiah Desborough?" exclaimed the settler, with rage manifested in the clenching of his teeth and the tension of every muscle of his iron frame, "and that for jist tryin' to save a countryman—well, we'll see who'll have the best of it."

Before Grantham could anticipate the movement, the active and powerful Desborough had closed with him in a manner to prevent his making use of his pistol, had he even so desired. In the next instant it was wrested from him, and thrown far from the spot on which he struggled with his adversary, but at fearful odds, against himself. Harry Grantham, although well and actively made, was of slight proportion, and yet in boyhood. Desborough, on the contrary, was in the full force of a vigorous manhood. A struggle, hand to hand, between two combatants so disproportioned, could not, consequently, be long doubtful as to its issue. No sooner had the formidable Yankee closed with his enemy, than, pressing the knuckles of his iron hand which met round the body of the officer, with violence against his spine, he threw him backwards with force upon the sands. Grasping his victim with one hand as he lay upon him, he seemed, as Grantham afterwards declared, to be groping for his knife with the other. The settler was evidently anxious to despatch one enemy, in order that he might fly to the assistance of his son, for it was he whom Middlemore, with a powerful arm, had dragged from the canoe to the beach. While his right hand was still groping for the knife, an object which the powerful resistance of the yet unsubdued, though prostrate, officer rendered somewhat difficult of attainment, the report of a pistol was heard, fired evidently by one of the other combatants. Immediately the settler looked up to see who was the triumphant party. Neither had fallen, and Middlemore, if anything, had the advantage of his enemy; but, to his infinite dismay, he beheld a horseman, evidently attracted by the report of the pistol, urging his noble steed, with the rapidity of lightning, along the firm sands, and advancing with wild cries and vehement gesticulations to the rescue.

Springing with the quickness of thought from his victim, the settler was in the next moment at the side of Middlemore. Seizing him from behind by the arm within his nervous grasp, he pressed the latter with such prodigious force as to cause him to relinquish, by a convulsive movement, the firm hold he had hitherto kept to his adversary.

"In, boy, to the canoe, for your life," he exclaimed hurriedly, as, following up his advantage, he spun the officer round, and sent him tottering to the spot where Grantham lay, still stupified and half throttled. The next instant saw him heaving the canoe from the shore, with all the exertion called for by his desperate situation. And all this was done so rapidly, in so much less time than it will take our readers to trace it, that before the horseman, so opportunely arriving, had reached the spot, the canoe, with all its inmates, had pushed from the shore.

Without pausing to consider the rashness and impracticability of his undertaking, the strange horseman, checking his rein, and burying the rowels of his spurs deep into the flanks of his generous steed, sent him bounding and plunging, like a deer, into the lake, in pursuit of the fugitives.

He himself evinced every symptom of one in a state of intoxication. Brandishing a stout cudgel over his head, and pealing forth shouts of defiance, he rolled from side to side on his spirited charger, like some labouring bark careening to the violence of the winds, but ever, like that bark, regaining an equilibrium that was never thoroughly lost. Shallow as the lake was at this point for a considerable distance, it was long before the noble animal lost its footing, and thus had its rider been enabled to arrive within a few paces of the canoe, at the very moment when the increasing depth of the water, in compelling the horse to the less expeditious process of swimming, gave a proportionate advantage to the pursued. No sooner, however, did the centaur-like rider find that he was *losing ground* than, again darting his spurs into the flanks of his generous charger, he made every effort to reach the canoe. Maddened by the pain, the snorting beast half rose upon the calm element, like some monster of the deep, and, making two or three desperate plunges with his fore feet, succeeded in reaching the stern. Then commenced a momentary but extraordinary conflict. Bearing up his horse as he swam, with his teeth, the bold rider threw his left hand upon the stern of the vessel, and brandishing his cudgel in the right, seemed to provoke both parties to the combat. Desborough, who had risen from the stern at his approach, stood upright in the centre, his companion still paddling at the bows; and, between these two, a singular combat now ensued. Armed with the formidable knife which he had about his person, the settler made the most desperate and infuriated efforts to reach his assailant; but, in so masterly a manner did his adversary use his simple weapon, that every attempt was foiled, and more than once did the hard iron-wood descend upon his shoulders, in a manner to be heard from the shore. Once or twice the settler stopped beneath some falling blow, and, rushing forward, sought to sever the hand which still retained its hold of the stern;

but, with an activity remarkable in so old a man as his assailant, for he was upwards of sixty years of age, the hand was removed —and the settler, defeated in his object, was amply repaid for his attempt, by another severe collision of his bones with the cudgel. At length, apparently enjoined by his companion, the younger removed his paddle, and, standing up also in the canoe, aimed a blow with its knobbed handle at the head of the horse, at a moment when his rider was fully engaged with Desborough. The quick-sighted old man saw the action, and, as the paddle descended, an upward stroke from his own heavy weapon sent it flying in fragments in the air, while a rapid and returning blow fell upon the head of the paddler, and prostrated him at length in the canoe. The opportunity afforded by this diversion, instantaneous as it was, was not lost sight of by Desborough. The horseman, who, in his impatience to save and avenge the injury offered to the animal, which seemed to form a part of himself, had utterly forgotten the peril of his hand; and before he could return from the double blow that had been so skilfully wielded, to his first enemy, the knife of the latter had penetrated his hand, which, divided and powerless as the muscles now were, had relinquished its grasp. Desborough, whose object — desperate character as he usually was — seemed now rather to fly than to fight, availed himself of his advantage to hasten to the bows of his canoe, where, striding across the body of his insensible companion, he, with a few vigorous strokes of the remaining paddle, urged the lagging bark rapidly a-head. In no way intimidated by his disaster, the courageous old man, again brandishing his cudgel, and vociferating taunts of defiance, would have continued the pursuit — but, panting as he was, not only with the exertion he had made, but under the weight of his impatient rider, in an element in which he was supported merely by his own buoyancy, the strength and spirit of the generous steed began now perceptibly to fail him, and he turned, despite of every effort of his rider to prevent him, towards the shore. It was fortunate for the latter there were no arms in the canoe, or neither he nor his horse would, in all probability, have returned alive; such was the opinion, at least, pronounced by those who were witnesses of the strange scene, and who remarked the infuriated but impotent gestures of Desborough, as the old man, having once more gotten his steed into depth, slowly pursued his course towards the shore, but with the same wild brandishing of his enormous cudgel, and the same rocking from side to side, until his body was often at right angles with that of his jaded but sure-footed beast. As he is, however, a character meriting rather more than the casual notice we have bestowed, we may take an early opportunity of again introducing him to our readers.

Brian, the Still Hunter

Susanna Moodie

O'er mem'ry's glass I see his shadow flit,
Though he was gathered to the silent dust
Long years ago: — a strange and wayward man,
Who shunn'd companionship, and lived apart.
The gleamy lakes, hid in their gloomy depths,
Whose still dark waters never knew the stroke
Of cleaving oar, or echoed to the sound
Of social life — contained for him the sum
Of human happiness. With dog and gun,
Day after day he tracked the nimble deer
Through all the tangled mazes of the forest:

AUTHOR.

It was early day, in the fall of 1832. I was alone in the old shanty, preparing breakfast for my husband, and now and then stirring the cradle with my foot, to keep little Katie a few minutes longer asleep, until her food was sufficiently prepared for her first meal — and wishing secretly for a drop of milk to make it more agreeable and nourishing for the poor weanling — when a tall, thin, middle-aged man walked into the house, followed by two large, strong dogs.

Placing the rifle he carried across his shoulder in a corner of the room, he advanced to the hearth, and, without speaking or seemingly looking at me, lighted his pipe, and commenced smoking. The dogs, after growling and snapping at the cat, who had not given the strangers a very courteous reception, sat down on the hearth-stone on either side of their taciturn master, eyeing him from time to time, as if long habit had made them understand all his motions. There was a great contrast between the dogs: the one was a brindled, grey and white bull-dog, of the largest size, — a most formidable and powerful brute; the other, a stag-hound tawny, deep-chested, and strong-limbed. I regarded the man and his hairy companions with silent curiosity. He was between forty and fifty years old: his head, nearly bald, was shaded at the sides by strong, coarse, black, curling hair. His features were high, his complexion brightly dark, and his eyes, in size, shape, and color, resembled the eye of a hawk. The expression of his face was sorrowful and taciturn; and his thin, compressed lips looked as if they were not much accustomed to smiles, or, indeed, often served to hold communication with any one. He stood at the side of the huge hearth, silently smoking, his keen eyes fixed on the fire; and now and then he patted the heads of his dogs, and reproved their exuberant expressions of attachment with — "Down, Chance! Down, Music!"

"A cold, clear morning," said I, in order to attract his attention and draw him into conversation.

A nod without raising his head or taking his eyes off the fire was my only answer; and turning from my unsociable guest, I took up the baby, who just then awoke, sat down on a low stool by the table, and commenced feeding her. During this operation, I once or twice caught the stranger's keen eye fixed upon me; but word spoke he none; and presently after, he whistled to his dogs, resumed his gun, and strode out.

When M——and Monaghan came in to breakfast, I told them what a strange visitor I had; and they laughed at my vain attempts to get him to talk.

"He is a strange, mysterious being," I said. "I must find out who or what he is."

In the afternoon, an old soldier called Layton, who had served during the American war and got a grant of land about a mile in the rear of our location, came in to trade for a cow. Now, this Layton was a perfect ruffian, a man whom no one liked, and whom all feared. He was a deep drinker, a great swearer, and a perfect reprobate, who never cultivated his land, but went jobbing about from farm to farm, trading horses and cattle and cheating in a pettifogging way. Uncle Joe had employed him to sell M——a young heifer, and he had brought her for him to look at.

When he came in to be paid, I described the stranger of the morning; and as I knew that he was familiar with every person in the neighborhood, I asked if he knew him.

"No one should know that better than myself," he said. "'Tis old Brian, the hunter, and a near neighbor of yourn. A sour, morose, queer chap he is, and as mad as a 'March hare'. He's from Lancashire in England, and came to this country some twenty years ago with his wife, Deb, who was a pretty young lass in those days. He had lots of money, too; and he bought four hundred acres of land just at the corner of the concession line where it meets the main road, and excellent land it is; and a better farmer, while he stuck to his business, never went into the bush. He was a dashing, handsome fellow too, and did not hoard the money either. He loved his pipe and his pot too well; and, at last, he left off farming, and stuck to them altogether. Many a jolly booze he and I have had, I can tell you. But Brian was an awful passionate man, and when the liquor was in, and the wit was out, as savage and as quarrelsome as a bear. At such times, there was no one but Ned Layton dared go near him. We once had a pitched battle, and I whipped him; and ever after he yielded a sort of sulky obedience to all I said to him. After being on the spree for a week or two, he would take fits of remorse, and return home to his wife—would go down upon his knees, and ask her forgiveness, and cry like a child. At other times, he would hide himself up in the woods, and steal home at night, and get what he wanted out of the pantry, without speaking a word to any one. He went on with these pranks for some years, till he took a fit of the 'blue devils'.

" 'Come away, Ned, to the Rice Lake with me,' said he. 'I'm weary of my life, and I want a change.'

" 'Shall we take the fishing tackle?' says I. 'The black bass are in prime season, and F——will lend us the old canoe. He's got some capital rum up from Kingston. We'll fish all day, and have a spree at night.'

" 'It's not to fish I'm going,' says he.

" 'To shoot then? I've bought Reckwood's new rifle.'

" 'It's neither to fish nor to shoot, Ned: it's a new game I'm going to try; so, come along.'

"Well, to the Rice Lake we went. The day was very hot, and our path lay through the woods and over those scorching plains for sixteen miles; and I thought I should have dropped by the way but all that distance my comrade never opened his lips. He strode on before me at a half run, never once turning his hard leather face.

" 'The man must be the devil,' says I, 'and accustomed to a warmer place, or he must feel this. Hollo, Brian! stop there! Do you mean to kill me?'

" 'Take it easy,' says he; 'You'll see another day after this. I've business on hand, and cannot wait.'

"Well, on we went, at this awful rate; and it was mid-day when we got to the little tavern on the lake shore, kept by one F——, who had a boat for the convenience of strangers who came to visit the place.

"Here we had our dinner, and a good stiff glass of rum to wash it down. But Brian was moody; and to all my jokes, he only made a sort of grunt; and while I was talking with F——, he slips out, and I saw him crossing the lake in an old canoe.

" 'What's the matter with Brian?' says F——; 'all does not seem right with him, Ned. You had better take the boat, and look after him.'

" 'Phoo!' says I, 'he's often so, and grows so glum now-a-days that I will cut his acquaintance altogether if he does not improve.'

" 'He drinks awful hard,' says F——; 'there's no telling what he may be up to at this minute.'

"My mind misgave me, too; so I e'en takes the oars and pushes out right upon Brian's track; and, by the Lord Harry! if I did not find him, upon my landing on the opposite shore, lying, wallowing in his blood, with his throat cut!

" 'Is that you, Brian?' says I, giving him a kick with my foot. 'What upon earth tempted you to play F—— and me this dirty, mean trick; to go and stick yourself like a pig — bring such a discredit on the house — and so far from home, too, and those who should nurse you!'

"I was so wild with him, that, saving your presence, ma'am, I swore awfully, and called him names which would be undacent to repeat here; but he only answered by groans and a horrid gurgling in his throat.

" 'It's choking you are,' said I; 'but you shan't have your own way, and die so easily either, if I can punish you by keeping you alive.' So I just turned him upon his belly, with his head down the steep bank; but he still kept choking and growing black in the face. I then saw that it was a piece of the flesh of his throat that had been carried into his wind-pipe. So, what do I do but puts in my finger and thumb and pulls it out, and bound up his throat with my handkerchief, dipping it first in the water to stanch the blood. I then took him, neck and heels, and threw him into the bottom of the boat, and pushed off for the tavern. Presently, he came to himself a little, and sat up in the boat, and, would you believe it? made several attempts to throw himself into the water. 'This will not do,' says I; 'you've done mischief enough already by cutting your wizzand; if you dare to try that again, I will kill you with the oar.' I held it up, threatening him all the while; and he was scared, and lay down as quiet as a lamb. I put my foot upon his breast. 'Lie still now, or you'll catch it.' He looked piteously at me, but he could not speak; but he seemed to say — 'Have pity upon me, Ned; don't kill me' Yes; this man, who had cut his throat, and who, twice after that, tried to drown himself, was afraid that I should knock him on the head, and kill him. Ha! ha! I never shall forget the work F—— and I had with him.

"The doctor came, and sewed up his throat; and his wife — poor crater! — came to nurse him; and he lay bad there for six months and did nothing but pray to God to forgive him; for he throught the devil would surely have him for cutting his own throat. And when he got about again — which is now twelve years ago — he left off drinking entirely, and wanders about the country with his dogs, hunting. He seldom speaks to any one, and his wife's brother carries on the farm for him and the family. He is so shy of strangers that it is a wonder he came in here. The old wives are afraid of him; but you need not heed him; his troubles are to himself, he harms no one."

Layton departed, and left me brooding over the sad tale he had told me in such an absurd and jesting manner. It was evident, from the account he had given of Brian's attempt at suicide, that the hapless hunter was not wholly answerable for his conduct — that he was a harmless monomaniac.

The next morning, at the very same hour, Brian again made his appearance; but instead of the rifle across his shoulder, a large stone jar was suspended by a stout leathern thong. Without speaking a word, but with a truly benevolent smile that flitted slowly over his stern features, and lighted them up like a sunbeam breaking from beneath a stormy cloud, he advanced to the table and, unslinging the jar, set it down before me, and in a low, gruff, but not unfriendly voice, said:

"Milk for the child," and vanished.

"How good it was of him! — how kind!" I exclaimed, as I poured the precious gift of four quarts of pure, new milk out into a deep pan — "and I never asked him, never said that the poor babe wanted milk. It was the courtesy of a gentleman, of a man of benevolence and refinement."

For weeks did my strange friend steal silently in, take up the empty jar, and supply its place with another, replenished with milk. The baby knew his step, and would hold out her hands to him, and cry, "Milk!" and Brian would stoop down and kiss her, and his two great dogs lick her face.

"Have you any children, Mr. B——?"

"Yes, five; but not like this — "

"My little girl is greatly indebted to you for your kindness."

"She's welcome, or she would not get it. You are strangers, but I like you all. You look kind, and I would like to know more about you."

M—— shook hands with the old hunter, and assured him that he should always be glad to see him.

After this invitation, Brian became a frequent guest. He would sit and listen with delight to M——, while he described to him elephant hunting at the Cape, grasping his rifle with a determined air, and whistling an encouraging air to his dogs. I asked him one evening what made him so fond of hunting?

" 'Tis the excitement," he said; "it drowns thought; and I love to be alone. I am sorry for the creatures, too, for they are free and happy; but I am led, by an impulse I cannot restrain, to kill them. Sometimes, the sight of their dying agonies recalls painful feelings; and then I lay aside the gun, and do not hunt for days. But 'tis fine to be alone, with God, in the great woods—to watch the sunbeams stealing through the thick branches — the blue sky breaking in upon you in patches; and to know that all is bright and shiny above you, in spite of the gloom which surrounds you."

After a long pause, he said, with much solemn feeling in his look and tone:

"I lived a life of folly for years — for I was well born and educated before I left home for the woods, and should have known better; but if we associate long with the depraved and ignorant, we learn to become even worse than them. I felt I had become a slave to low vice and sin. I hated myself; and in order to free myself from the hateful tyranny of evil passions, I did a very rash and foolish action. I need not mention the manner in which I transgressed God's laws — all the neighbors know it, and must have told you long ago. I could have borne reproof, but they turned my sorrow into indecent jests; and, unable to bear their ridicule, I made companions of my dogs and gun, and went forth into the wilderness. Hunting became a habit—I could no longer live without it—and it supplies the stimulant which I lost when I renounced the cursed whisky bottle.

"I remember the first hunting excursion I took alone in the forest, how sad and gloomy I felt. I thought there was no creature in the world so miserable as me; I was tired and hungry, and I sat down upon a fallen tree to rest. All was still as death around me; and I was fast sinking to sleep, when my attention was aroused by a long wild cry. My dog—for I had not Chance then, and he is no hunter—pricked up his ears, but instead of answering with a bark of defiance, he crouched down, trembling, at my feet. 'What does this mean?' I said; and I cocked my gun, and sprang upon the log. The sound came nearer upon the wind. It was like the deep baying of a pack of hounds in full cry. Presently, a noble deer rushed madly past me, and fast upon his trail—I see them now, like so many black devils—swept by, a pack of ten or fifteen large fierce wolves, with fiery eyes and bristling hair, and paws that seemed scarcely to touch the ground in their eager haste. I thought not of danger, for, with their prey in view, I was safe; but

I felt every nerve within me tremble for the poor deer. The wolves gained upon him at every step: a close thicket intercepted his path; and rendered desperate, he turned at bay. His nostrils were dilated; his eyes seemed to send forth long streams of light. It was wonderful to witness the courage of the beast—how bravely he repelled the first attack of his deadly enemies—how gallantly he tossed them to the right and left, and spurned them from beneath his hoofs; yet all his struggles were useless, and he was quickly torn to pieces by his ravenous foes. At that moment, he seemed more unfortunate than me; for I could not see in what manner he had deserved his fate. All his speed and energy, his courage and fortitude, had been given to him in vain. I had tried to destroy myself; but he, with every effort vigorously made for self-preservation, was doomed to meet the fate he dreaded. Is God just to his creatures?"

With this sentence in his throat, he started abruptly from his seat, and left the house.

One day he found me painting some wild flowers, and was greatly amused in watching the progress I made in the group. Late in the afternoon of the following day, he brought me a large bunch of splendid spring flowers.

"Draw these," he said; "I have been all the way to the Rice Lake Plains to find them for you."

"Oh! pretty, pretty flowers," lisped Katie, grasping them with infantine joy, and kissing, one by one, every lovely blossom.

"Those are God's pictures," said the hunter; "and the child, who is all nature just now, understands them in a minute. Is it not strange, Mrs. M——, that these beautiful things are hid away in the wilderness, where no eyes but the birds of the air, and the wild beasts of the woods, and the insects that live upon them, ever see them? Does God provide, for the pleasure of such creatures, these flowers? When I am alone in the forest, these things puzzle me."

Knowing that to argue with Brian was only to call into action the slumbering fires of his fatal malady, I asked him why he called the dog Chance?

"I found him," he said, "forty miles back in the bush. He was a mere skeleton. At first I took him for a wolf, but the shape of his head undeceived me. I opened my wallet, and called him to me. He came slowly, stopping and wagging his tail at every step, and looking me wistfully in the face. I offered him a bit of cooked venison, and he soon became friendly, and followed me home, and has never left me, night or day, since. I called him Chance, after the manner I happened with him; and I would not part with him for twenty dollars."

Alas! for poor Chance! he had, unknown to his master, contracted a private liking for fresh mutton; and one night he killed no less than eight sheep belonging to Mr. D——, on the front road, who, having long suspected, caught him in the very act; and this mischance cost him his life. Brian was very sad and gloomy for many weeks after his favourite's death.

"I would have restored the sheep, four-fold," he said, "if he would but have spared the life of my dog."

All my recollections of Brian seem more particularly to concentrate in the adventures of one night, when I happened to be left alone for the first time since my arrival in Canada. I cannot now imagine how I could have been such a fool as to give way for four and twenty hours to such childish fears; but so it was, and I will not disguise the truth from my readers. M——had bought a very fine cow of a black man named Mollineux, who lived twelve miles distant through the woods, and one fine, frosty spring day, he and John Monaghan took a rope and the dog to fetch her home. M——said that they should be back by six o'clock in the evening, and to mind and have something cooked for supper when they returned, as their long walk and the sharp air would give them a great appetite. This was during the time that I was without a female servant, and lived in old Mrs. H——'s shanty.

The day was so bright and clear, and Katie was so full of frolic and play, rolling about the floor or toddling from chair to chair, that the day passed on without my feeling remarkably lonely. At length the evening drew nigh, and I began to expect the return of my beloved, and to think of the supper I was to prepare for his reception. The red heifer came lowing to the door to be milked, but I did not know how to milk in those days, and was terribly afraid of the cattle. Yet as I knew milk must be had for the tea, I ran across to Mrs. Joe, and begged that one of her girls would be so kind as to milk for me. My request was greeted with a rude burst of laughter from the whole set.

"If you can't milk," says Mrs. Joe, "it is high time you should learn. My gals are above being helps."

"I would not ask you but as a favor; I am afraid of cows."

"*Afraid of cows!*" Here followed another hoarse laugh; and indignant at the refusal of the first request I had ever made, when they had all borrowed so much from me, I shut the door, and returned home.

After many ineffectual attempts I succeeded at last, and bore my half pail of milk in triumph to the house. Yes! I felt prouder of that milk than the best thing I ever wrote, whether in verse or prose; and then it was doubly sweet when I considered that I had procured it without being under any obligation to my ill-natured neighbors.

I fed little Katie and put her to bed, made the hot cakes for tea, boiled the potatoes, and laid the ham cut in nice slices in the pan, ready to cook the moment I saw the men enter the clearing, and arranged the little room with scrupulous care and neatness. A glorious fire was blazing on the hearth, and everything was ready for their supper, and I began to look out anxiously for their arrival. The night had closed in cold and foggy, and I could no longer distinguish any object a few yards from the door. Bringing in as much wood as I thought would last me for a few hours, I closed the door, and for the first time in my life, found myself in a house entirely alone. Then I began to ask myself a thousand torturing questions as to the reason of their unusual absence. "Had they lost their way in the woods? could they have fallen in with wolves? — one of my early bugbears — could any fatal accident have befallen them?" I started up, opened the door, held my breath, and listened. The little brook lifted up its voice in loud hoarse wailing, or mocked, in its bubbling to the stones, the sound of human voices. As it became later, my fears increased in proportion. I grew too superstitious to keep the door open, and not only closed it, but dragged a heavy box in front of it. Several ill-looking men had asked their way to Toronto during the day; and I felt alarmed lest such rude wayfarers should come to-night, and find me alone and unprotected. Once I thought of running across to Mrs. Joe and asking her to let one of the girls to stay with me till M——returned; but the way in which I had been repulsed in the evening deterred me.

Hour after hour wore away, and the crowing of the cocks proclaimed midnight, and yet they came not. I had burnt out all my wood, and I dared not open the door to fetch in more. The candle was expiring in the socket, and I had not courage to go up into the loft, before it went finally out, to set up another. Cold, heart-weary, and faint, I sat in the middle of the floor, and cried. The furious barking of the dogs at the neighboring farms, and the cackling of the geese on our own place, made me hope they were coming; and then I listened, till the beating of my own heart excluded all other sounds. Oh! that weary brook! how it sobbed and moaned, like a fretful child! What unreal terrors and fanciful illusions my too active mind conjured up, while listening to its mysterious tones!

Just as the moon rose, the howling of a pack of wolves, from the great swamp in our rear, filled the whole air. The yells were answered by the barking of all the numerous dogs in the vicinity; and the geese, unwilling to be behind hand in the general confusion, set up the most discordant screams. I had often heard, and even been amused, during the winter, particularly on thaw nights, by the howls of these formidable wild beasts; but I had never before heard them alone, and my fears reached a climax. They were directly on the track that M——and Monaghan must have taken, — and I now made no doubt that they had been attacked and killed on their return and I wept and cried, until the grey cold dawn looked in upon me through the small dim windows. I have passed many a long, cheerless night; but that was the saddest and longest I ever remember. Just as the day broke, my friends, the wolves, set up a parting benediction, so loud and wild, and so near the house, that I was afraid that they would come through the windows, or down the chimney, and rob me of my child. But the howls died away in the distance; the bright sun rose up, and dispersed the long horrors of the night; and I looked once more timidly around me. The sight of the uneaten supper for a few minutes renewed my grief, for I could not divest myself of the idea that M——was dead. I opened the door, and stepped forth into the pure air of the early day. A solemn and beautiful repose still hung, like a veil over the face of nature. The mists of night still rested upon the majestic woods; and not a sound but the flowing of the waters went up in the vast stillness. The earth had not yet raised her matin hymn to the Throne the Creator. Sad at heart, and weary and worn in spirit, I went down to the spring, and washed my face and head, and drank a deep draught of its icy waters. On returning to the house, I met, near the door, old Brian the hunter, with a large fox across his shoulder, and the dogs following at his heels.

"Good God! Mrs. M——, what is the matter? You are early up, and look dreadfully ill. Is anything wrong at home? Is the baby or your husband sick?"

"Oh, no!" I cried, bursting into tears; "I fear he is eaten by the wolves."

The man stared at me as if he doubted the evidence of his senses, and well he might; but this one idea had taken such strong possession of my mind that I would admit no other. I then told him, as well as I could, the cause of my alarm, to which he listened very kindly and patiently.

"Set your heart at rest, Mrs. M —— ; he is safe. It is a long journey, on foot, to Mollineux's, and they have stayed all night at his shanty. You will see them back at noon."

I shook my head, and continued to weep.

"Well, now, in order to satisfy you, I will saddle my mare, and ride over to Mollineux's, and bring you word as fast as I can."

I thanked him sincerely for his kindness, and returned in somewhat better spirits to the house. At ten o'clock, my messenger returned with the glad tidings that M——was safe, and on his way home.

The day before, when half the journey was accomplished, John Monaghan had let go the rope by which he had led the cow, and she had returned to her old master; and when they again reached his place, night had set in, and they were obliged to wait until the return of day.

Brian's eldest son—a lad of fourteen—was not exactly an idiot, but what, in the Old Country, the common people designate a *natural*. He could feed and assist himself and even go on errands to and from the town, and to the neighboring farm-houses; but he was a strange creature, who evidently inherited, in no small degree, the father's malady. During the summer months he lived entirely in the woods near his father's house, and only returned to obtain food, which was generally left for him in an out-house. In the winter, driven home by the severity of the weather, he would sit for days together moping in the chimney corner, without taking notice of anything passing around him. Brian never mentioned this boy—who had a strong active figure, and rather a handsome, though perfectly inexpressive, face—without a deep sigh; and I feel certain that half his own dejection was caused by painful reflections occasioned by the mental aberrations of his child.

One day he sent the lad with a note to our house to know if we would purchase the half of an ox he was about to kill. There happened to stand in the corner of the room an open wood-box, into which several bushels of apples had been thrown; and while M—— was writing an answer to the note, the eyes of the idiot were fastened, as if by some magnetic influence, upon the apples. Knowing that they had a very fine orchard, I did not offer him any, because I thought it would be useless so to do.

When the note was finished, I handed it to him. The boy grasped it mechanically, without removing his fixed gaze from the apples.

"Give that to your father."

The lad answered not; his ears, his eyes, his whole soul were concentrated in the apples. Ten minutes elapsed; but he stood motionless, like a pointer at a dead set.

"My good boy, you can go."

Still, he did not stir.

"Is there anything you want?"

"I want," said the lad, without moving his eyes from the object of his intense desire, and speaking in a slow, pointed manner, which ought to have been heard to be fully appreciated—"I want apples."

"Oh! if that's all; take what you like."

The permission once obtained, the boy flung himself upon the box with the rapacity of a hawk upon its prey, after being long poised in air to fix its certain aim. Thrusting his hands to the right and left in order to secure the finest specimens of the coveted fruit, scarcely allowing himself time to breathe, until he had filled his old straw hat and all his pockets. To help laughing was impossible; while this new "Tom o' Bedlam" darted from the house and scampered across the field for dear life, as if afraid that we should pursue him to rob him of his prize.

It was during this winter that our friend Brian was left a fortune of three hundred pounds per annum; but it was necessary for him to return to his native country and county in order to take possession of the property. This he positively refused to do; and when we remonstrated with him upon the apparent imbecility of this resolution, he declared that he would not risk his life in crossing twice the Atlantic for twenty times that sum. What strange inconsistency was this, in a being who had three times attempted to take away that life which he dreaded so much to lose accidentally!

I was much amused with an account, which he gave me, in his quaint way, of an excursion he went upon with a botanist, to collect specimens of the plants and flowers of Upper Canada.

"It was a fine spring day, some ten years ago; and I was yoking my oxen to drag in some oats I had just sown, when a little, fat, punchy man with a broad, red, good-natured face, and carrying a small black leathern wallet across his shoulder, called to me over the fence, and asked me if my name was Brian. I said, 'Yes; what of that?'

" 'Only, you are the man whom I want to see. They tell me that you are better acquainted with the woods than any person in these parts; and I will pay you anything in reason, if you will be my guide for a few days.'

" 'Where do you want to go?' said I.

" 'No where in particular,' says he. 'I want to go here, and there, in all directions, to collect plants and flowers.'

" 'That is still-hunting with a vengeance,' said I. 'To-day I must drag in my oats. If to-morrow will suit, we will be off.'

" 'And your charge?' said he: 'I like to be certain of that.'

" 'A dollar a day. My time and labor just now upon my farm is worth that.'

" 'True,' said he. 'Well, I will give you what you ask. At what time will you be ready to start?'

" 'By day-break, if you wish it.'

"Away he went; and by day-light next morning, he was at my door, mounted upon a stout French pony.

" 'What are you going to do with that beast?' said I. 'Horses are of no use on the road that you and I are to travel. You had better leave him in my stable.'

" 'I want him to carry our traps,' said he. 'It may be some days that we shall be absent.'

"I assured him that he must be his own beast of burden, and carry his axe and blanket and wallet of food upon his own back. The little body did not much relish this arrangement; but as there was no help for it, he very good-naturedly complied. Off we set, and soon climbed the hills at the back of your farm, and got upon the Rice Lake Plains. The woods were flush with flowers; and the little man grew into such an extasy that at every fresh specimen he uttered a yell of joy, cut a caper in the air, and flung himself down upon them, as if he were drunk with delight.

" 'Oh! what treasures! what treasures!' he cried. 'I shall make my fortune!'

" 'It is seldom I laugh,' quoth Brian; 'but I could not help laughing at this odd little man; for it was not the beautiful blossoms that drew forth these exclamations, but the queer little plants which he had rummaged for at the roots of old trees, among the moss and long grass. He sat upon a decayed tree, which lay in our path, for an hour, making a long oration over some greyish things which grew out of it, which looked more like mould than plants; declaring himself repaid for all the trouble and the expense he had been at, if it were only to obtain a sight of them. I gathered him a beautiful blossom of lady's slipper; but he pushed it back when I presented it to him, saying:

" 'Yes, yes; 'tis very fine; I have seen that often before; but these lichens are splendid!'

"The man had so little taste that I thought him a fool, and left him to talk to his dear plants while I shot partridges for our supper. We spent six days in the woods; and the little man filled his wallet with all sorts of rubbish, as if he wilfully shut his eyes to the beautiful flowers, and chose only to admire the ugly, insignificant plants that even a chipmunk would have passed without noticing, and which, often as I had been in the woods, I never had observed before. I never pursued a deer with such earnestness as he continued his hunt for what he called 'specimens'. When we came to the Cold Creek, which is pretty deep in places, he was in such a hurry to get at some plants that grew under the water that he lost his balance, and fell, head over heels into the stream. He got a thorough ducking, and was in a terrible fright; but he held on to the flowers which had caused the trouble, and thanked his stars that he had saved them, as well as his life. Well, he was an innocent man," continued Brian—"a very little made him happy; and at night he would sing and amuse himself, like a little child. He gave me ten dollars for my trouble, and I never saw him again; but I often think of him when hunting in the woods we wandered through together; and I pluck the wee plants he used to admire, and wonder why he preferred them to the fine flowers."

When our resolution was formed to sell our farm and go upon our grant of land in the backwoods, no one was so earnest in trying to persuade us from our ruinous plan as our friend Brian, who became quite eloquent in his description of the trials and troubles which awaited us. During the last week of our stay, he visited us every evening, and never bade us good-night without a tear moistening his eyes. We parted with the hunter as with an old friend, and we never saw him again.

His fate was a sad one. He fell into a moping melancholy, which ended in self-destruction — but a kinder or warmer-hearted man, while he enjoyed the light of reason, has seldom crossed our path.

Alice Sydenham's First Ball

Mrs. Rosanna Leprohon

> Fill the bright goblet, spread the festive board
> Summon the gay, the noble and the fair;
> Through the loud hall, in joyous concert pour'd,
> Let mirth and music sound the dirge of care —
> But ask not thou if happiness be there.

SCOTT.

"MAMMA, dear mamma, may I not go to Mrs. Belmont's party to-morrow night?" exclaimed Alice Sydenham, awakening from the revery in which she had been absorbed for the previous half hour.

The lady, at whose feet she sat, laid down the book which had engrossed her attention, and replied with gentle earnestness:

"My dear child, wherefore should you wish to go? The Belmonts are people entirely out of our present sphere, and though Mrs. Belmont herself, remembering your early school girl friendship, may have extended you this invitation, her memory refreshed, as it has lately been, by meeting you some few weeks since, on your return from the country; believe me, she has no serious intention of keeping up your revived acquaintance. She knows our circumstances perfectly well, knows that, whatever our condition may at one time have been, at present we have barely the means of subsistence, and she doubtless supposes you will regard the card you have received in the same light as that in which it was sent, an unmeaning compliment. Where would a poor, portionless girl, like you, find means for procuring the splendid dress necessary to your appearing in her fashionable and gorgeous drawing rooms?"

A long pause followed, broken at length by her young companion, who exclaimed, whilst a very perceptible cloud passed over her countenance:

"And to think, mamma, — to think that you have a rich uncle, who is surrounded by all the luxuries of life, an uncle who possesses no other living relative, save yourself."

"True, Alice, but by his own patient, unremitting industry

alone has he amassed his wealth, and it is but just he should dispose of it as best pleases him. I never was a favourite with him. How could I be? Brought up from earliest childhood at a boarding school, miles from home, I never saw him but three times in my life."

"Did you ever see him after your marriage?"

"Never; your father brought me immediately to my new home, in a distant part of England, and thus effectually precluded all further intercourse. However, about a month after your poor father's death, I received a letter from him, enclosing the sum of twenty pounds, which he has regularly transmitted to us, every new year, till the last. He must be either ill, or abroad; but doubtless we will speedily receive the usual sum, for surely he cannot be so cruel as to deprive us so suddenly, without any plausible pretext, of what has for years proved our chief, I may say, our only support."

"And has he never written to you but once, mamma?"

"Never — the letter enclosing his earliest remittance was his first and last. It was a cold, formal missive indeed, informing me, in measured terms, that he had heard of Mr. Sydenham's decease, and of my destitution, a natural consequence of wedding a young gentleman whose only possessions were a graceful address, and high lineage, concluding by assuring me the annuity should be continued as long as I remained deserving of it, and peremptorily forbidding my seeking further intercourse with him, either in person or by letter."

"Well! we will talk of him no more, mamma; I am sure 'tis anything but a pleasant topic. I will sing some lively ballad to chase away any sad thoughts which the remembrance of this open-hearted uncle of ours may have excited."

And she advanced towards the piano forte, but notwithstanding the seeming cheerfulness of her tones, there was a slight quivering of the lip, and an almost imperceptible shade of sadness in the full, soft eye, which the observant mother at once detected.

"Come here, Alice," she said, pointing to the stool her daughter had quitted.

The latter silently obeyed.

"You cannot deceive me, my child. You feel this deprivation more acutely than you are willing to avow; but Alice, Alice—this is childish," she continued, as her daughter, whose assumed fortitude suddenly deserted her, burst into tears. "You are sixteen years of age, and to weep thus, like a child, for so trivial a disappointment."

There was a kind smile, however, hovering round the mother's lips, which contradicted the seeming reproof her words conveyed.

"But 'tis my first ball," sobbed the young girl; "and you know now long and earnestly I have desired to go to one. You remember, in the winter evenings, how I have listened to you for hours, describing those at which you assisted in your youth, and the first years of your marriage; scarcely daring to indulge a hope that I might ever have the happiness of witnessing such a scene of brilliancy; and now, when I have the opportunity, 'tis too hard to be disappointed."

"You shall not be disappointed, my child, for you shall go; but dry up those tears. Really I would scold, only 'tis so very seldom you indulge in them. Ah! sunshine is restored," she added, as, with a radiant smile, Alice looked up into her mother's face. "Now tell me, dearest, what are the pleasures you expect at this ball? Let me see if their loss is worth weeping for."

The young girl's cheek flushed.

"Why, dear mother, novelty, gaiety, and — and — "

"Admiration," subjoined her mother, quietly.

"And admiration too," was the low-toned reply.

A pause succeeded, when Alice, suddenly raising her dark, lustrous eyes to her mother's face, exclaimed:

"And why not admiration, mamma? I have been always told I am a graceful dancer, and am I not handsome?"

"Yes, you *are* handsome," replied Mrs. Sydenham gravely, and for a moment her glance rested with earnestness on the brilliant complexion and raven tresses of her beautiful daughter. "You are handsome and graceful; yet, Alice, possessing both these qualifications, as I have often told you, you may find yourself greatly neglected, and feel very miserable at a ball."

"Let me make the experiment, mamma dear," was the girlish rejoinder.

"You shall, dear Alice," smilingly returned Mrs. Sydenham, who, as she looked on the sparkling eyes and sweet smile dimpling the rose-bud mouth of her companion, felt how improbable it was that her forebodings would be realized. "And may it prove satisfactory—but away and prepare your gay attire. You have not much time."

With the sparkling delight of a child, the young girl bounded from the room to enter on her task; and a difficult task it was indeed, for poor Alice's wardrobe contained not one single one of the many articles indispensable to that of any ball-going young lady. However, Mrs. Sydenham ventured on the unusual extravagance of purchasing a white tarlatane dress, whilst Alice expended a little hoard she had been for months accumulating for the purchase of new books and music in the absolute requisites of kid gloves, shoes, flowers, &c. The important night at length arrived, and long before any of the fashionable invited had thought of entering on the duties of the toilet, Alice, her preparations nearly completed, sat in her mother's room, awaiting her new dress, which had not yet arrived—half reclining in an easy chair, her dreamy gaze fixed on the carpet, as if absorbed in contemplating its dull, faded pattern; for one long hour she sat without proffering a word. Suddenly Mrs. Sydenham, who had been regarding her some time in silence, exclaimed:

"Why, Alice, you are unusually, wonderfully pre-occupied. What are you thinking of?"

A flood of vivid carnation instantly dyed her cheek and brow, as, after a second's hesitation, she murmured:

"Of to-night and its pleasures, dear mamma."

Ah! Alice! Alice! That answer, though partly true, was not what it should have been. The ball indeed occupied those thoughts, but only as connected with a still more engrossing subject. It was of Henry St. John, the handsome and elegant brother of Mrs. Belmont, a being she had never met but once, and that only for a few minutes in the company of his sister, but whose high-bred politeness, and evident admiration of herself, had left a deep and durable impression on her mind. 'Twere hard to say how many aëriel castles she had constructed during the hour she had sat wrapped in silent revery; but however wild or improbable they may have been, she ever finished the construction of each by the sober, natural thought:

"I shall at least see him, for he will be there, and surely he will ask me *once* to dance."

But her mother's address dispelled, at least for the moment, her fleeting visions, and after replying to her question, she suddenly remembered that her dress, that dress whose vast importance she alone could thoroughly appreciate, had not yet come home. Looking at the timepiece, however, she saw it was still early, and after reviewing again every article to see that all was complete, she sat down to her instrument to wile away the time, and practise a few songs and pieces in case she should be called on to play; but hour after hour passed on, and still the priestess of fashion with her priceless treasure, the dress, came not. Poor Alice, who had long previously abandoned her instrument, and endeavoured to dispel her nervous impatience by pacing the room with rapid steps, felt her hopefulness gradually ebbing, and at length, when ten o'clock struck, her fortitude completely overcome, she flung herself on the sofa in a paroxysm of tears. Mrs. Sydenham, really sympathizing with her natural distress, kindly endeavoured to soothe her, reminding her it was not yet too late for fashionable hours, and that Mrs. Graham, the lady who had undertaken to *chaperone* her, being an ultra-fashionable, would not probably call for some time to come.

"Dry your tears, my own Alice," she said, raising carefully the rich tresses of her daughter, which the latter in her emotion had entirely forgotten. "See, your curls are already commencing to droop; they are positively damp, and your eyes, my dear child, will be quite red."

" 'Tis useless! mother, useless!" was the sobbing reply; "and there is Mrs. Graham's ring," she added, starting, as the hall bell pealed violently, from the sofa, on which she however immediately threw herself again with a fresh burst of grief. "Go, and tell her 'tis impossible for me to go."

With a slow step Mrs. Sydenham left the room, but she almost immediately returned, and, with a beaming countenance, exclaimed:

" 'Tis not Mrs. Graham, Alice, but the girl with your dress. Quick, quick, here it is!"

Her daughter sprang to her feet with a bright smile, though the tears yet hung on her long lashes, and proceeded to try on the dress. But alas! fresh disappointments! slight, graceful as Alice's figure was, the milliner had thought fit to improve on it, and accordingly had made the dress so tight that, when strained to the utmost, the lower hooks were still nearly an inch apart.

"Positively, this is too provoking!" exclaimed Mrs. Sydenham, almost as much annoyed as her daughter. "Why, it would not fit an infant. 'Tis no use," she added as the girl, after another superhuman effort, fell on a chair in sheer exhaustion, her face scarlet with her exertions. "Take it off again," said Alice quietly, seating herself with the calmness of despair. A solemn pause succeeded during which the spectators looked at each other in funereal silence, when suddenly a bright idea entered the head of Alice's humble tirewoman:

"Sure, Miss, you can hide it with your sash." The suggestion was like the plank to the drowning mariner, the well-spring in the desert, and was promptly, eagerly acted upon; but many a crease and ungraceful fold was the sad consequence. This, however, was of minor importance, as the milliner, who was anything but a proficient in her art — poor Alice could not afford to procure the services of a better — had left so many proofs of her skill in the shape of numberless awkward discrepancies and creases that those formed by the subterfuge of the sash passed undistinguished, if not unobserved. The dress, however, was at length adjusted; and now the gloves had to be tried, but they were certainly many removes from French kid, for with the first effort made to draw them on, one finger tore from top to bottom. Poor Alice was by this time, however, inured to misfortune, and the only additional evidence of annoyance perceptible was in the deepening of her former faint flush into intense scarlet. The glove, however, was at length mended, the white rose placed in the dark hair, and the last act of the drama, the large cloak thrown over her, when a furious peal at the bell announced the arrival of her *chaperone.*

With a hasty kiss from her mother, Alice, without a parting look at her mirror, hurried down stairs, sprang into Mrs. Graham's carriage, and, secure in the consciousness that all her dreams, her hopes, were now on the point of fulfilment, sank back with a sigh of relief on its cushioned seat. Mrs. Graham happened to be in a very ill temper, and it was not therefore in the most amiable of tones she exclaimed: "I hope you will excuse me, Miss Sydenham, for being so late; but I have only just returned from the Opera, and I scarcely waited to change an article of dress. Indeed, had it not been for my promise to Mrs. Sydenham and yourself, I should have dismissed all thought of appearing in Mrs. Belmont's rooms to-night."

Her young companion, who felt greatly disconcerted by this communication, murmured some inarticulate words about gratitude, thanks, and a long pause followed. Suddenly, Mrs. Graham asked, "if she were acquainted with any of the expected guests."

"I know none but Mrs. Belmont herself — and Mr. St. John," she added, after a moment's hesitation.

"Both passable people in their way," rejoined the lady in a careless tone; "but Mrs. Belmont is one of the most capricious, uncertain women I know of, and Henry St. John is — but what do you think of him?"

It was well for Alice that the darkness hid from Mrs. Graham's penetrating eye the vivid flush that overspread her cheek. The consciousness, however, that her companion could not read her countenance enabled her to reply with the most perfect calmness.

"Indeed, I am scarcely competent to pass any opinion on Mr. St. John, as I have never spent more than a half hour altogether in his society."

"Well! I will give you his character, and in a few words too, for I *pique* myself on my brevity and clearness, at least in describing the weaknesses of my friends. Henry St. John is a young gentle-man, strikingly like most of his class, very handsome, very elegant, and very conceited. Passing rich, and well-born too, he thinks so many qualifications exempt him from the necessity of ever troubling himself in the slightest degree about any body, or even stooping to be polite to any one, unless he have some peculiar end in view. Then he can render himself almost irresistible."

Alice remembered at the moment with gratitude, and it must be confessed a slight tincture of vanity, that this well-born, handsome, haughty individual had thought it worth while to be not only polite, but particularly attentive to herself. She did not however reply, and Mrs. Graham, after a few additional remarks of the same charitable nature, suddenly awoke to the consciousness that she was wasting her powers of satire and comment on one of the *uninitiated,* an individual who, being out of her sphere, could not appreciate them. She therefore relapsed into silence, which remained unbroken till they stopped before Mrs. Belmont's elegant mansion. The brilliantly illuminated windows, before which light indistinct figures were perpetually passing and repassing, the rich strains of music, the confused sounds of voices and laughter, betokened that mirth and festivity were in full flow.

"We are very late!" was Mrs. Graham's exclamation, as, after ascending the wide staircase, she threw herself on a couch in the elegent but deserted drawing room. "However, we shall have the mirrors entirely to ourselves. That is some consolation. Really," she added, as the waiting maid divested her of her cloaks and shawls, "I never felt less disposed for gaiety. Carelessly dressed, looking so shockingly ill," and she cast anything but a pleasant glance at her figure, which a superb mirror opposite reflected at full length. Alice turned, and that toilette, so slightingly spoken of, fairly dazzled her — a light gossamer fabric of delicate pink over rich white satin, looped up with bows of delicate beauty; and then the exquisite wreath encircling the plain, glossy hair, the splendid bracelets and rings. The heart of poor Alice sank within her; and as the reflection: "Perhaps they are all dressed like her, even more elegantly," presented itself, she was conscious for the first time of an almost involuntary wish that she could transport herself at once to her mother's quiet happy room; but she had little time to indulge in aspirations of any sort, for Mrs. Graham, who had just despatched the maid on some commission, turned, exclaiming:

"And, now, Miss Sydenham, let me examine you; but, my heavens!" she added, as a rapid change came over her countenance; "is that the dress you intend to wear? Who on earth could have made such a thing? Such a waist! and such fitting sleeves!" Poor Alice bowed her head, but spoke not. "And do inform me," she added, in a still sharper tone, for her ill humour had completely gained the ascendancy over her politeness, "do inform me what this heavy band on your arm is intended for? Surely not a bracelet?"

As her companion made no reply, she had no answer to cavil at, and she impatiently exclaimed:

"In pity to yourself, take it off, and here, clasp this on." As she spoke, she presented the jewel which she had just taken from her own arm, and Alice, fearing to remonstrate, silently obeyed. It was an ornament indeed of excessive beauty—a rare and magnificent opal, surrounded by splendid rubies.

"And now," added Mrs. Graham, giving a last impatient twist to her sash; "I can do no more for you. We will go—but, are you ill?" she asked, perceiving that Alice trembled from head to foot.

"'Tis nothing," was the murmured reply. "I feel a little faint."

Mrs. Graham signed the servant, who had just entered, to hand a glass of water, and the young girl, fearing to put her companion's patience to any further trial, hastily swallowed it, and rose to follow her. With the first glance at the large and glittering saloon they were entering, her self-possession, her very sense of perception, seemed to desert her, and when at length she recovered, she found herself seated in a corner, near a large table covered with magazines and engravings. Almost opposite her was a young and pretty lady, leaning on the arm of a gentleman, and both were attentively regarding her. The lady stooped and whispered something, with a smile, to her companion, who replied by a light laugh; but, observing that they had attracted the attention of their victim, they turned away. With a strange feeling of loneliness, mortification and fear, she surveyed the brilliant scene before her. All seemed happy, cared for, but her. Those who were not dancing conversed in groups, partook of refreshments, or promenaded, in couples, the lofty apartments. How painfully, too, did the contrast between herself and the other, faultlessly attired girls, who flitted before her with their graceful draperies and delicate ornaments, strike upon her heart. Suddenly, while glancing from group to group, with a feeling of sickly despair, her eye fell on the elegant figure of Henry St. John, who was dancing with a haughty-looking but fashionable girl. Entirely engrossed by his partner, he of course saw not Alice, who was almost concealed by the heavy draperies of the window on one side, and, on the other, by the shadow of a large lamp on the table beside her. From that moment, however, things appeared in a new, a roseate light. There was, at least, one person present who knew her, and who would surely ask her once to dance. That person would introduce others, and—in fine, Alice had already arrived at the second story of one of her aërial edifices, when Mrs. Belmont passed her with a rapid step. She would not have perceived Alice, but her *bouquet* happened to fall at the feet of the latter, who immediately bent to raise it.

"What! you, my dear Miss Sydenham — not dancing! but I must get you a partner."

She turned and beckoned apparently to someone in the crowd, whilst her young companion, ready to sink with shame at the idea of being thus forced in a manner on a partner, cast down her eyes in speechless confusion. She raised them, however, as a light step approached, and saw Henry St. John before her.

"I have reserved a partner for you, Henry," said Mrs. Belmont, in her soft voice.

"Miss Sydenham!" exclaimed the young man, springing forward with much *empressement*. "This is, indeed, an unexpected pleasure; but how is it I have not seen you before?"

"We arrived very late," rejoined Alice, crimsoning to her temples.

"And you were dancing in the next apartment nearly all the time, Henry!" quickly interposed Mrs. Belmont, who, with ready tact, at once divined that her guest, failing a partner, had not left as yet the quiet corner in which she had sought refuge on her entrance. After a few additional words of silvery courtesy, the hostess gracefully turned away, whilst Alice, leaning on the arm of her handsome and distinguished partner, her heart beating with mingled fear and delight, joined the quadrille now forming, inwardly congratulating herself that she was now, indeed, participating in the pleasures of a ball. For a few moments, Henry St. John was all gaiety and devotion, but gradually his tones grew colder, his mirthful sallies and compliments became fewer and fewer, and, before the end of the third figure, had entirely ceased. Poor Alice, who had replied to him heretofore only by smiles and blushes, instantaneously perceived the desolating change, and for the first time raised her eyes from the ground, to discover, if possible, the cause. As she did so, the whispered words:

"Ciel! quelle tournure!" and then, in a still lower tone: "What on earth could have induced Henry St. John to select such a partner?" fell on her ear. With what volumes of horror were those short sentences fraught! For a moment she actually gasped for breath, but her positive terror enabled her quickly to subdue her emotions, and she cast a stolen glance from beneath her long lashes at her partner. He was looking studiously in a distant direction of the room, but his deepened colour, and a certain nameless air of embarrassment pervading his whole figure, told her that he too had heard the comments which had just been uttered. Involuntarily she turned her glance on one of the large mirrors lining the sides of the apartment, and she almost started at the figure it reflected. True, it gave back many figures, all light and graceful, all faultlessly attired, but *one* stood out pre-eminent to the horrified gaze of Alice. One ill-dressed, flushed, awkward-looking girl, with long, black hair, hanging in immense uncurled masses around her neck and shoulders. Oh! how fearful seemed to her, her vast inferiority to all around her, and the consciousness of that inferiority was accompanied by a pang so bitter that the colour which had hitherto equally dyed cheek and brow retreated, leaving her pale as a statue, and with a haggard

worn-out, look which certainly appertained not to a girl of six-teen. Her confusion was further increased by the contemptuous scrutiny with which the lady opposite (the same with whom St. John had been dancing when she had first perceived him) re-garded her. Though fully twelve or thirteen years older than Alice, with a dark, colourless complexion, and haughty, irregular features, yet her air of dignity, of fashionable repose, combined with an elegant and faultless toilette, gave her a strange and wonderful advantage over the latter, with all her youth and beauty. What an hour of torture was that quadrille to Alice; and when her now silent and inanimate partner, after leading her to her seat, and uttering a few words of cold, common-place civility, left her, she felt too unhappy, to disheartened, to wish for his return. Nor did he return. The film which had invested, even for a few moments, the poor and portionless girl with winning charms, had fallen from his eyes, and he saw again, with his usual faultless clear-sightedness. The young and beautiful crea-ture, with the aristocratic name and graceful address — for Alice was then at her ease — who had attracted his admiration when he had first met her in the company of his sister, was a very different being from the unfashionable, neglected, unknown girl, whom he had been entrapped into dancing with. Inwardly vowing it would be his last folly of the like nature, and muttering, we will charitably suppose, only a doubtful sort of benediction on his sister's officiousness, which had led to such a result, Henry St. John, the hero of the ball-room, immediately sought out the lady with the faultless toilette, and engaged her hand for the ensuing dance, endeavouring, by increased devotion and graceful flat-tery, to obliterate any evil impression his late ill-directed choice of a partner might have left on her mind. The lady was placable, and to Henry St. John's great delight, for Miss Aberton was a wealthy heiress, he succeeded. Meanwhile, poor Alice was nearly half dead with agitation and inanition, for she had as yet taken no refreshment whatever, save one jelly, which a tall, grave-looking gentleman with a bald head had presented, chancing to observe her glance at the tray which he was setting down on the table beside her. This abstinence was the more acutely felt, as she had not tasted food that day, her excitement and the bright hopes and anticipations which had thronged upon her effectually precluding such a thing. It had been with the greatest difficulty Mrs. Sydenham had prevailed upon her to take a cup of tea an hour or two before leaving. What would she not have given now for that, or any other refreshment. She looked around in despair; no one knew, noticed, or saw her, and she was too young and timid to think of asking.

At length, beginning to feel really ill, she formed the desperate determination of seeking Mrs. Graham, and begging her to send her home immediately. Twice she rose to cross the brilliantly lighted room, and twice her courage failed her; but finally taking advantage of the confusion of a rapid *galop,* she succeeded in gliding unobserved into the next apartment. It was a small sitting-room, opening on the conservatory, and was empty at the time, but, ere she had half crossed it, the sound of laughter and voices approaching filled her with dismay. Hastily raising the purple draperies which hung before a recess at the other end, she sprang behind them, and had hardly time to readjust their folds when the party entered.

"Do let us rest here a moment," exclaimed a fashionable and not unmusical voice. "I am completely exhausted! The heat is *so* oppressive in that dancing room."

"Permit me, then, to bring you some refreshments," rejoined the clear, yet soft accents of Henry St. John. "I will not be absent a moment."

Alice glanced through a small opening in the fold of the curtain, which commanded a full view of the room. Thrown negligently but gracefully on a crimson couch was her disagreeable *vis-à-vis,* the object of Henry St. John's devotion; whilst two or three young ladies were sitting or standing round; St. John himself, and the other gentlemen of the party, had gone in quest of refreshments.

"My ringlets are all out," exclaimed the youngest and prettiest of the group; as she twined a glossy auburn tress round her white fingers. "They are positively straight."

"Yes, something like the abundant locks of Henry St. John's

partner," was the laughing rejoinder. "Where on earth did he contrive to find her? He may certainly pride himself on having had a partner who, if she possessed no other attraction, had at least the rare one of being *unique* of her kind. But, seriously, Miss Aberton," she continued, addressing the lady on the couch, "do you know who she is? I would never have noticed her, nor I dare say would any of us, but for the circumstances of the usually exclusive and over-fastidious Henry St. John having chosen her for a partner. Who can she be?"

"I for one know nothing about the girl," returned Miss Aberton, closing her haughty eyelids; "but I rather suspect she came with Mrs. Graham. Perhaps some country cousin."

"Who is paying the usual penalty of the absent now?" gaily interrupted St. John, who entered at the moment. "I hope that I am not the hapless one."

"Not exactly," returned the former speaker, with a mischievous smile. "Still, there is no material difference — for 'tis your whilom partner. Pardon me, but as I really feel a friendly solicitude regarding your peace of mind, I must inquire her name," and she raised her sparkling eyes with a pretty air of gravity to his face. St. John's brow instantly became scarlet, and he bit his lip as if to restrain his impatience.

"Surely, Mr. St. John, *sur ce chapitre on peut se rapporter à vous*," said Miss Aberton, with a somewhat sarcastic smile curling her lip. "A guest of your sister's, and a partner of your own choice."

"Her name is Sydenham," rejoined the young man with ill-dissembled annoyance. "That is all I know of her, beyond exchanging a few words when introduced to her by Mrs. Belmont."

"Oh! fie, fie, Mr. St. John," interrupted his former tormentor, the Honourable Miss Templeton. "Do you count for nothing all the flattering smiles and compliments you showered upon her, during that short but blissful dance? A dance, too, of your seeking, for 'tis to be presumed, the lady did not solicit your hand."

"Not exactly, Miss Templeton," was the cool reply; "but when my sister, who was a schoolfellow of Miss Sydenham's, gave her to me as a partner, I could scarcely, even to win Miss Templeton's priceless approbation," here he bowed low, "be sufficiently ungallant to inform the young lady I had no particular desire for the honour."

"Dear Mrs. Belmont has so warm a heart," sweetly lisped the Lady Helena Stratton. "How few of us are so faithful to those delightful things, school-girl friendships."

"Sydenham is a good name, though," said another, in a more matter of fact tone; "and Miss Aberton says she came with Mrs. Graham."

"I said I supposed so, from the circumstances of perceiving on her arm a rare and magnificent bracelet, the only passable thing the young girl had on her person, which I am convinced belongs to Mrs. Graham."

"An opal set in rubies," exclaimed Lady Helena. "I have seen it on her several times, and 'tis a very rare ornament. I also saw Mrs. Graham address a few words to her at the beginning of the evening."

"But Mrs. Graham has not troubled herself much about her since," rejoined Miss Templeton.

"How could she? Mrs. Graham, ethereal soul! being, as she herself says poetically, a creature whose whole being is devoted to sweet sounds. I really believe she has been in the music room all night, and hush! I hear her full tones at the present moment."

"She certainly has a beautiful voice," said St. John, sincerely delighted with the change the conversation had taken. "We can distinguish the words partly from here, 'I'll hang my harp on a willow tree.' "

"I sincerely wish she would 'hang her harp on a willow tree', for I am heartily sick of its strains," said Miss Aberton, as she rose from the couch; "but, come, let us leave Mrs. Graham and her charming *protégé,* to their fate. The subject is worn out."

"Nay, do not let us leave this sweet spot so soon," returned Miss Templeton. "I really shall change the hangings of my morning room, and adopt this beautiful shade. And what a charmingly mysterious recess! Do you remember the words of the old song.

> I'm weary of dancing now, she cried,
> Here tarry a moment, I'll hide, I'll hide.

Shall I follow her example?" and with the graceful *étourderie* of a child, she sprang forward, and grasped the purple draperies in her small hand. What a moment of fearful, of breathless agony must that have been for the trembling being they screened! For a second, Miss Templeton held the curtains, and then with a gay laugh, she turned away, exclaiming: "No! I had better not be too rash. Who knows but yonder draperies conceal some solemn mysteries? There never was such a thing heard of in a romance as a recess without its grisly skeleton, or mysterious portrait, making awful descents from its frame and taking short pedestrian excursions through the halls and passages. Really, I appeal to you, Miss Aberton, does it not look like the nooks we read of in old-fashioned novels? Dark, rich folds hanging from the lofty ceiling!"

"It looks like a nook marvellously well adapted to play the eaves-dropper in," drily returned Miss Aberton, who concealed with difficulty the disgust which the *enfantillage* of her friend excited.

"Nay, do not check Miss Templeton's delightful enthusiasm," said Henry St. John, in a tone whose doubly refined politeness savoured strongly of sarcasm. "Really, such freshness, such *naïve* eagerness is a charming deviation from our customary monotonous insipidity."

Miss Templeton saw at once that Mr. St. John was "paying her off" for her former unwelcome jests at his expense, and, resolving not to leave him "victor of the field," she rejoined:

"You are too complimentary, Mr. St. John. I am not the only one who does occasionally display traits of a better nature. What greater example could we require of unworldly enthusiasm, of heroic indifference to the world's opinion, than that with which you edified us to-night in your selection of the being to whom you doubtless offered your heart as well as hand. Ah! she indeed is a bright specimen of that sweet, silent sensibility, that fascinating, rural timidity, so highly euologized by boarding-school teachers and middle-aged people, and so signally distinguished by Mr. St. John."

"But, really, St. John," said a tall, affected-looking young gentleman, who rejoiced in the appellation of Viscount Howard. "Really, you, whom the lady promoted to the dignity of her *preux chevalier*, are bound by all the laws of chivalry and knighthood to go in search of her. She is doubtless at the present moment making signals of distress for an ice, or calling on you to rescue her from some remote corner, where no other partner can penetrate."

"Had you not better make the experiment yourself, my lord? As your fancy is so very lively in conjuring up scenes of distress, probably your generosity is equally prompt in relieving them."

There was a very perceptible tone of sarcasm in the words, and a slight contraction of the high brow of the speaker, which told that further jesting on the subject would prove anything but conducive to mirth or friendship, and Lord Howard, taking the hint, drew the fair Lady Helena's arm in his own, and passed on to the adjoining saloon. The others followed in like order—Miss Aberton and St. John last. The latter had lingered to gather a blossom from a superb Indian jasmine that stood in the conservatory, which he presented, repeating in a tone half playful, half serious, the sentiment it imaged: "I attach myself to thee." It was graciously accepted, and the delicate compliments, the words of homage he whispered as they slowly followed their companions, proved that Henry St. John was a proficient in the science of flattery.

Meanwhile, what were the feelings of the young and sensitive girl, who, an unsuspected listener to that long dialogue, with all its bitter contemptuousness, its heartless egotism, had thus received her first terrible lesson in the world's ways. For an hour, a long hour after the thougtless revellers had passed out, she stood leaning against the tapestried wall, her eyes closed, her small hand pressed on her heart as if to still its wild, convulsive throbbing. At length a feeling of strange bewildering weakness crept over her, and, conscious that she was on the point of fainting, she left the recess, and, with some difficulty, reached the table on which fortunately stood a vase of water, a glass of which somewhat revived her, and a few moments rest on the couch on which Miss Aberton had late reclined in all the pride of wealth and rank comparatively restored her. But, with returning force returned her old fear that some gay party, if not the same one that had lately passed, might enter and see her sitting there, so lone, so neglected. That would have been indeed the last drop in her cup of bitterness; but what was she to do? There was no alternative save to seek Mrs. Graham, and entreat her to return; but where was she to be found, and how could Alice summon courage to approach her before a crowded room, and importune her, perhaps at a time where she might be totally engrossed by some other subject.

"Oh! that I might go home myself," murmured Alice, clasping her hands. "How willingly would I set out on foot in damp and darkness. Yet alas! I have no resource save patience. But I must seek my former place of refuge. There at least I may remain unobserved, unseen—how happy I shall feel if I can but reach it without meeting any of those heartless fashionables. I will not be tempted to leave it again."

With a beating heart and timid step she reentered the ball-room, and was quietly and unobservedly gliding back to her former seat when directly in her path, advancing towards her, was Henry St. John, Miss Aberton leaning on his arm. Alice stood transfixed with positive terror; but she was at least spared that mortification, for without having perceived her, they turned off in another direction. With renewed hope she continued to advance, when something soft, crushing beneath her foot, caused her to stoop. It was the white rose, now soiled and discoloured, which her fond mother had placed with such maternal pride, some hours before, amid her dark tresses. The sight brought back in all their vivid bitterness the mortifications, the humiliations, which had been her portion that night. What a contrast to the roseate visions, the soft hopes, that had flitted before her when that rose, white and lovely, had been placed amid her hair. The hot tears of acute mental suffering gushed to her eyes; spite of her efforts, they fell faster and faster. Half blinded by them, she hurried on. At length her haven was all but won, when suddenly — how closely is the sublime blended with the ridiculous, the mournful with the mirthful, in this changing world of ours—in her feverish haste, she stepped on the outstretched foot of an old gentleman, with venerable white hair and rather choleric face, who was reclining in solitary dignity on a couch adjoining her former seat. The injured individual instantly sprang to his feet with a muttered apostrophe, in which the name of a certain sovereign, whose dominions are not on the earth, nor yet above the earth, was distinctly audible. But the soft, entreating voice, the pale, tearful face of the young girl, as she earnestly apologized, calmed his ire, and he fell back in his former position, murmuring:

"Never mind, ma'am! Accidents will happen to the best-intentioned persons."

With a heart full to bursting, Alice glided past him, and sank on her chair. Secure in the grateful shade of the lamp, she covered her face with her hands, and gave free vent to the passionate emotion she could no longer control or restrain. Suddenly a slight noise caused her to look up. The old gentleman was standing before her, and regarding her with a very benevolent expression of countenance.

"Forgive the meddling impertinence of an old man," he kindly said; "but you seem unhappy, my dear young lady; surely, you are too young for that."

"Oh! I am very, very miserable," sobbed poor Alice, feeling it was useless to attempt controlling her grief.

"No! That can scarcely be at your age; 'tis but a summer shower, heavy while it lasts but of short duration. The sunshine will be brighter after. But, you look very pale! Let me get you some refreshments?" She gratefully bowed, and he hastened off on his kind mission. Ere many minutes had elapsed, he returned with a cup of fragrant coffee, and some cold chicken, — we beseech our romantic readers to close their eyes to this passage, for 'twill shock every sentiment of their exquisitely refined na-tures—which our heroine not only accepted, but heartily partook of. Thankful for the old man's kindness, and greatly refreshed she endeavoured effectually to calm her still excited feelings, and in answer to his question: "If she felt better," replied, with an effort at cheerfulness: "Yes; a great deal. Thanks to your double kindness."

"You are a good girl," he returned, "and more sensible than I expected; but if you do not think it too great a liberty for an old man like me to take, may I ask the cause of your sorrow?"

A pause followed, during with the rich colour mounted to her very temples, and, at length, she replied with downcast eyes:

"Wounded vanity, and self-love. I came here expecting gaiety, attention, admiration; and I have met nothing but contempt and neglect."

"Just so, my child," said her companion; "you expected too much, and you must not repine that your expectations have been disappointed."

"But, surely, I have not deserved the entire, the bitter contempt I have met with. I am neither old nor ugly."

"You are indeed neither, but beautiful, very beautiful," he rejoined as he gazed earnestly on the deep truthful eyes now raised to his: "but you have yet to learn that beauty and grace, when ill dressed or obscure, will meet with nothing but neglect in a ball-room. And now, tell me your name as frankly as you have told me the rest of your story."

"Alice Sydenham."

"Sydenham!" he repeated reflectively. "A high name."

"'Tis all is left us of former grandeur," said Alice sadly. "Poor, unpretending as we are, how wrong, how foolish of me to thrust myself into a scene so utterly removed from our present sphere; but I acted contrary to mamma's wishes, her earnest remonstrances, and I have been justly punished."

"Your mother—is she here?" said the old man quickly. "And neglect you thus!"

"No, no! she is at home. I came with a Mrs. Graham."

"A lady very youthfully dressed with a parterre of roses scattered about her robes? She has been screaming Italian *canzonets* in the music room all night."

"The same," said Alice, the first smile that had illumined her pale features that night stealing over them.

"Hem!" coughed her companion; "but who have we here?"

This exclamation was called forth by the approach of the lady Helena Stratton, leaning on the arm of the Viscount Howard, both of whom Alice had seen with Miss Aberton's party in the ante-room. Deeply engrossed in conversation, they slowly advanced towards the table, as if to examine the engravings upon it.

"Hollo!" suddenly exclaimed a loud voice. "Look where you're going to, young lady!"

Lady Helena, who was unconscious of the sofa's having an occupant, had nearly deposited her delicate satin shoe on the irritable toes of the old gentleman, who seemed as if in very malice to keep them extended in the way. The lady thus cavalierly addressed sprang round with a violent start, widely different from her usual languid movements, whilst her partner angrily said:

"I think, Sir, you might show a little more regard for the young lady's nerves."

"Let the young lady then shew a little more regard for other people's toes," was the unceremonious rejoinder.

The young viscount turned fiercely upon him, but there was something so very irascible in his venerable antagonist's face, whose hue had now deepened to a fiery red, that he thought it wiser to forbear. A duel with a man sufficiently old to be his father would be anything but creditable, and, whispering something to his fair partner, who replied by smilingly elevating her shoulders, they turned away.

"We have disposed of them at last," he said, turning with his former benevolent smile to Alice, who was actually trembling to find herself in such close proximity with so very fiery a neighbour. "What! you are afraid of me," he continued in a kind tone. "Why, you little simpleton, that scene was half got up to give yon supercilious young lady, with her foppish companion, a lesson, and to deliver us from their company. And now, preparatory to returning to our former topic, I must inform you of my name, as freely as you gave me yours. 'Tis Hammersly, a plain name, but one never sullied, I believe, by falsehood or dishonesty. Now, my dear child, tell me, have you no brother or cousin whose attentions would shield you from the slights you have experienced to-night?"

"No; I had three brothers, but they all died in infancy. The only living relative I possess is an uncle of mamma's, but he lives in a distant part of England."

"What county?"

"Cumberland."

"What name?"

"Weston—James Weston, I think—but to tell you the truth, I know very little about him."

"And care still less," said the old man, interpreting aright an almost imperceptible smile that curved the rosy lips of his companion. "But, have you ever seen him?"

"Never, in person — but I have seen his miniatures; a stern, grave-looking man, with raven hair and black eyes. Mamma says I strongly resemble him."

"That were paying him indeed a compliment; but if I am not mistaken, I know this same Mr. Weston, and without further preamble, a more egotistical, churlish being, never existed."

"Oh! shame! shame!" exclaimed Alice, really indignant at hearing her relative thus unceremoniously condemned by a stranger.

"Pardon me! I speak truth; but, however, I can also say, he has a good heart, though its better qualities are nearly choked up by selfishness. You need not speak, young lady," he continued, raising his hand to silence the warm remonstrance hovering on Alice's lips. "Were he not selfish, he would not have left you and your mother—Pardon me!—in the comparative destitution you are in, whilst he, himself, is surrounded by all earth's luxuries, rolling in wealth."

"That is his own affair," was the somewhat cold reply; "and, notwithstanding we have no real claims upon him, since the death of my father, he has regularly transmitted to us, every year, a considerable sum."

"Well, that is something; however, the generosity of the act depends greatly on the extent of the gift. But, I think, my dear child," he added, glancing at his gold repeater, as the strains of the band suddenly ceased, preparatory to commencing some new dance: "I think you had better prepare for leaving. You look very pale, indeed worn out."

"But not with pleasure," said poor Alice, the cheerful smile which had lately animated her features fading away, as the recollection arose that the night to which she had so eagerly looked forward, which was to have witnessed her first essay in the brilliant gaieties of the world, had come and passed away, leaving nought but bitter remembrances behind.

"Wait, I will bring you a glass of wine first," said her kind companion. "Remain here a moment."

He soon returned and, in compliance with his entreaties, she tasted the refreshments he offered.

"And now," he exclaimed; "take my arm, and we will go in quest of your very attentive and thoughtful *chaperone*."

With a feeling of comparative ease and confidence, to which she had as yet been a stranger, Alice obeyed, and they proceeded together to the music room. The crowd near the door was so great they were forced to stand aside for a moment, and during the time, she noticed many polite bows and smiles directed to her companion, whilst as many scrutinizing, impertinently inquisitive glances were bent on herself. To the courtesies showered upon him, Mr. Hammersly replied only by an abrupt nod or careless smile; and when Miss Aberton, in sweeping past, accidentally dropped her handkerchief at his very feet, he never bent himself, and by pressing Alice's arm, restrained her first involuntary impulse to raise it. The haughty girl glanced at him with a look of indignant surprise, which he returned by one of the most provoking unconsciousness; but fortunately for her, a gentleman standing in the crowd perceived her embarrassment, and springing forward to the rescue, gracefully presented it. That gentleman was Henry St. John.

Courteously saluting Alice's companion, he turned to him, as if to address a few words, but the latter, with a stiff bow, passed out. Mr. St. John was equally unsuccessful in an effort which he made to attract the glance of Alice, which was instantly averted from him. In the adjoining apartment they encountered Mrs. Graham, who, at the centre of a small *coterie*, was vehemently discussing the merits and demerits of the last new Opera.

"Why, where have you been all this time, Miss Sydenham?" immediately exclaimed the lady, on the entrance of her charge. "I have been searching for you in every direction."

"Either your researches did not extend beyond the music room, or you will soon require spectacles, madam, for Miss

Sydenham has never left the adjoining room, the whole night."

Mrs. Graham drew herself up, with a lightning glance, but the hostess, who at the moment joined the group, foreseeing the impending storm, instantly interposed.

"Ah! my sweet young friend!" addressing Alice, after bestowing a beaming smile on her companion, "I hope you have enjoyed yourself."

"Vastly, madam; I can vouch for the truth of that," drily rejoined the old man, who seemed to have taken on himself the task of answering for Alice on all occasions. "Complete neglect, entire isolation, is so delightful, not to speak of the facility thus afforded of indulging in philosophical meditations, undisturbed by such vanities as dancing or attention. Oh! 'twas all doubtless charming for a girl of sixteen."

Mrs. Belmont would not see the very palpable cut thus given her, but continued to chat pleasantly with him, whilst Alice glided after Mrs. Graham to the dressing room. It was crowded with ladies, all eagerly conversing together, discussing the pleasures of the night, or planning future amusements. A group of these immediately surrounded Mrs. Graham, and Alice was again left, as she had been the greater part of the evening, entirely alone. She was soon cloaked and veiled, and leaning against the large mirror at the deserted end of the apartment where she had attired herself, she gazed sadly, upon the pale, haggard face it reflected. But her thoughts dwelt not long there; they wandered soon back to the bitter events of the night, the slights, the humiliations showered on one whose birth was equal to the proudest there, whose only inferiority was in the paltriest of earth's distinctions, wealth. Suddenly the voice of Mrs. Graham sharply exclaimed.

"Miss Sydenham, are you ready yet?"

Conscious that her pre-occupation had been observed, the latter quickly turned, but as she did so, she heard Miss Aberton whisper to her neighbour.

"'Tis cruel of Mrs. Graham to disturb so blissful a revery. We are all fond of meditating on our conquests."

Alice, irritated beyond expression, fixed her eyes upon the

speaker with a glance of such profound, unutterable contempt, that the lady, to the secret delight of her companions, with whom she was no favourite, turned away her head in silent embarrassment. Arrived at the landing place, Mrs. Graham stopped to exchange a few parting words with a friend, whilst her young companion shrank timidly behind her. Sometime after, her *chaperone*'s carriage was announced, when Mr. St. John, who had been leaning listlessly over the staircase, sprang forward, and with his most fascinating smile, "begged the honour of handing Miss Sydenham in."

Alice raised her eyes in wondering astonishment at this unaccountable change, when she suddenly encountered the glance of her kind friend of the evening. Instantly comprehending his quick, but meaning look, she coldly thanked Mr. St. John for the intended favour, and with a stiff bow, turned away.

To fill the measure of the latter's mortification, the old man unceremoniously pushed past him, exclaiming:

"'Tis rather late to renew your acquaintance with Miss Sydenham now," and presenting his arm to Alice, they moved off, leaving him biting his lips with vexation.

"St. John, do tell us who that old bear is?" asked a fashionable-looking young man who had witnessed the whole scene, with very lively demonstrations of satisfaction.

"Some rich old Hottentot whom my sister made acquaintance with during her travels. She says he is worth thousands. In payment alone of some kind of forfeit, or jesting bet, he presented her with a brooch worth at the least eighty guineas."

"Well! he is a fiery old gentleman, and I suspected it was something of that sort when I witnessed the lamb-like gentleness with which you suffered his onset. St. John, St. John, gold is then thy god."

"A god whom we all worship, you among the rest," rejoined the other, peevishly, as he turned away. Meanwhile Alice and her friend had reached the carriage, in which Mrs. Graham was already seated. Warmly pressing her hand, he assisted her in, and then turning to her *chaperone,* exclaimed:

"I resign your charge, madam, but before doing so, allow me to congratulate you on the tender solicitude, the scrupulous fidelity, with which you have discharged your trust."

Ere the lady addressed had time to recover from the breathless astonishment in which his audacity had thrown her, he had disappeared.

"Upon my word!" she exclaimed, "this is something novel," and she again relapsed into silence; but suddenly she resumed, in a much louder key: "Will you have the goodness, Miss Sydenham, to inform me who this new and singular acquaintance of yours is?"

"I—I really forget," stammered poor Alice, who had but little heeded the information which the stranger had imparted to her concerning himself.

"Forget his name!" was the indignant rejoinder. "Really, Miss Sydenham, you surprise me. Forget his name! and, yet, you took his arm, conversed with him, treated him with all the familiarity of an old acquaintance."

"Because he was the only being who seemed to possess one spark of kindness, or feeling for me," vehemently replied Alice, to whom the remembrance of her wrongs imparted a sudden and unusual courage.

"That has no connexion with the subject, whatever, Miss Sydenham. I allude to the strange and unaccountable error you have committed in thus receiving and encouraging the attentions of a nameless individual; I am certain, were Mrs. Sydenham to know it, she would feel deeply pained. How do you know but your acquaintance may be some old tradesman? or — or," she continued, evidently seeking for some term of suitable degradation — "a pickpocket!"

"In that case, he would scarcely be admitted into Mrs. Belmont's saloons," said her companion gently.

"I am not so sure of that," rejoined Mrs. Graham, with increased asperity. "Mrs. Belmont is not so remarkably select. We meet many persons in her circles whom we would not dream of finding there."

Oh! how deeply Alice felt the ungenerous, the unkind insinuation, but she made no retort. She was reflecting that this was but her first essay in the bitter path of dependence, and she vowed, in her inmost heart, that as far as lay in her power it should be her last. At the moment, her handkerchief fell, and as she bent forward to raise it, the light of the lamps shone full upon her figure. Whiter than marble instantly became her cheek, and clasping her hands, she murmured in accents of horror: "Good God!"

"How! what is the matter?" quickly exclaimed Mrs. Graham, springing from her seat. But she heard her not. Gazing with an air of total supefaction upon her small white arms, she ejaculated in the same thrilling tone, "*the bracelet!*" Yes! the opal bracelet, the rare, costly jewel, which had called forth the admiration of even the supercilious children of wealth, was gone. Her companion understood at once the meaning conveyed in Alice's one exclamation, and she rapidly repeated, sinking back on the cushion:

"What! my bracelet? You do not mean to say, Miss Sydenham, that you have lost it?"

"'Yes! I have been indeed so utterly unfortunate," murmured poor Alice, who, overwhelmed with agonized shame and regret, would have gladly welcomed death at the moment to deliver her from this last climax of misery.

"Did you lose it in Mrs. Belmont's rooms?" was the sudden and eager query.

"Alas! no. I must have lost it in getting into the carriage. 'Tis by this time broken to atoms, or appropriated by some foot passenger."

"Unless your new acquaintance anticipated them, and performed that duty himself," exclaimed Mrs. Graham, who, even in the midst of her trouble, could not resist the temptation of launching a sarcasm at the head of the audacious meddler, who had presumed to question so insolently her conduct. But her satire fell unmarked. Alice was too wretched to heed it, and the lady might, with equal impunity, have styled the old gentleman a robber, or a murderer. An ominous pause followed, broken by the young girl's saying in a low tone:

"And it was so very valuable, too?"

"It only cost three hundred guineas," rejoined Mrs. Graham sarcastically.

"But you value it for its own sake only," said Alice eagerly, a ray of joy lighting up her haggard face, which already bore the marks of care, the first that had ever rested there. "'Tis no *souvenir*, no cherished remembrance! Oh! there is yet hope!" And already in fancy, she had rapidly pictured to herself the sacrifices she would make, the unwearying diligence with which she would toil night and day, denying herself every comfort, even necessary, till she had discharged her fearful obligation. Her companion, who instantly comprehended the meaning conveyed in her hurried words, exclaimed in a cold, stiff tone:

"I hope, Miss Sydenham, you do not intend insulting me by ever talking about restitution. It was entirely an accident. You are in no manner accountable, and you will oblige me by waiving the subject for ever."

Even had she possessed the strength and voice, what could Alice say? In total silence they arrived at her humble home: in total silence, the footman let down the steps, pulled the bell, and then, Mrs. Graham frigidly exclaiming: "Good night," the carriage drove off. It was Mrs. Sydenham who answered the summons, her one domestic having hours before retired to rest, and an exclamation of horror escaped her as the pale, suffering face of her daughter met her view.

"Alice! Alice! You look dreadfully pale. What is the matter?"

"Oh! mamma, I am so wretched," sobbed the young girl, as she threw herself in a paroxysm of tears into the fond arms so eagerly opened to receive her. "I have been tried beyond my strength."

Mrs. Sydenham, seeing the inutility of attempting to restrain her emotion, permitted her daughter to indulge freely in it, her only token of sympathy a gentle pressure of her hand; but after a time, the violence of her sorrow began to subside, and the mother softly whispered.

"Then, my own Alice, your bright expectations have not been fulfilled."

"Alas! no!" she rejoined, raising her streaming eyes. "Would that I have never gone! Would that, by the sacrifice of half my existence, I could blot out from my happy life this last night of bitterness, of suffering, of agony."

"Hush! my child! this wild sorrow is sinful in the eyes of your Creator. He has not afflicted you so heavily as to call forth such vehement grief. Be patient, and bear as a Christian should this your first trial. Alas! my darling! you will through life, be that life ever so fortunate, have many such. Retire to rest now, and to-morrow you will tell me all."

"Oh! no, mother! let me tell you now. It will relieve my heart, which seems almost breaking."

"Well, as you will, my child! but throw off that foolish dress, and set yourself near the fire, whilst I get you some hot coffee, which you sadly need."

When Mrs. Sydenham returned, she found poor Alice seated in an easy chair, in her dressing gown, gazing on the bright coals in the grate, whilst she silently wiped away the burning tears which, notwithstanding her late outburst of emotion, continued to fall like rain. But loving tones and cheerful words are efficient aids in dispelling sorrow, and the young girl was soon able to relate, with tolerable calmness, the many bitter events of the night. Nothing did she omit, nothing did she equivocate, even to the episode of Henry St. John, and the vain fancies she had wasted on him. We will pass over the gentle, yet forcible, counsels imparted by Mrs. Sydenham to her daughter—the moral she drew from the bitter lessons she had received; suffice it to say, they sank into her heart, and in after life, bore noble fruit.

The following day, after a sleepless, tearful night, Alice was seated in the sitting-room, despoiling her festal robe, which she inwardly vowed never to wear again, of the ribands adorning it, which she intended converting to some more useful purpose; but though the white fingers moved with strange rapidity, they often desisted to dash aside the glittering drops that fell upon them. The door unclosed, but she heard it not; a step approached, and the next moment Alice was clasped in the arms of the old gentleman, her friend of the preceding night.

Ere she could disengage herself from his warm, heartfelt embrace, the voice of Mrs. Sydenham, who had entered at the moment, exclaimed, in tones of startled surprise:

"Good Heavens! Uncle Weston! Is it possible!"

It was indeed the wealthy but eccentric James Weston, her indifferent, cold-hearted relative.

"Well! my own little Alice!" said the old man, drawing tenderly towards him the young girl, whose changing colour betokened her astonishment. "Tell me, are you willing to acknowledge the relationship?"

"But—but,"—she at length stammered; "how can you be my uncle? You are not like the miniature. You have neither raven hair nor dark eyes?"

"Not now, but I had twenty years ago," he returned, bursting into a merry laugh. "You do not imagine I was to have remained always in the same state of preservation I happened to be in when I sat for the portrait in your mother's possession."

"And you told me your name was—was—" Alice paused, for though she felt assured it was not Weston, yet she could not recall the appellation he had given.

"Yes, I told you my name was Hammersly, and that was no great departure from truth, for I was christened James Hammersly Weston."

Her doubts all dispelled, with a confused though happy smile, she threw herself in his arms, murmuring:

"My dear, good uncle! How different are you to the stern, unkind being my traitorous imagination had painted."

"And whose cause you nevertheless so warmly, so nobly defended. Oh! how grateful should I feel! I, the solitary, isolated old man, thus suddenly enriched by the gift of two beloved children, blessed by the certainty that I may end my days among you. Truly, Alice, may it be said that out of seeming evil springeth good, and but for that ball, painful, trying as it has proved, I would never have known or loved you half as well as you deserve. Had I come here to you, formally announced, as I had intended, suspicious as I am by nature, I might have mistaken your sweetness, your girlish frankness, for the refinement of art; a plan to secure the good will of an old man, tolerated only for his riches."

"But, tell me, uncle, did you know from the first I was your own Alice?"

"No, dear, but I had strong suspicions. In truth, from the moment I saw your gentle face, its wonderful resemblance to your mother struck me. You were just what she was at your age, when I beheld her, on her return from school. When I left you a moment, in quest of refreshments, I carelessly asked Mrs. Belmont who you were. Supposing it was merely an old man's curiosity, she instantly informed me. Wishing to obtain a further insight into your character, I dissembled my secret, resolving to keep the explanation for to-day. You may judge, Alice, whether I was pleased or not with your appearance, when I assure you that even had I found you were in no manner related to me I would have still found you out, and in as delicate a manner as I could, bestowed on you many and substantial proofs of my good will."

We will not weary the reader with further details. Better than we can portray them, can they imagine the heartfelt gratitude of Mrs. Sydenham, the delight of Alice, and the perfect happiness of Mr. Weston. The latter immediately procured an elegant mansion in one of the most fashionable localities, purchased a splendid carriage and superb horses, engaged a retinue of servants, whilst he daily showered money, jewels, the costliest gifts on Alice, who retained in prosperity the sweet gentleness which characterised her in cloudier days, and which justly rendered her the idol of her old uncle's heart. The first care of Mr. Weston, to whom she had soon recounted the mishap of the bracelet, was to set out for the jeweller's. He returned, after some delay, and handing a casket to Alice, exclaimed:

"There, Mrs. Graham's bracelet cost three hundred guineas—that cost nearly double the sum."

It was a magnificent jewel, surpassing far in beauty the one she had lost — the opal being replaced by a diamond. Mr. Weston proposed enclosing it in a sheet of paper with the words: "In discharge of Miss Sydenham's debt to Mrs. Graham," but yielding to the entreaties of Alice, he consented to abandon his first project. Taking another sheet, he wrote: "From Mr. Weston to Mrs. Graham, as a token of his deep gratitude for the care and attention she has displayed towards his niece, Miss Sydenham."

"There! Alice," said the old man smiling, "if that does not bring a blush to her cheek, I do not know what will."

The gift was duly received, and the intelligence of Miss Sydenham's sudden change of fortune circulated with lightning rapidity. The invitations and the cards hourly heaped upon the table almost bewildered Alice. First among these was that of Henry St. John, who immediately decided on abandoning Miss Aberton, who possessed neither the beauty nor brilliant prospects of her rival, and laying close siege to the niece and professed heiress of the individual he had classically designated as "an old Hottentot". To Henry St. John, however, for a long period, Alice was never "at home", and when at length, constrained to receive him by the frequency of his visits and the affectionate attentions of his sister, Mrs. Belmont, the cold civility with which she ever treated him shewed that she had profited of her first bitter lesson. That lesson proved indeed a blessing, doubly precious, preceding as it did, her sudden elevation to a sphere where she was the object of unceasing homage and adulation. It taught her to value according to their proper worth the flatterers who immediately surrounded her; and when listening to the praises of her grace, her beauty, so often now poured into her ear, she ever found an antidote against the vanity the silvery words might have excited in the remembrance of the trials and humiliations of her FIRST BALL.

A Legend of the Lake

Mrs. Harriet V. Cheney

When the viceroy, M. D. Roberval, came out to Canada about the year 1549, with a royal commission to settle the country, and establish colonies on the St. Lawrence, or in the territory of New France, as it was then called, it is well known he brought with him a numerous train of adventurers, many of them from distinguished families, whom interest, ambition, or a mere love of novelty and adventure tempted to the savage shores of the New World. Among them was a young artist, —Eugene St. Foy, —an especial favorite of the Viceroy, and distantly connected with his house. Eugene was descended from a younger branch of the same noble family, and though fortune had not showered her golden favors on him, he had powerful relations to make interest for him at court, and the army— the road to advancement in the days of the warlike Henry, —was open to him, with the certainty of rapid promotion.

But Eugene prized an artist's life above all things; he would not bind his free will to conventional forms, nor bring down his roving fancy to the dull routine of military tactics. Already his talents, his handsome person, and his versatile and graceful intellect had gained him distinction in Parisian society, and won the heart of a fair young girl, whose sweetness and virtue were the theme of every tongue. But ever and again he broke from the trammels of society, and with his *port-feuille* in his hand, and a knapsack on his shoulder, he wandered on foot through every country of Europe, a worshipper of nature at each shrine of grandeur and of beauty, and a student of art in the temples of her ancient glory. When he returned from these long rambles, Madeline would receive him with a sad sweet smile that seemed to chide while it welcomed him; and then his heart smote him that he could ever leave her — that he could ever choose any happiness but that of being near to her. Yet even as he kissed away her tears, he felt that there was a chord within his heart which she had never touched, — that lovely and dear as she was to him, the enthusiasm of his soul could find no response in hers.

History has recorded the adventurous voyages of Jacques Cartier, and of the Sieur De Roberval, the earliest pioneers of Canadian settlement. Their names and deeds enrich the early annals of these provinces, but they are referred to here only in connexion with the expedition of De Roberval, out of which arose the incidents of our simple legend.

Eugene St. Foy, as we have said, was one of the adventurous company of "cavaliers and gentlemen" who sailed from France with the Viceroy to take possession of a new country beyond the great western ocean, which was then almost an unknown pathway to the navigator. It was midsummer when they left the pleasant shores of sunny France; and as St. Foy cast a parting look on the vine-clad hills of his native land, fast receding while the ocean spread before him in its grandeur and infinity, the lingering regrets which had fondly clung to him, binding his heart to home and kindred, and to one, dearer than all the world beside— all yielded to the spirit of romantic adventure, and to his artist-eye the ocean in its endless changes and the clouds in their ever shifting hues and combination of forms were sources of perpetual interest and delight.

Various delays, and the tedious navigation of the period, retarded their progress, so that autumn was advancing when the little fleet cast anchor at Quebec, just above the natural fortress which has since been world-renowned for feats of daring, and for dear-bought victory. What a blaze of unimagined grandeur burst on the dazzled eye of the young artist, as he gazed for the first time on the vast outlines of that new world! Those primeval forests, gorgeous with their thousand tinted autumn trees! Those awful solitudes, that breathed no whisper of the past — that mighty river, rolling its flashing waves hundreds of leagues from the great reservoir of Lakes, —as yet known only by traditions of the roving savage, — and still rushing on a hundred leagues to seek the ocean flood—in this untrodden world where sublimity and beauty walked hand in hand like the first pair in the bowers of paradise — here the artist's eye could revel in new forms of beauty, and the poet's soul mount upward in a loftier inspiration!

Months passed on, and St. Foy's enthusiasm knew no abatement, and the monotony of his life caused no weariness. M. D. Roberval built a fort at Quebec, large enough to contain his little colony, and having brought out an ample supply of all things needful for their comfort, the winter passed away rapidly and not without enjoyment. The neighboring Indians came to the Fort on friendly terms to traffic, and were always entertained with cordial hospitality, and the young Frenchmen, for whom novelty had a powerful charm, delighted to dress in the rich furs purchased from the Indians with bartered trifles, and to follow the savages to their wigwam homes, or travel with them over the dazzling snows on the hunting excursions. Eugene St. Foy, whose life was more dreamy and imaginative than his companions, delighted to witness every phase of savage life, though seldom an active participator in it, and the vivid impressions he received were grouped in graceful combinations, and transferred with a graphic pencil to the pages of his *port-feuille.*

Spring broke upon the little settlement, — the brief northern Spring, soon melting into golden Summer, and the earth, as if disenchanted by a magic touch, threw off its ιcy fetters; the trees burst into leaf, a tender green appeared on hill and plain, and the broad river, free and majestic, again bounded on its course, sparkling in the cheerful sunlight. Those only who have experienced the rapid transitions of a northern climate can realize the thrill of delight which pervaded the colony at Quebec when nature thus suddenly resumed her crown of verdure, and arrayed herself as a goddess on the throne of her sylvan empire. The cheerful sounds of life again rung through the forest and floated on the wave, — busy hands were seen refitting the ships that had lain so long encrusted with ice, while savages in fantastic attire came swarming in their bark canoes, dimpling the waters that were scarce parted by the slender keels.

Eugene St. Foy caught the inspiration of the scene, and with untiring ardor pursued his favorite art, tracing his lonely way through forest wilds, — happy in the ambitious dreams of sanguine youth which marked no cloud arising to dim the brightness of the future. Following the course of the little river St. Charles he stood, one day, awe-struck and with admiring wonder, before the graceful cataract, long since famed as the Falls of Montmorency. Age after age that stream had poured its waters from the giddy height, and chimed its solemn anthem in the solitary wild! Never before had foot of civilized man approached, or an artist's eye gazed upon its wondrous beauty.

Eugene sketched with rapid hand; but hour after hour passed away, and the setting sun was shimmering through the forest leaves, and spanning the leaping flood with a brilliant rainbow, when he threw aside his pencil, and exclaimed with proud satisfaction, "This surely shall win for me a name!" Close to him a slight rustling as of a startled fawn caught his ear, and looking up he saw a pair of bright dark eyes peering from behind a bush, and directly a young Indian girl sprang to her feet, and stood timidly before him, her eyes still bent on his, as if transfixed by curiosity and wonder. Her attitude was the perfection of unstudied grace; her figure tall and delicately formed, and her features regular and finely moulded, expressed the simplicity of childhood and the blushing consciousness of early womanhood. Her gay, savage attire relieved the dark hue of her olive complexion, — a tunic of beaver skins edged with scarlet cloth, and confined at the waist by a belt, wrought with porcupine quills; — deerskin moccasins, richly embroidered, displayed the symmetry of her limbs, while a tuft of scarlet feathers mingled with her jet-black hair, which fell in silken masses on her neck and shoulders.

Eugene gazed on the sudden apparition with intense delight; "surely," he thought, "this is the crowning glory of the scene — the beautiful goddess of this wild domain" — and again seizing the pencil, he began to sketch her as she there stood, her eyes following the motion of his hand, but otherwise immoveable as a statue. Presently, like a bashful child, she came step by step towards him, and glanced over his shoulder; but when the picture met her eye, she started, as if surprised and delighted by the feats of a magician, and clapping her hands uttered a wild, but musical cry, pointing to the water-fall, the trees, and to herself, as if to identify them all with the subjects of his artistic skill.

"Pretty savage, from whence comest thou?" — began St. Foy,

taking her hand, and quite unmindful that his refined dialect was lost on her untutored ears; but she sprang from him with the bound of a young doe, and but once pausing to look back, pursued her flight and was soon hid in the dense shadows of the wood.

In another week the young artist had joined an expedition sent by the Viceroy to explore the country bordering on the great St. Lawrence. The party, consisting mostly of young men filled with a romantic spirit of adventure, sailed from Quebec in bark canoes, attended by Indian guides, to whom every path of the wilderness was well known. At the entrance of the Sorel, the party separated, and St. Foy with a few others proceeded to the present village of Chambly, where the charming scenery tempted them to encamp for a few days, and enjoy the pleasures of hunting and of fishing in the fairy little lake. St. Foy took no delight in these amusements, but spent his time in solitary rambles in which he found rich subjects for his favorite art. He at first rarely ventured without a guide; but familiarity with forest life rendered him daring, and he one day found himself bewildered by a labyrinth of paths, alone, and totally unable to identify the one which he had followed from the encampment. Night was approaching, and the land-marks of the forest were unkown to him. Dreamily he had wandered on, he knew not where, carving the name of Madeline on many a tree, — when suddenly he observed the lengthening shadows, and the deep gloom settling on the forest—and the silence was more profound, for the birds had ceased their warbling, and the little wild wood animals had sought their nightly coverts.

Eugene was fearless and light of heart; all his efforts to escape only involved him more and more in the intricacies of the forest, —he shouted aloud, hoping his voice would reach some friendly ear, and echo caught the sound and repeated it from rock and dell, but brought no answer, and all was silent as before. Eugene next kindled a fire and piled high the blazing branches, thinking it would at least keep off the beasts of prey who might soon be prowling abroad, and the grateful warmth was welcome even under a summer's sky in those thick forest shades. Scarcely had the fire begun to blaze when at some distance, beyond a level greensward, an answering flame leaped high into the air, spreading a ruddy glow around, and disclosing several groups of tawny figures sitting or standing near it. The young artist stood a few moments admiring the picturesque effects of this animated scene, which seemed to have sprung from the earth before him, then hastened to the spot, relying on the friendly disposition of the Indians for a hospitable reception. As he approached nearer, he found the party consisted of some twenty savages, who were probably abroad on a hunting excursion, and had just encamped there for the night. Most of the men were sitting on the ground smoking their rude pipes, while several squaws appeared busied at the fire, engaged in culinary preparation.

St. Foy's sudden appearance produced an evident sensation, though the Indians seldom express surprise, or allow the gravity of their countenances to be disturbed by any emotion. They were, in fact, returning from the Fort, where they had been to traffic; and as Eugene approached them with friendly signs, and endeavoured to make them comprehend that he had lost his way, they made room for him within their circle, and offered a pipe, which is always a pledge of amity. The women gathered about him with more unrestrained curiosity, but a few words of command, as it appeared, from an old warrior of the tribe, sent them hastily back to their occupations. Close beside the warrior stood a young girl of perhaps fifteen summers, who seemed exempted from household drudgery; and as Eugene met her flashing eye, he recognized the striking features and the graceful form that had won his admiration at the Falls of Montmorency. With the habitual gallantry that was extended to all her sex, the young Frenchman saluted her by a courteous gesture, and the recognition was acknowledged by a crimson flash that dyed her tawny cheek, and gave a softened grace to her expression.

Oneidava, the Sachem's daughter, — the Lily of the Lake, as she was fondly styled, — had indeed been tenderly cared for, and reared with a gentle love that is rarely extended to savage woman. Safe under her father's powerful protection, she had grown up beautiful and beloved, — the young men of the tribe worshipped her in silence, but none ventured to offer her the homage of affection, she seemed so elevated above them; and among the bravest, she had not yet found one worthy to receive her love. Eugene St. Foy enjoyed a romantic adventure in the true spirit of careless and ardent youth; frank and genial in his manners, he at once won the confidence of his savage entertainers, and was hospitably pressed to share their rude repast. Some among them could utter a few words of his own language, which they had learned in their intercourse with the white strangers, and aided by expressive signs, he made them comprehend his situation and received from them assurances of aid whenever he wished to regain his companions. Fasting and exercise had given him a keen appetite, and the venison, roasted on coals, and the baked cakes of maize, which were placed before him, if not very tempting to the palate, could not be refused when offered by the graceful hand of Oneidava.

On the following morning he awoke at an early hour, and found the Indians already prepared to pursue their onward journey, which they gave him to understand was some degrees farther south, to their hunting grounds on the borders of a great lake. St. Foy hastily decided to follow out the adventure, satisfying his doubts by the ready logic of a strong inclination which suggested that he could but learn the habits of that singular race among their own forest homes, and also that the opportunity would afford rich subjects for his artistic skill. He prevailed on a young savage, by some tempting reward, to carry back a message to his companions at Chambly; and *he* never knew that his messenger was unfaithful, while *they* waited long and vainly for his return, and day after day scoured the neighbouring woods in hopeless search for him.

Weeks passed into months, — Summer was waning, and still St. Foy remained a willing captive among the red men of the forest. The old Sachem of the tribe looked on him as an adopted son, but the young warriors regarded him with secret envy, believing that the Lily of the Lake would surely become the wife of the pale face stranger. Yet Eugene still wore a talisman near his heart, — the miniature of the gentle Madeline — and his better nature revolted from the thought of treachery to his early vows. Why did he not fly when temptation pressed upon him, and whispered bland falsehoods, sapping the foundation of his virtuous resolution!

Wherever he went, Oneidava attended on his steps. Like a beautiful spirit she flitted around his path, and if he sought the depths of the forest shade, to commune alone with his heart, and still its rebellious throbbing, — there she followed with step lighter than a bounding fawn; and timid as a gentle child, she would wait in silence, watching him with eyes so full of love and tenderness that he could not cast her from him, or resist her fascination. The wild enthusiasm of her nature captivated him no less than her more gentle moods. She seemed instinctively to appreciate the refinement of his mind, and to sympathise in all his emotions. The creations of his pencil filled her with wild delight—she would gaze on them, and clap her hands, and often tears rushed into her eyes when words failed to express her admiration. Her ardent feelings met a full response in his own heart, and satisfied every wish — never had the calm and too sensitive Madeline awakened emotions so passionate and absorbing.

The bridal feast was prepared, and amidst the festivities of savage rejoicing, the dark-eyed daughter of the Iroquois was given in marriage to the stranger youth. And was St. Foy happy in the accomplishment of his wishes? Did no pale remembrance cast a shadow on his joy? Alas! the faithless lover had already marred the integrity of his soul, and a broken vow is surely followed by a righteous retribution. Yet for a time Eugene revelled in the happiness which he had so dearly bought by a sacrifice of principle. Still, in the shadows of the old forest, he pursued his favorite art, and whispered his tale of love. Oneidava learned from his lips the words of his native tongue, and never had they sounded so sweetly in his ear as when breathed in the music of her voice. Away from all jarring sounds, and from every curious eye, they wandered along the wooded shores of the lovely lake, which now bears the name of Champlain, or floating in a frail bark canoe, glided over its quiet waters, and choosing some lonely isle, they would make it, for a time, the resting place of love, till roving fancy allured them to some brighter spot.

The early frosts of Autumn again tinged the forest with a thousand brilliant hues, and the crisped grass and falling leaves gave melancholy token of approaching Winter. The Indian party were preparing to remove farther to the west, and St. Foy, on learning their intentions, for the first time realized the thought that he must go with them, he knew not whither, or else return to the abodes of civilization, and carry with him his Indian bride. Was there no alternative? What would the Viceroy say to *him,* the protégé whom his favor had placed in the path of fortune, from which he had so recklessly turned aside!

Torn by contending emotions, Eugene sought the deepest solitude, vainly hoping to calm the tumult of his feelings. There Oneidava came to him with flying footsteps, joy sparkling in her eye, the bearer, she fondly hoped, of happy tidings. With a playful gesture, she held up a packet, which a friendly savage, charged to seek St. Foy wherever an Indian trail could lead him, had just brought from the Viceroy at Quebec. His eye caught the well-known writing on the superscription, and with a frantic hand he snatched it from her, and gazed upon it, while a mortal paleness overspread his features, which became rigid as a marble statue.

With a wild cry, Oneidava threw herself on his breast, and twining her arms around his neck, in the most endearing accents of affection sought to win from him the secret of his sudden change. For the first time he recoiled from her caresses, and cast her rudely from him. The Indian girl started to her feet, and looked at him with a proud, searching gaze, but wounded tenderness chased away resentment, and she burst into a passionate flood of tears. Eugene, touched to his inmost heart, caught her in his arms, and in the earnest tones of sincere affection sought to calm and reassure her. But the golden chain of confidence was rudely shivered, and its broken links could never become reunited.

When St. Foy found himself again alone, he opened his letters and read them with indescribable emotion. M. de Roberval, in the confident hope that he still lived, and that the Indian messenger would overtake him in his wanderings, entreated Eugene to place himself under his guidance and return without delay to the settlement. The season, he said, was fast advancing, and already their vessels were in readiness and waited tidings from him to depart on their homeward voyage. Despatches had been received from France during his absence, and letters from Madeline were enclosed. With a pang of bitter self-reproach Eugene cut the silken threads, and read there words of deep, maidenly affection, which had once thrilled, like tones of sweetest music, on his wayward and fickle heart.

From that moment, firmly as he sought to veil his feelings, the eye of constant and watchful love detected the sorrow and the vain regret that constantly corroded him. Oneidava breathed not a word of reproach, nor betrayed a jealous fear, but a shadow had fallen on the sunshine of her love, and her heart was wrung with sorrow. She saw him afterwards in conference with the Indian guide, and fear sharpened the vigilance of her natural sagacity, and impelled her to watchfulness and secrecy.

But if St. Foy meditated escape, he found himself surrounded on all sides by the most determined obstacles. The eyes of the warriors were upon him, for he had been adopted into their tribe, and they would not suffer him to depart. There was no outward restraint, but he knew that his steps were watched, and he inwardly reproached Oneidava for the abridgement of his freedom. But whatever were her sufferings, she endured them with savage stoicism; her eyes still followed him with mournful tenderness, and his capricious coldness was answered only by more devoted expressions of affection. Often his love for her revived with passionate fondness, and the dream of their former happiness was transiently renewed. Remorse and pity melted his heart, but with all his generous impulses, his nature was selfish, and his spirit rebelled against the very shadow of restraint. . . .

It was a dark, stormy night. On the morrow the Indians were to depart westward, and the bustle of preparation throughout the encampment had given place to deep repose. Oneidava slept, or seemed to sleep, soundly on her couch of skins, and St. Foy, not daring to cast on her one parting look, rose softly, and lifting a mat which closed their leafy tent, passed forth into the outer air. There he was joined by the Indian guide, and with swift and noiseless steps they entered the forest depths. But behind them was a step lighter than their own, and an eye which pierced through the gloom followed their stealthy flight. Oneidava's loving heart could not be deceived, and throughout that day she had noted the secret council, and the hasty preparation. With a beating heart, and eyes closed but sleepless, she lay, seemingly wrapped in repose, for she knew that other eyes were watching, and that in the hour of need she alone could save him. Her presentiment was just; and as she still followed Eugene, like an unseen guardian spirit, a cry was raised from the encampment, and the savage warriors came swarming on his track.

The treacherous guide uttered a shrill cry and darted from him, hiding himself in the intricacies of the wood.

Eugene, bewildered, knew not where to turn; but a soft hand clasped his own, and the sweet voice of his forsaken Lily whispered to him to keep silence and follow her. Passively he submitted to her gentle guidance; the storm raged, flashes of lightning showed him the pale, agitated face of Oneidava, but on they passed, turning from the path which their pursuers had taken, till their voices were almost lost in the distance. Presently the broad lake lay before them, and a bark canoe was moored upon its margin. Oneidava looked with an anxious eye upon the tossing waves,—a moment she hesitated, a slight sound, unheard by St. Foy, caught her practised ear — she laid her head upon the ground to listen — then starting up, whispered hurriedly.

"They are coming — it is our only chance of safety," she stepped into the frail canoe, still leading her bewildered lover, and loosing it from the mooring, dipped the paddles lightly into the waves.

Scarcely had they parted from the shore when a savage band rushed to the spot, and a loud shout of rage mingled hideously with the rushing of the storm. A vivid flash of lightning revealed the fugitives, beyond their reach; the rain poured in torrents, the thunder roared, and the wind, sweeping over the waves in sudden blasts, whirled the little bark in circling eddies — another flash, and then midnight darkness, and again the lightning gleamed like a fiery spirit across the angry waves—an empty bark floated passively towards the shore, but the young artist and his Indian bride were never seen again. . . .

Madeline pined long and faithfully for her absent lover, but happily his infidelity never reached her ears. When all hope of his return failed, after years of patient waiting, she retired from the world, and devoted the remnant of her days to the religious duties of a conventual life.

Many long years passed away, when some succeeding adventurers, in exploring the borders of Champlain, discovered melancholy traces of the ill-fated Eugene St. Foy. The descendants of the old Sachem, Oneidava's father, preserved his *port-feuille,* as a sacred relic, and the almost obliterated traces of his pencil, and his name, written by his own hand, painfully recalled his sad history to the memory of his countrymen. Tradition still cherishes his name among the scattered Iroquois, and from father to son is handed down the melancholy Legend of the Lake.

Coming of Age: Stories of the New Domain

Old Man Savarin

E. W. Thompson

Old Ma'ame Paradis had caught seventeen small doré, four suckers, and eleven channel-catfish before she used up all the worms in her tomato-can. Therefore she was in a cheerful and loquacious humor when I came along and offered her some of my bait.

"Merci; non, M'sieu. Dat's 'nuff fishin' for me. I got too old now for fish too much. You like me make you present of six or seven doré? Yes? All right. Then you make me present of one quarter dollar."

When this transaction was completed, the old lady got out her short black clay pipe, and filled it with *tabac blanc.*

"Ver' good smell for scare mosquitoes," said she. "Sit down, M'sieu. For sure I like to be here, me, for see the river when she's like this."

Indeed the scene was more than picturesque. Her fishing-platform extended twenty feet from the rocky shore of the great Rataplan Rapid of the Ottawa, which, beginning to tumble a mile to the westward, poured a roaring torrent half a mile wide into the broader, calm brown reach below. Noble elms towered on the shores. Between their trunks we could see many whitewashed cabins, whose doors of blue or green or red scarcely disclosed their colors in that light.

The sinking sun, which already touched the river, seemed somehow the source of the vast stream that flowed radiantly from its blaze. Through the glamour of the evening mist and the maze of June flies we could see a dozen men scooping for fish from platforms like that of Ma'ame Paradis.

Each scooper lifted a great hoop-net set on a handle some fifteen feet long, threw it easily up stream, and swept it on edge with the current to the full length of his reach. Then it was drawn out and at once thrown upward again, if no capture had been made. In case he had taken fish, he came to the inshore edge o his platform, and upset the net's contents into a pool separated from the main rapid by an improvised wall of stones.

"I'm too old for scoop some now," said Ma'ame Paradis, with a sigh.

"You were never strong enough to scoop, surely," said I.

"No, eh? All right, M'sieu. Then you hain't nev' hear 'bout the time Old Man Savarin was catched up with. No, eh? Well, I'll tol' you 'bout that." And this was her story as she told it to me.

"Der was fun dose time. Nobody ain't nev' catch up with dat old rascal ony other time since I'll know him first. Me, I'll be only fifteen den. Dat's long time 'go, eh? Well, for sure, I ain't so old like what I'll look. But Old Man Savarin was old already. He's old, old, old, when he's only thirty; an' *mean*—*baptême!* If de old Nick ain' got de hottest place for dat old stingy—yes, for sure!

"You'll see up dere where Frawce Seguin is scoop? Dat's the Laroque platform by right. Me, I was a Laroque. My fader was use for scoop dere, an' my gran'fader—the Laroques scoop dere all de time since ever dere was some Rapid Rataplan. Den Old Man Savarin he's buyed the land up dere from Felix Ladoucier, an' he's told my fader, 'You can't scoop no more wisout you pay me rent.'

" 'Rent!' my fader say. '*Saprie!* Dat's my fader's platform for scoop fish! You ask anybody.'

" 'Oh, I'll know all 'bout dat,' Old Man Savarin is say. 'Ladoucier let you scoop front of his land, for Ladoucier one big fool. De lan's mine now, an' de fishin' right is mine. You can't scoop dere wisout you pay me rent.'

" '*Baptême!* I'll show you 'bout dat,' my fader say.

"Next mawny he is go for scoop same like always. Den Old Man Savarin is fetch my fader up before de magistrate. De magistrate make my fader pay nine shillin'!

" 'Mebbe dat's learn you one lesson,' Old Man Savarin is say.

"My fader swear pretty good, but my moder say: 'Well, Narcisse, dere hain' no use for take it out in *malediction*. De nine shillin' is paid. You scoop more fish—dat's the way.'

"So my fader he is go out early, early nex' mawny. He's scoop, he's scoop. He's catch plenty fish before Old Man Savarin come.

" 'You ain't got 'nuff yet for fishin' on my land, eh? Come out of dat,' Old Man Savarin is say.

" '*Saprie!* Ain' I pay nine shillin' for fish here?' my fader say.

" '*Oui*—you pay nine shillin' for fish here *wisout* my leave. But you ain't pay nothin' for fish here *wis* my leave. You is goin' up before de magistrate some more.'

"So he is fetch my fader up anoder time. An' de magistrate make my fader pay twelve shillin' more!

" 'Well, I s'pose I can go fish on my fader's platform now,' my fader is say.

"Old Man Savarin was laugh. 'Your honor, dis man tink he don't have for pay me no rent, because you'll make him pay two fines for trespass on my land.'

"So de magistrate told my fader he hain't got no more right for go on his own platform than he was at the start. My fader is ver' angry. He's cry, he's tear his shirt; but Old Man Savarin only say, 'I guess I learn you one good lesson, Narcisse.'

"De whole village ain't told de old rascal how much dey was angry 'bout dat, for Old Man Savarin is got dem all in debt at his big store. He is grin, grin, and told everybody how he learn my fader two good lesson. An' he is told my fader: 'You see what I'll be goin' for do wis you if ever you go on my land again wisout you pay me rent.'

" 'How much you want?' my fader say.

" 'Half de fish you catch.'

" '*Monjee!* Never!'

" 'Five dollar a year, den.'

" '*Saprie*, no. Dat's too much.'

" 'All right. Keep off my lan', if you hain't want anoder lesson.'

" 'You's a tief,' my fader say.

" 'Hermidas, make up Narcisse Laroque bill,' de old rascal say to his clerk. 'If he hain't pay dat bill to-morrow, I sue him.'

"So my fader is scare mos' to death. Only my moder she's say 'I'll pay dat bill, me.'

"So she's take the money she's saved up long time for make my weddin' when it come. An' she's paid de bill. So den my fader hain't scare no more, an' he is shake his fist good under Old Man Savarin's ugly nose. But dat old rascal only laugh an' say, 'Narcisse, you like to be fined some more, eh?'

" '*Tort Dieu*. You rob me of my place for fish, but I'll take my platform anyhow,' my fader is say.

" 'Yes, eh? All right—if you can get him wisout go on my land. But you go on my land, and see if I don't learn you anoder lesson,' Old Savarin is say.

"So my fader is rob of his platform, too. Nex' ting we hear, Frawce Seguin has rent dat platform for five dollar a year.

"Den de big fun begin. My fader an Frawce is cousin. All de time before den dey was good friend. But my fader he is go to Frawce Seguin's place an' he is told him, 'Frawce, I'll goin' lick you so hard you can't nev' scoop on my platform.'

"Frawce only laugh. Den Old Man Savarin come up de hill.

" 'Fetch him up to de magistrate an' learn him anoder lesson,' he is say to Frawce.

" 'What for?' Frawce say.

" 'For try to scare you.'

" 'He hain't hurt me none.'

" 'But he's say he will lick you.'

" 'Dat's only because he's vex,' Frawce say.

" '*Baptême! Non!*' my fader say. 'I'll be goin' for lick you good, Frawce.'

" 'For sure?' Frawce say.

" '*Saprie!* Yes; for sure.'

" 'Well, dat's all right den, Narcisse. When you goin' for lick me?'

" 'First time I'll get drunk. I'll be goin' for get drunk dis same day.'

" 'All right, Narcisse. If you goin' get drunk for lick me, I'll be goin' get drunk for lick you'—*Canadien* hain't nev' fool 'nuff for fight, M'sieu, only if dey is got drunk.

"Well, my fader he's go on old Marceau's hotel, an' he's drink all day. Frawce Seguin he's go cross de road on Joe Maufraud's hotel, and *he's* drink all day. When de night come, dey's bose stand out in front of de two hotel for fight.

"Dey's bose yell an' yell for make de oder feller scare bad before dey begin. Hermidas Laronde an' Jawnny Leroi dey's hold my fader for fear he's go 'cross de road for keel Frawce Seguin dead. Pierre Seguin an' Magloire Sauve is hold Frawce for fear he's come 'cross de road for keel my fader dead. And dose men fight dat way 'cross de road, till dey hain't hardly able for stand up no more.

"My fader he's tear his shirt and he's yell, 'Let me at him!' Frawce he's tear his shirt and he's yell, 'Let me at him!' But de men hain't goin' for let dem loose, for fear one is strike de oder ver' hard. De whole village is shiver 'bout dat offle fight—yes, seh, shiver bad!

"Well, dey's fight like dat for more as four hours, till dey hain't able for yell no more, an' dey hain't got no money left for buy wheeskey for de crowd. Den Marceau and Joe Maufraud tol' dem bose it was a shame for two cousins to fight so bad. An' my fader he's say he's ver' sorry dat he lick Frawce so hard, and dey's bose sorry. So dey's kiss one anoder good—only all their close is tore to pieces.

"An' what you tink 'bout Old Man Savarin? Old Man Savarin is just stand in front of his store all de time, an' he's say: 'I'll tink I'll fetch him *bose* hup to de magistrate, an' I'll learn him *bose* a lesson.'

"Me, I'll be only fifteen, but I hain't scare 'bout dat fight same like my moder is scare. No more is Alphonsine Seguin scare. She's seventeen, an' she wait for de fight to be all over. Den she take her fader home, same like I'll take my fader home for bed. Dat's after twelve o'clock of night.

"Nex' mawny early my fader he's groaned and he's groaned 'Ah—ugh—I'm sick, sick, me. I'll be goin' for die dis time, fo' sure.'

" 'You get up an' scoop some fish,' my moder she's say, angry 'Den you hain't be sick no more.'

" 'Ach—ugh—I'll hain't be able. Oh, I'll be so sick. An' I hain't got no place for scoop fish now no more. Frawce Seguin has rol' my platform.'

" 'Take de nex' one lower down,' my moder she's say.

" 'Dat's Jawnny Leroi's.'

" 'All right for dat. Jawnny he's hire for run timber to-day.'

" 'Ugh—I'll not be able for get up. Send for M'sieu le Curé—I'll be goin' for die for sure.'

" '*Misère*, dat's no *man*! Dat's a drunk pig,' my moder she's say, angry. 'Sick, eh? Lazy, lazy—dat's so. An' dere hain't no fish for de little chilluns, an' it's Friday mawny.' So my moder she's begin for cry.

" Well, M'sieu, I'll make de rest short; for de sun is all gone now. What you tink I do dat mawny? I take de big scoop-net an' I'll come up here for see if I'll be able for scoop some fish on Jawnny Leroi's platform. Only dere hain't nev' much fish dere.

"Pretty quick I'll look up and I'll see Alphonsine Seguin scoop, scoop, scoop on my fader's old platform. Alphonsine's fader is sick, sick, same like my fader, an' all de Seguin boys is too little for scoop, same like my brudders is too little. So dere Alphonsine she's scoop, scoop for breakfas'.

"What you tink I'll see some more? I'll see Old Man Savarin. He's watchin' from de corner of de cedar bush, an' I'll know ver' good what he's watch for. He's watch for catch my fader go on his own platform. He's want for learn my fader anoder lesson. *Saprie!* dat's make me ver' angry, M'sieu!

"Alphonsine she's scoop, scoop plenty fish. I'll not be scoop none. Dat's make me more angry. I'll look up where Alphonsine is, an' I'll talk to myself: —

" 'Dat's my fader's platform,' I'll be say. 'Dat's my fader's fish what you catch, Alphonsine. You hain't nev' be my cousin no more. It is mean, mean for Frawce Seguin to rent my fader's platform for please dat old rascal Savarin.' Mebby I'll not be so angry at Alphonsine, M'sieu, if I was able for catch some fish; but I hain't able — I don't catch none.

"Well, M'sieu, dat's de way for long time—half-hour mebby. Den I'll hear Alphonsine yell good. I'll look up de river some more. She's try for lift her net. She's try hard, hard, but she hain't able. De net is down in de rapid, an' she's only able for hang on to le hannle. Den I'll know she's got one big sturgeon, an' he's so big she can't pull him up.

" *Monjee!* what I care 'bout dat! I'll laugh me. Den I'll laugh good some more, for I'll want Alphonsine for see how I'll laugh big. And I'll talk to myself: —

" 'Dat's good for dose Seguins,' I'll say. 'De big sturgeon will pull away de net. Den Alphonsine she will lose her fader's scoop wis de sturgeon. Dat's good 'nuff for dose Seguins! Take my fader platform, eh?'

"For sure, I'll want for go an' help Alphonsine all de same — she's my cousin, an' I'll want for see de sturgeon, me. But I'll only just laugh, laugh. *Non, M'sieu;* dere was not one man out on any of de oder platform dat mawny for to help Alphonsine. Dey was all sleep ver' late, for dey was all out ver' late for see de offle fight I told you 'bout.

"Well, pretty quick, what you tink? I'll see Old Man Savarin goin' to my fader's platform. He's take hold for help Alphonsine an' dey's bose pull, and pretty quick de big sturgeon is up on de platform. I'll be more angry as before.

"Oh, *tort Dieu!* What you tink come den? Why, dat Old Man Savarin is want for take de sturgeon!

"First dey hain't speak so I can hear, for de Rapid is too loud. But pretty quick dey's bose angry, and I hear dem talk.

" 'Dat's my fish,' Old Man Savarin is say. 'Didn't I save him? Wasn't you goin' for lose him, for sure?'

"Me — I'll laugh good. Dass *such* an old rascal.

" 'You get off dis platform, quick!' Alphonsine she's say.

" 'Give me my sturgeon,' he's say.

" 'Dat's a lie — it hain't your sturgeon. It's *my* sturgeon,' she's yell.

" 'I'll learn you one lesson 'bout dat,' he's say.

"Well, M'sieu, Alphonsine she's pull back de fish just when Old Man Savarin is make one grab. An' when she's pull back she's step to one side, an' de old rascal he is grab at de fish, an' de heft of de sturgeon is make him fall on his face, so he's tumble in de Rapid when Alphonsine let go de sturgeon. So dere's Old Man Savarin floating in de river — and *me*! I'll don' care eef he's drown one bit!

"One time he is on his back, one time he is on his face, one time he is all under de water. For sure he's goin' for be draw into de *culbute* an' get drown' dead, if I'll not be able for scoop him when he's go by my platform. I'll want for laugh, but I'll be too much scare.

"Well, M'sieu, I'll pick up my fader's scoop and I'll stand out on de edge of de platform. De water is run so fast, I'm mos' 'fraid de old man is boun' for pull me in when I'll scoop him. But I'll not mind for dat, I'll throw de scoop an' catch him; an' for sure, he's hold on good.

"So dere's de old rascal in de scoop, but when I'll get him safe, I hain't able for pull him in one bit. I'll only be able for hold on an' laugh, laugh—he's look *ver'* queer! All I can do is to hold him dere so he can't go down de *culbute*. I'll can't pull him up if I'll want to.

"De old man is scare *ver'* bad. But pretty quick he's got hold of de cross-bar of de hoop, an' he's got his ugly old head up good.

"'Pull me in,' he say, *ver'* angry.

"'I'll hain't be able,' I'll say.

"Jus' den Alphonsine she come 'long, an' she's laugh so she can't hardly hold on wis me to de hannle. I was laugh good some more. When de old villain see us have fun, he's yell: 'I'll learn you bose one lesson for this. Pull me ashore!'

"'Oh! you's learn us bose one lesson, M'sieu Savarin, eh?' Alphonsine she's say, 'Well, den, us bose will learn M'sieu Savarin one lesson first. Pull him up a little,' she's say to me.

"So we pull him up, an' den Alphonsine she's say to me: 'Let out de hannle, quick' — and he's under de water some more. When we stop de net, he's got hees head up pretty quick.

"'*Monjee!* I'll be drown' if you don't pull me out,' he's mos' *cry*.

"'*Ver'* well — if you's drown, your family be *ver'* glad,' Alphonsine she's say. 'Den they's got all your money for spend quick, quick.'

"M'sieu, dat scare him offle. He's begin for cry like one baby.

"'Save me out,' he's say. 'I'll give you anything I've got.'

"'How much?' Alphonsine she's say.

"He's tink, and he's say, 'Quarter dollar.'

"Alphonsine an' me is laugh, laugh.

"'Save me,' he's cry some more, 'I hain't fit for die dis mawny.'

"'You hain't fit for live no mawny,' Alphonsine she's say. 'One quarter dollar, eh? Where's my sturgeon?'

"'He's got away when I fall in,' he's say.

" 'How much you goin' give me for lose my big sturgeon?' she's ask.

" 'How much you'll want, Alphonsine?'

" 'Two dollare.'

" 'Dat's too much for one sturgeon,' he's say. For all he was not feel fit for die, he was more 'fraid for pay out his money.

" 'Let him down some more,' Alphonsine she's say.

" 'Oh, *misère, misère!* I'll pay de two dollare,' he's say when his head come up some more.

" 'Ver' well, den,' Alphonsine she's say; 'I'll be willin' for save you, *me*. But you hain't scooped by *me*. You's in Marie's net. I'll only come for help Marie. You's her sturgeon'; an' Alphonsine she's laugh an' laugh.

" 'I didn't lose no sturgeon for Marie,' he's say.

" 'No, eh?' I'll say mysef. 'But you's steal my fader's platform. You's take his fishin' place. You's got him fined two times. You's make my moder pay his bill wis *my* weddin' money. What you goin' pay for all dat? You tink I'll be goin' for mos' kill mysef pullin' you out for noting? When you ever do something for anybody for noting, eh, M'sieu Savarin?'

" 'How much you want?' he's say.

" 'Ten dollare for de platform, dat's all.'

" 'Never—dat's robery,' he's say, an' he's begin to cry like *ver'* li'll baby.

" 'Pull him hup, Marie, an' give him some more,' Alphonsine she's say.

"But de old rascal is so scare 'bout dat, dat he's say he's pay right off. So we's pull him up near to de platform, only we hain't big 'nuff fool for let him out of de net till he's take out his purse an' pay de twelve dollare.

"*Monjee,* M'sieu! If ever you see one angry old rascal! He not even stop for say: 'T'ank you for save me from be drown' dead in the *culbute!*' He's run for his house an' he's put on dry clo'es, an' he's go up to de magistrate first ting for learn me an' Alphonsine one big lesson.

"But de magistrate hain' ver' bad magistrate. He's only laugh an' he's say: —

" 'M'sieu Savarin, de whole river will be laugh at you for let two young girl take eet out of smart man like you like dat. Hain't you tink your life worth twelve dollare? Didn't dey save you from de *culbute*? *Monjee!* I'll tink de whole river not laugh so ver' bad if you pay dose young girl one hunder dollare for save you so kind.'

" 'One hunder dollare!' he's mos' cry. 'Hain't you goin' to learn dose girl one lesson for take advantage of me dat way?'

" 'Didn't you pay dose girl yoursef? Didn't you took out your purse yoursef? Yes, eh? Well, den, I'll goin' for learn you one lesson yoursef, M'sieu Savarin,' de magistrate is say. 'Dose two young girl is ver' wicked, eh? Yes, dat's so. But for why? Hain't dey just do to you what you been doin' ever since you was in beesness? Don' I know? You hain' never yet got advantage of nobody wisout you rob him all you can, an' dose wicked young girl only act just like you give dem a lesson all your life.'

"An' de best fun was de whole river *did* laugh at M'sieu Savarin. An' my fader and Frawce Seguin is laugh most of all, till he's catch hup wis bose of dem anoder time. You come for see me some more, an' I'll tol' you 'bout dat."

The Pantekalidescopenecropolis Coffee-Maker

"Jamix"

The following paper was found inside of a volume that formed a part of a tied-up parcel of books knocked down to me at a New York auction. It was written in a small crabbed hand, on fine foreign paper, and the writer had dotted every *i* and crossed every *t* with the most perfect regularity. The auctioneer could give me no satisfaction as to the author, beyond stating that "he guessed the lot had remained over from Pyncheon's or Morlack's pile." In answer to gentle enquiry, I found that Pyncheon was a clergyman of the Congregational body, lately deceased; and that Morlack was "a fool of an old bachelor that cut his throat". Following up the trail of Morlack by further enquiries, I was told that there was an account of his death in some issue of the *New York Times* of March, 1877. A visit to the office of that paper somewhat disappointed me, as there was nothing more on record than a short paragraph stating that a Coroner's inquest had been held on Mr. Morlack, that the verdict was temporary insanity, that the deceased was known to a few friends as a gentle, inoffensive man, chiefly remarkable for his hatred of all the improvements of modern life and for writing magazine articles that were religiously rejected by all editors. Beyond this, I never heard anything of Mr. Morlack; but the oftener I studied his paper, the more I saw marks of that insanity, which developing into a hankering after razors, ended in an incurable sore throat. I give the paper now to the public, feeling sure that that was the defunct Morlack's intention when he wrote it: —

MORLACK'S PAPER

Once upon a time, in a certain house in a suburban region, there was an old-fashioned silver coffee-pot, in which the household coffee had been made for years. Unfortunately, some fiend in human shape bewitched the head of the establishment, Mr. Fashionsetter, to buy a new coffee-pot called The Pantekalidescopenecropolis coffee-maker. This engine was a marvel of mechanical ingenuity, worked by weights, wheels, and cranks, and warranted to make coffee for forty people in three minutes. Well, it came home, and the old coffee-pot was consigned to an honourable tomb on the upper shelf of the pantry press, and forty friends were asked to a small coffee-party on the strength of the new investment. After receiving her guests Mrs. Fashionsetter slipped out of the room; in a few moments Fashionsetter himself followed her example, and then Fashionsetter, his wife, two servants, and the boy page got around the Grecian instrument (which was placed on the kitchen table), and put in the coffee. Off went the wheel with a whir-r-r-r, on went the whole apparatus for three minutes, making a noise like a well-to-do sawmill, a railway engine at a crossing, and a nursery in an infants' home, and at long last (for the three minutes seemed like an hour) the coffee was made, and in due time brought up to the guests. Well, it was horrible coffee. In the first place, it was cold. In the second, it was full of gritty matter, defiant of all chemical analysis; and in the third place, it was bitter as gall. "How do you like the coffee?" asked Mrs. Fashionsetter, "I am really anxious to know for it is the first time we have tried our Pantekalidescopenecropolis coffee-maker." With a face on which agony was written—internal agony, deep, vital, and searching, — the lady nearest to her replied, "it's perfectly beautiful." "Oh, dear Mrs. Fashionsetter," said another verging on sudden death, and evidently a member of the defunct Washington family, who could not lie, "dear Mrs. Fashionsetter, I never tasted anything like it." "Oh," said a gentleman throwing his eye heavenward—possibly in gratitude, probably in pain—"what coffee." That gentleman was preparing to run as a member of Parliament, and was practising oracular expressions full of daring dubiousness. Well, the upshot of that party was, that, in spite of sick headaches, sick stomachs, sick morals (for an amount of ejaculations the reverse of blessings that lay round that drawing-room floor was awful); in spite of all these things, that coffee-pot became fashionable, and every guest invested in one, and that suburban region was cursed with vile coffee for at least one season. It came to pass, however, that one night I happened to drop in on Fashionsetter without any notice, and found him drinking coffee made in the old coffee-pot. Lovely coffee—coffee with an aroma sweet as a Persian garden—coffee worthy of a Mohammedan's Paradise. "Why Fashionsetter," I asked, "what has become of your infer—endowed Pantekalides-copenecropolis coffee-maker?" "Oh," said Mrs. Fashionsetter, coming to the aid of her husband, who was a poor hand at telling a quick, common lie, "we only keep that for our friends, the fact is, it makes the coffee too strong for the dear children." Here Billy (a godchild of mine, and fully able to bring me to the bishop as far as necessary knowledge is concerned) became communicative, stating that his mother had called it " a nuis—," but was cut short in his eloquence by being ordered out of the room; Fashionsetter scowling, his wife's face blazing, Billy's knuckles excavating the corners of his eyes, and the boy page on a broad grin.

Now why should reasonable men and women enter into a voluntary slavery such as this? If Fashionsetter had asked me to spend that evening with him, on which Billy was disgraced for telling the truth, he would have gulped down bad coffee, and so would I, and probably both would have complimented Mrs. F. on the perfection to which she had attained as a coffee-maker. The coffee-pot trouble, however, is a very small part of the evil, for the real trouble lies in the fact that fashion will be followed anywhere, even when its sole object appears to be that of making laughing-stocks of us, turning us into ridicule, making us thoroughly miserable.

Take public singing for instance. A crowd of English, Irish, Scotch, and Canadian people get together to enjoy a musical entertainment; admission, reserved, one dollar; unreserved, seventy-five cents; humility seats one quarter. The majority come out to enjoy themselves to gratify their musical tastes, and please their musical ear. Not one in fifty of them are first-class musicians, but all have a keen taste and relish for melody.

If it became fashionable to slip in a small dose of castor oil between the first and second course of a private dinner-party, and a spoonful of senna and salts between the pie and the nuts and almonds, would the guests put up with it? Certainly. What is it? Not as bad surely as badly rendered and worse understood Italian songs, hauled into English programmes, made up for the benefit and comfort and enjoyments of ordinarily educated English-speaking people. Out comes an amateur, a lady never out of Canada in her life, a lady that believes that what she is singing is Italian, but beyond that knows nothing of the language, and off she starts in this unknown tongue, out into the unknown regions of musical geography. Now shaking on a high note as if she had the palsy, now balancing a note till her eyes get very large and her face very red, now up in the sky, now down in a coal pit, and finally ending with a mournful cry as if something had snapped inside, and that she had hurt herself — poor girl. I turn round to my friend Fashioncopy who is sitting beside me in the reserved seats, and say, "Fashioncopy, you are musical, you play the flute, you sing in a choir, what do you think of that?" "It is exquisite," he replies. "Fashioncopy," I say, "look me straight in the face and from the depths of your heart and intellect, tell me the honest truth, what do you think of that?" "I think it is horrible, Sir." "Then why did you applaud and cry *encore,* and injure the floor, and the small toe of my left foot with the ferule of your walking stick?" "Because," whispers Fashioncopy, "it's fasionable to do so. Miss So-and-so is all the rage just now in Italian music."

Now, unfortunately for fashion, I had heard real Italian artists sing that song, and real artists, English born, soul artists, and every note seemed laden with a message of beauty, and the effect of the whole was as if some fairy vessel, rich freighted with spicery and balm, had anchored in the harbour of my soul. Such SOUL (thus in MS.). Singers are as much beyond fashion as an angel, whose lips tremble beneath its message of Divine praise, is superior to a lifeless butterfly. You may set any words, Tartar, Mohawk, Cherokee, to Soul music, it makes no matter to what barbarian you wed the child of beauty, you cannot seal her lips, or snap the magic chord that binds heart and lip together, — the music thrills out its loving notes careless of earth and earthliness, soaring aloft to gain its destiny of universal admiration. Neither can you imitate Soul music; as well expect the galvanized corpse to blush your cheek with thoughts of love as it presses your trembling hand, or the painted canvass to give forth the sound of rippling water or roar of awful thunder.

And yet though I have no soul to throw into a foreign song, I may have a rich ripe soul that I can throw into some simple ballad or old-fashioned melody. It has been my fate more than once to sit on the platform during public concerts, and I have often felt amused in watching the faces of the audience — those tell-tale faces, those true indexes of spontaneous criticism. Out comes the singer, with the soulless song, and before the first verse is over, all sense of enjoyment has passed away from ninety per cent of the faces present. Out comes the same singer half an hour after, and the first notes of "Kathleen Mavourneen" or "Coming thro' the Rye" or "Home they brought her warrior dead" lights up the singer's face with such a glory of soul life, that the faces of ninety per cent are baptized with the reflection of its radiance. Ten per cent (these are the gods, great Jove and Juno) shrug their fair or manly shoulders, and talk of a low school of music—but high or low or broad it matters not, for real music, after all is said and done, is like real speaking, real preaching, real love, real any-thing; it should touch the heart, a touch that fashion hates, for it has no heart about it.

(The next paragraph seems to give the first plain evidence of that morbid feeling which finally blossomed into the actual mad-ness of the author. — EDITOR.)

A "High School of Music" with its harmonious discords and marvellous fugues may touch the high-strung souls of the highly educated, but why force them on the masses who are only fairly educated? Why should organists, who are supposed to play in aid of worship, destroy the plain simple music of divine service by the introduction of harmonious discords that are perfectly revolting to the uneducated ear? As a rule, three parts of the congregation put down such trophies of art to gross negligence, to want of taste, to actual bad playing, and hence the musical genius who presides at the organ is as much out of his element in an ordinary American church as a fish would be out of water. The day may come (we hardly know if we can say, God speed it) when the public taste shall be so educated that this strong meat will suit them, but it is not now so educated, and it is not fair to a magnificent organist, that he should gain the reputation of being a bad player, because he gives a crowded congregation, Sunday after Sunday, these classical performances. But the fashion says he must, and where is the Reformer who will dare to say her, Nay? Come ye organists, children of another world, musical prodigies, born before your time, authors of the jarring discord and murdered melody, come here—all of you, under my hands of benediction till I bless you. Go my children, go from this rough world of common melody, to some cool grot,—anywhere, so as you go. Emigrate where lofty winds will prize your every note. Try Boston, and if that fails, stand together my children, apart from vulgar mankind, and wait the openings of the glorious future.

(The next paragraph has madness in every word of it.—EDITOR.)

But singers and organists are nothing, the terrible evil worked by fashion yet has to be described. If I were going to cultivate some lots that I possess in the Moon, at the base of the Appennines, fourth concession of the County of Herschel, I would like previous to emigration to gather a tremendous audience round me, and assault, like a brave coward, the tyranny of fashion over the dress of women. I would not be very hard on men for the simple reason that taken at their best they are a poor awkward lot. I do not wonder at them trying anything that will make them better looking. But I would be hard on women. God has made them as a rule, pretty. It is not an uncommon thing to find them beautiful, and almost always graceful. Why women so formed and made should allow fashion to mar their prettiness, and injure their beauty, and destroy their gracefulness, it is to me amongst all the enigmas of womankind the strangest.

A witty writer (American of course) has fancied how puzzled one of the pilgrim passengers in the old *Mayflower* would be if he came back into the world and saw its changes. Amongst other questions the Puritan Warran is represented as asking the following: —

> Once more we stepped into the street
>   Said Warran — 'What is that,
> Which moves along, across the way,
>   Like a badly injured cat?
>
> 'I mean that thing upon two feet
>   With feathers on its head,
> With monstrous lump bedecking it,
>   Like an infant's feather bed.
>
> 'It was the gift of speech I hear,
>   But sure it can't be human?'
> 'My resurrected friend,' said I,
>   'That's what we call a WOMAN.'

Now nature never meant a woman to walk "like a badly injured cat". There is nothing so beautiful as the free, easy, ladylike carriage of a well-made woman "in whose step the goddess stands confessed". Nature never distorted the female form with a feather bed appendage, or intended that the graceful spinal curve should look like a fishing rod with a twenty-pound salmon tugging at the line; and surely nature never meant that that exquisitely shaped head, arched and dome-like, should be degraded into the position of a hay-cart, with a load of hay toppling to the fall. Not from nature came the order that woman should encase herself in coloured sacks so tightly drawn in warp and woof across the form as to destroy, once, forever and finally, the easy graceful carriage, the majestic and — yes, out with it — the modesty of the fair sex. Nay, nature intended woman to be, what she is, a fool, if she is not, the loveliest, the most graceful, the most perfectly moulded, of all the living things of God's creation.

O ye women — O deadly fashion! O —

Here the manuscript of Morlack came to a sudden end. I fancy that he never ended it, or can it be (awful thought!) that the terrible picture of womankind that his own morbid fancy had created so acted on his fevered imagination that he laid down his pen, and taking up the deadly razor gave it its final strapping. "Morlack?" replied the auctioneer, "he was a fool of an old bachelor that cut his throat."

The Chase of the Tide

Norman Duncan

The enviable achievement in his sight was a gunwale load snatched from a loppy sea; he had never heard of a pirate or a clown or a motorman. From the beginning, he was committed to the toil of the sea; for he was a Newfoundlander of the upper shore—the child of a grey, solemn waste-place: a land of artifical graveyards. The lean rocks to which the cottages of Ragged Harbour cling like barnacles lie, a thin, jagged strip, between a wilderness of scrawny shrubs and the sea's fretful expanse. Hence, inevitably, from generation to generation, the people of that barren match their strength against the might of tempestuous waters, fighting with their bare hands—great, knotty, sore, grimy hands; match, also, their spirit against the invisible terrors which the sea's space harbours, in sunshine and mist, by all the superstition of her children. He had been brought forth and nurtured into hardy childhood — into brown, lithe, quick strength — no more for love than for the labour of his hands. Obviously, then, he was committed to the toil of the sea.

This was disclosed to him—this and the sea's enmity—while he was yet in a pinafore of a hardtack sacking, months distant from his heritage of old homespun clothes.

"I 'low I cotches moare fish 'n Job Luff when I grows up," he boasted to Sammy Arnold, who had fished out of Ragged Harbour for sixty years and was then past his labour. "I 'low I salts un better, too."

Sammy chuckled.

"I 'low," the child pursued, steadily, "I cotches moare'n you done, Uncle Sammy."

"Hut, b'y!" the old man cried in a rage. "They be moare quintals t' my name on Manuel's books 'n they be—'n they be—folk in the — the warld!"

They were on Lookout Head, waiting for the fleet to beat in from a thickening night; from this vantage Uncle Sammy swept his staff over the land, north to south, to comprehend the whole world.

"Iss?" said Jo, doubtfully. It was past his understanding; so he crept to the edge of the cliff to watch the black waves roll ponderously out of the mist, and shatter and froth over the lower rocks.

"The say do be hungry for lives this even," Uncle Sammy sighed.

"For me?" the boy screamed. "Is un?" He shrank from the abyss, quivering.

"He do be hungry this day."

Jo strode forward, as in wrath; then boldly he faced the sea, bearding it, with clinched hands and dilated nostrils.

" 'Tis good for un," Uncle Sammy laughed.

"The say woan't cotch me!" the boy cried. "I woan't let un cotch me!"

"He've not cotched *me*," Sammy said, serenely. He peered seaward; and for him it was as though the mist were the dust of past years.

"I woan't let un cotch me!" the boy cried again. He stumbled, in blind fright, to Uncle Sammy, and took his hand. "I woan't!" he sobbed. "I woan't . . . I woan't!"

It was the Mystery! "Skipper Jo, b'y," the old man whispered, "you be one o' they poor folk that can't 'bide the say. Little Skipper," he said, crooking his arm about the lad's waist, "never care. Iss, sure — you be one o' they the say cotches — like your fawther — iss, sure."

Thereafter Jo knew the sea for his enemy. But the perception was not always present with him; it was, indeed, to his spirit, like the eternal sound of the breakers to his senses—overshadowing, obscured, lost. For, as of course, in the years of idleness — numbering, from the suckling months, five — he had all the wisdom of children to glean and winnow and store; and that, in but small part, concerns many things—the ways of lobsters and tom cod, the subtle craft of dories, the topography of the wilderness under the broad flakes, the abiding place of star-fish and prickly sea-eggs, the significance of squid-squalls, and the virulence of squids. In the years that browned his face and yellowed his hair and brought him boots of goatskin, a jew's harp, and a slicker, he had to learn of the activities of life much of a kind with this: In the morning—soon as the light spreads from the inland hills — men go out to fish, and, when they have fished many days, their wrists are swollen and festered, and the cracks in the palms of their hands are filled with hard, black blood; women never go out to fish, but, rather, stay ashore to milk goats, make boots, spin the sheep's wool, split wood, tend babies, spread the fish on the flakes, gather soil for the gardens, keep the stages clean, and cook potatoes and broose; children stand on tubs at the splitting table, to cut the throats of cod, and when, in the depths of night, they nod, through weariness, a man with a bushy white beard cries, "Hi, b'y! I'll heave a head at ye if ye fall asleep"—a cold, slimy, bloody cod head.

"They be a time comin'," was the burden of his thought in those days, "when I can't bide awake." So thinking, he would shudder.

Thence, to his tenth year, when all things were suddenly revealed, he wondered concerning many things; and chief among his perplexities was this: Where did the tide go? Where did the waters bide until they ran back through the tickle to cover again the slimy harbour bottom? It was a mocking mystery; ultimately, as shall be set down, it was like a lure to adventure cast by the sea. He wondered, also, what lay beyond the hills that rose, softly blue, far, far beyond the rocks where the bake-apples and juniper berries grew. The land was undiscovered; the wilderness between impenetrable. Who made God? God was uncreated, said the parson. That was incomprehensible. Did they use squid or caplin for bait in the storied harbour called New York? Heigh, oh! The stranger had gone. Where did the tide go? Day after day it slipped out and crept back; and as, returning, it gurgled over the bottom, it mocked him again; and, as it turned and stole away, it enticed him to follow—far as need be. Oh, well! How could flour grow on blades of grass, as the stranger had said? Again, the stranger had gone. Was a horse as big as two dogs put together—big as Bob and Bippo? Tom Jearce, who had seen a horse in Green Bay, was with Manuel's schooner on the

Labrador. Nobody else knew. But where did the tide go? Where did the waters bide? That was the nearest mystery. Truth, it was like a scream in the night.

"Hut, b'y!" said Uncle Sammy. "They be a hape o' curious things about the say. Sheer off from they. Iss, sure. The tide do goa in a hoale in the bottom."

Jo had abandoned that theory months ago; and so he puzzled, until, one day, when he and Ezekiel idled together, the punt slipped, at the turn of the tide, from under the laden flake, where the shadows are deep and cold, into the fading sunshine of the open harbour. Her shadow wriggled to the dull, green depths where the starfish and sea-eggs lay; and the wary dories darted, flashing, into the security of the black waters beyond. She tugged at her painter like a dog at the leash—swinging fretfully, reaching, slacking with a petulant ripple; it was as though she panted to join the waters in the race through the tickle to the wide, free open. Now, the sea was here restrained from treacherous violence by encircling rocks; so, with rocking and ripple and amorous glitter, Jo was lured from the absent observation of a lost kid —which, bleating, picked its way up the cliff to a ragged patch of snow—to a deeper contemplation of the mystery that lay beyond the placid harbour. The sea's ripple and glitter and slow, mighty swell; her misty distances, expanse, and hidden places; the gulls, winging, free and swift, in her blue heights; the fresh, strong wind blowing—these are an enticement to the thoughts of men. They soothe all fear of the sea's changeful moods, excite strange dreams, wake soaring, fantastic longings; and to those who look and hearken comes the impulse, and hot on the heels of the impulse the deep resolve, and after the deep resolve the perilous venture. It was so with the boy in the shute of the punt, lying with his head on a slicker and his eyes staring vacantly through the tickle rocks to the glistening distance.

"Now, b'y," Jo said, abruptly, "I knows!"

"Iss, b'y?" little Ezekiel answered from the bow.

"I 'low he heaps hisself up; an' 'twill be like climbin' a hill t' paddle t' the top."

"Iss, b'y?" Ezekiel was patiently sure of Jo's wisdom.

"The tide — he do."

"They be nar a hill t' the say," Ezekiel cried with scorn.

"You be oan'y a lad," Jo persisted. "I 'low he heaps hisself up."

"Where do he?"

"T'other side o' the Grapplin' Hook grounds, where he've no bottom."

"'Tis barbarous far." Ezekiel regretfully glanced at the little schooner he had made. He had just rigged the jib with pains; he wanted to try the craft out in the light wind.

"'Tis not so far as the sun's hoale."

"Huh! 'Tis not so handy as Tailor's Nose."

Jo stirred himself. "Be your caplin spread, all spread on the flake t' dry, b'y?"

"Iss,"

"Be un *all* spread, b'y?"

"Iss," plaintively.

"Us'll goa. Cast off!"

Ezekiel hesitated. "Be *your* caplin spread?" he demanded. Then, stern as a prophet, "God'll damn you t' everlastin' fire 'n you lie."

"You be cursin' God, Ezekiel Sevior!" Jo exclaimed. "God'll damn *you*. 'Tis marked down this minute — iss, sure." With impatience, "Us'll goa. Cast off!"

Ezekiel loosed the painter and sprang to the rowing seat; and Jo bent his strength to the scull-oar, and sent the punt clear of a jutting rock. Now, in these parts the tide has a clutch; the water gripped the boat and drew her out — swift and sly as a thief's hand. Soon the grip was fast; had the young strength—that now spent itself in guiding, to escape wreck on the Pancake — been turned to flat resistance, it would have wasted itself in vain. The waters hurried, leaping, eddying, hissing; they tightened their grip as they ran past Aunt Phoebe's flake, where Aunt Phoebe herself was piling her fish, against the threat of rain over night— past the skipper's stage and net-horse, where the cod-trap was spread to dry in the sun, with a new and unaccountable rent exposed—past Jake Sevior's whitewashed cottage, set on a great rock at Broad Cove, where the pigs and chickens were amicably rioting with the babies in the kitchen. And the tide as it ran may here be likened to the hand of a woman on a victim's arm: to her winks and empty chatter as she leads him from a broad thoroughfare to an alley that is dark, whence a darker stair leads to a place where thieves and murderers wait; for the north wind was heaping up a bank of fog behind Mad Mull, which stretched far out into the sea, and would soon spread it the length of the coast below. But to the children's sight the sea was fair; so they were swept on, singing:

> *The fire bust out in Bonavist' Bay.*
> Fol de rol, fol de rol!
> *Where was the fish and the flake nex' day?*
> Fol de riddle rol, de-e-e-e!

> *An' 'tis Nick, bully Nick, Mister Nicholas;*
> *An' 'tis Nick, Mister Nicholas, O!*
> *An' 'tis Nick, Mister Nick, Skipper Nicholas;*
> *An' 'tis Cap-tain Penny, heigh oh!*

> *Who made the fish for the fire to eat?*
> Fol de rol, fol de rol!
> *Whose was the room what the fire swep' neat?*
> Fol de riddle rol, de-e-e-e!

> *An' 'tis Nick, bully Nick, Mister Nicholas;*
> *An' 'tis Nick, Mister Nicholas, O!*
> *An' 'tis Nick, Mister Nick, Skipper Nicholas;*
> *An' 'tis Cap —*

"Lookit!" Ezekiel exclaimed, pointing to the shore. He was scared to a whisper.

"'Tis Bob," Jo said, "Hark!"

Bob, a frowsy old dog with the name of a fish-thief, was in the shadow of a flake, howling and madly pawing the shingle.

"'Tis the sign o' death!" Jo gripped the gunwale.

The dog howled for the third time; then he slunk off down the road with his clog between his legs.

"Josiah Butts — 'tis he, sure!" Ezekiel exclaimed.

"Noa; 'tis — "

"Iss; 'tis Josiah. He've handy t' five yards too much t' the spread o' his mains'l."

"'Tis Uncle Job Luff, b'y," Jo said, knowingly. "I heered un curse God last even."

Ezekiel started. "What did un say, b'y?" he insinuated.

"I heered un say—" Jo came to a full stop. "Huh!" he went on, cunningly. "Think o' all the cursin' you ever heered."

"Noa!" Ezekiel said, quickly. "Sure 'tis a sin t' think o' cursin'."

Jo grinned. Then, sadly, he said: " 'Tis Uncle Job—iss, sure. Poor Aunt 'Melia Ann!"

Ezekiel mused. "I 'low 'tis Uncle Job," he agreed at last. "He've a rotten paddle to his punt."

Jo spread the sail, stretched himself in the stern, with his feet on the gunwales and a lazy hand on the scull-oar, and took up the song again:

> An' 'tis Nick, bully Nick, Mister Nicholas;
>   An' 'tis Nick, Mister Nicholas, O!
> An' 'tis Nick, Mister Nick, Skipper Nicholas;
>   An' 'tis Cap-tain Penny, heigh oh!

The sun was dropping swiftly, puffing himself up in his precipitate descent to the ragged black clouds that were mounting the sky, taking on a deepening, glowing crimson, the colour of flame in dense smoke. The woolly clouds in the east were flushed pink, mottled like a salmon's belly — a borrowed glory that, anon, fled, leaving a melancholy tint behind. Soon the whole heaven, from the crest of the black hills, far in the unknown inland, to the black horizon in the mysterious expanse beyond the Grappling Hook fishing-grounds, was aglow: spashes of pink and grey and blue, thin streaks of pale green, heaps of smoky black and of gold, glowing, and of purple and violets and fiery red. The coast, high and rugged, with a low line of frothy white, and a crest of stunted spruce sloping to the edge of the precipice, was changed from dull green and duller grey to blood-red and purple and black; but this glorious mantle was soon lifted. In the white line there was one black space, the harbour mouth, whence the tickle led to the basin; and that

space was like a rat-hole. On either side, from the tip of Mad
Mull to the limit of vision in the south, the coast rocks were like a
wall, sheer, massive, scowling, with here and there, at the base,
great shattered masses, over which the sea frothed. The boat
was headed for the sun; it was slipping over a gentle lop in a
light wind. The weird, flaring sky—its darkening colours—the
expanse of dull, red water, upon which the little boat bobbed as
upon an ocean of thick cod blood—the isolation and impending
night: all awed the boys. Their singing gave way to heavy
silence, long continued, and silence to the talk of twilight hours.

"Rede me a riddle," said Ezekiel.

The demand startled Jo. The great descending night oppressed him; and he had been thinking of the tide, now a cold,
frowning mystery. He eased the sheet and scanned the sea
ahead. The sea was flat; there was no hill to be seen. He sighed,
and asked this riddle in a distracted way:

> "As I went up t' London Bridge,
>   I met me brother Jan;
>   I cut off his head an' sucked his blood,
>   An' let his body stan'."

"Jewberry," said Ezekiel with lack of interest, giving the local
answer, which all lads knew.

"Uh-hugh!" said Jo. Then, bethinking himself:

> "As I went up t' London Bridge,
>   I saw a mighty wonder;
>   Twenty pots a-bilin',
>   An' no fire under."

It was a new riddle in Ragged Harbour! "Who give it you, b'y?"
Ezekiel cried.

"Granny Sevior," said Jo. "Iss, sure; when I took her some
trouts. She do say she heered un when she were a maid. 'Tis a
brook bubblin'."

Ezekiel marvelled.

From the body of fog that lurked behind Mad Mull, there
dammed in its course from the north, a thick, grey mass over-
flowed and settled to the surface of the sea. A cloud, high lying,

attenuated, impenetrable, rounded the point and crept seaward with the deviated current of the wind, its outmost parts swerving to the south, advancing slowly, impacably. Along shore, hugging the surface, a second silent cloud, impenetrable also, and immense, swept over the face of the waters to the Rocks of Three Poor Sisters. The light scud, detached from the main body and driven before it, obscured the breakers, which, hitherto, had been in sharp contrast with rock and sea; the body that dragged itself after absorbed the distinguishing colour altogether, and thereafter nothing remained to mark the place. I may write: It was as though the sea's ally were relentlessly about its business—the one division stealthfully intent on interposing its opacity between the punt and the lurid sky, which was now glowing like the embers of a conflagration; the other swiftly proceeding to give ambush to the breakers, and to hide the entrance to the harbour. Or, if you will, the fog was in the form of a gigantic hand, shaped like a claw, being passed cautiously over a table, to close on a careless fly.

"They be nar a hill t' the say, b'y" Ezekiel said, impatiently. He glanced apprehensively shoreward.

It had come to Jo that the abode of the tide was hidden of design —an infinite, terrible mystery. In the consciousness of presumption he quaked; but he gripped the scull-oar tighter and held the boat on her course for the sun.

"They be nar a hill 'tween here an' the sun," Ezekiel plainted.

They were sailing over the Grappling Hook grounds; and, as far as sight carried, the greying sea was flat.

"Us'll goa hoame, now, Jo," Ezekiel pleaded. "'Twill be barbarous hard t' find the goaats in the dark."

"They do be a hill further out," said Jo. "Keep a lookout, b'y."

A rift in the clouds disclosed the sun as it sank—as it went out like a candle in a sudden draught. The arm of fog closed in on the boat; the shoreward cloud crept past the harbour and reached for Gull's Nest Point, a mile to the south, the last distinguishable landmark. The boys were silent for a long time. Ezekiel watched a whale at play to leeward; he wondered concerning his fate if it should mistake the punt for its young, as had happened to Uncle

Sammy Arnold long ago, when there were more whales, and they were much, much bigger, as Uncle Sammy had said. Jo was sunk in the bitterness of realising failure; he saw nothing but a surface of water that was flat — flat as the splitting table.

"'Tis past the turn o' the tide," said Jo at last, like a man giving up hope.

"Iss, sure!" said Ezekiel, blithely. "Us'll come about."

"Us'll come about," said Jo.

The theory had failed. Jo headed the boat for shore. He shaped the course by Gull's Nest Point, measuring the shore from its fading outline to the probable location of the harbour; then he noted the direction of the wind, feeling it with his ear, his cheek, and the tip of his nose: fixing it, thus, in his mind. When he looked to Gull's Nest Point again, the black mass had vanished.

"Job Luff do say," said Ezekiel, "that the tide bides in a hoale in the say."

"Noa!" said Jo, sharply.

"I 'low," Ezekiel said with some deference, "he've a hoale t' goa to."

"Noa, b'y!" Jo exclaimed, fretfully.

"I 'low he do," Ezekiel persisted with deepening politeness.

"Huh!" said Jo. "What 'ud come o' the fires o' hell?"

"Iss, sure, b'y," Ezekiel said in awe. "The tide 'ud put un out."

"Put un out," Jo echoed, sagely.

Ezekiel accounted for the heresy of Job Luff's theory thus: "Huh! Job Luff do be Seven Days Adventist. Hell be for un—iss, sure."

The fog thickened. Night came on, an untimely dusk. Fog and night, coalescing, reduced the circumference of things material to a yet narrowing circle of black water. The feel of the fog was like the touch of a cold, wet hand in the dark. The night was heavy; it was, to the confusion of sense, *falling*; it seemed to have been strangely vested with the properties of density and weight; it was, in truth, like a great pall descending, oppressing, stifling. Here is an awesome mystery; for the night was no substance; the mist, also, is impalpable! The fog, like the dark, is a hiding-place for shadowy terrors; it covers up familiar places—headlands and hills and coves and starry heavens — and secludes, in known vacancy, all the fantastic monsters that enter into and possess the imaginings of children in lonely times. Ezekiel, cowering in the bow, searched the mist for ghostly dangers—for one, a gigantic lobster, with claws long as a schooner's spars and eyes like the Shag Rock light. But Jo had no time for terror; he was fighting a fight that was already old, of which the history was written on the hand on the steering oar—a hand too small to span the butt, but misshapen, black at the knuckles, calloused in the palms, with the blood of cod congealed under the nails, and festering salt-water sores on the wrist. Time for visions of frothing lobsters? Joe had none. He was true son of that shore, and he had the oar and the sheet in his hands.

"Thick's bags," Jo remarked, alluding to the fog.

Ezekiel was silent.

Jo was steering by the wind; but the wind veered, scarce perceptibly, and the boy did not perceive the change at all. A crafty enemy! Thus was his childish inexperience turned against him. He had laid his course cunningly for the harbour before Gull's Nest Point had been wiped out; the course was now to the north by half a mile. With the deviation and drift he would meet the coast at the Rocks of the Three Poor Sisters, where his father had struck in a blizzard years ago. The boy planned to take the punt within sound of the surf, then to ship the sail and creep along shore to the harbour. That was the one way; but it was a perilous way, for the surf, being hidden, and sounding near at hand, has no location. Its noise rises and subsides through long distances; its strength is here, there, elsewhere, everywhere, nowhere; it is elusive, confusing as a great noise. The surf also has a clutch; a foot beyond its grasp and it is to be laughed at; an inch within its eager fingers and it is irresistible. The breakers of the Rocks of the Three Poor Sisters are like long arms — their reach is great; their strength and depth and leap are great. There was no peril in the choppy sea over which the boat was now pushing; the peril was in the breakers. Watchfulness could evade it; but with every boat's length of progress Jo was plunged in deeper wonder. He was evolving a new theory of the tide, which was a subtle distraction. Was the spell of this mystery to undo him? Thus Jo; as for Ezekiel, he was afraid of the monsters he had conjured up in the mist, so—as his people invariably do in dread and danger — he turned to his religion for consolation. He thought deeply of hell.

"Is you been good the day, b'y?" Ezekiel asked, dreamily.

"Noa," Jo answered, indifferently. "I 'low I hasn't spread me caplin quite — quite straight."

The wind was stirring itself in the north. The dusk was thick and clammy. The sound of the surf had risen to a deep, harsh growl.

"Be you 'feared o' hell?"

"Noa," said Jo. "Lads doan't goa t' hell."

Momentarily Ezekiel thought himself in the company of the damned. He looked in new fright at the water, through which, his experience had taught him, most men found their exit from life.

"'Tis a sin," he cried, "t' say it!"

"Sure, o' such be the kingdom o' heaven," said Jo, in continued serenity, maintaining his position with the word of the Book.

"Iss, sure!" Ezekiel was comforted.

The breakers seemed very near. Jo peered long into the tumultuous darkness ahead. Soon they could hear the hiss of broken waves. Jo freed the sheet and sprang for the mast. They furled the sail and stowed the mast. Jo took his place in the shute; he propelled the boat by the scull. Then Ezekiel's sight did not reach seven oar-lengths from the bow.

"Be you sure—"

"You be not goain' t' hell, Ezekiel Sevior!" Jo exclaimed, lifting his voice above the sound of the surf. "Doan't worry me."

The boat was advancing slowly, for the strength in the oar was slight. They were secure for the time, and they were not unused to the predicament; but at such other times the oar had been in larger hands, the lookout kept by more discerning eyes. They thought the harbour tickle was ahead, perchance some fathoms to the south or to the north. The wind had confused them utterly; the breakers were not the breakers of the Pillar and the Staff, but

of the Rocks of the Three Poor Sisters. But they were not per-
turbed, so they fell again into thought and long silence; and for Jo
thought was the old, disquieting wonder.

"Ezekiel!" Jo's voice was husky, solemn; it had the thrill of
triumph in it.

"Iss, b'y? Does you see the shoare?"

"*Ezekiel!*" Jo was exultant, like an investigator who beholds in
wonder the beautiful issue of his research.

"Iss?"

Jo swung from side to side on the oar with a vigour stimulated
by his exultation.

"I knows — iss, sure," said he.

"Where the tickle be? Does you?"

"Where the tide goas."

"Where do un goa?" Ezekiel asked, in mournful disappointment.

Jo pointed to the wash in the bottom of the boat as it slipped
from stem to stern with the risen lop. Now the waters covered the
boy's feet and gurgled and hissed under the stern-seat; now they
swirled to Ezekiel's boots, sweeping along a chip and a spare
thole-pin. Now the stern looked like the harbour basin at flood-
tide, then the water receded, disclosing rusty nail-heads, which
may be likened to the uncovered rocks, and a brown, slimy
accumulation, which may be likened to sea-weed and ooze.

"'Tis like the tide — 'tis like un," Jo whispered.

The eyes of both boys were intent on the bottom of the punt,
straining through the dusk. Jo still swung from side to side on the
oar, an animate machine.

"Aye, b'y, sure," said Ezekiel.

"I found un out meself," Jo went on, solemnly. "I c'n tell Job
Luff, now. He thought un were a hoale." Jo laughed softly. "'Tis
noa hoale. 'Tis noa hill. 'Tis like *that*."

Ezekiel watched the water ebb and flow. Jo watched the water
ebb and flow. Both were in the grip of the mystery—of the great
solution which had been yielded to them of all the world.

"When 'tis ebb in Ragged Harbour," said Jo, "'tis the flood in
— in — other pairts."

The discovery had fascinated their attention. Lookout and headway were forgotten.

"Where, b'y?" said Ezekiel.

"Pa'tridge P'int," Jo answered, readily. "What you sees from the Lookout in a fine time."

"It do be too handy; it — "

"Twillingate, then, I 'low," said Jo. "Where Manuel's trader comes from. 'Tis further'n any place."

Ezekiel turned to resume the lookout. Jo gloated in a long, low chuckle.

"Port! Keep un off!" The ring of terror was in the scream. "Port! Port!"

"Aye, b'y," firmly spoken.

Ezekiel rose in the bow and raised his hands as though to push the boat back from a dang.

"Port! Port!"

"Aye, b'y."

The Rock of the Third Poor Sister took black, towering form in the mist, before and overhead. The punt paused on the crest of a declivity of rushing water. The white depths were like an abyss; she was like a man clinging to the fringe of a precipice. It was a time for the strength of men; in that swift pause the strength of a child's arms was as no strength.

"The sea've cotched us!" Jo muttered. "The sea — he've cotched us!"

The wave ran its course, broke with slow might, fell with a crash and a long, thick hiss.

Ezekiel sank to the seat and covered his eyes with his hands, but Jo dropped the oar, and bearded the rock and the wave as he had done in the days when he wore a pinafore of hard-tack sacking, and he clinched his hands, and his nostrils quivered.

"The sea—he've cotched me," he said again; and it was like a quiet admission of defeat at the hands of a long-fought enemy.

The returning body of water slipped like oil under the boat; it fastened its grip at the turn, lifted the boat, lost it, caught it again, swept it with full force onward and downward.

"Mother!"

Ezekiel had forgotten his God. He cried for his mother, who was real and nearer. God had been to him like a frowning shape in the mist.

How shall we interpret? Where is the poet who shall now sing the Sea's song of triumph? Who shall ascribe glory to her for this deed? Thus, in truth, she bears herself in the dark corners of the earth. These children had followed the lure of her mystery, which is, to the people of bleak coasts, like the variable light in false eyes, like a fair finger beckoning. It was as though the Sea had smiled at their coming, and had said to the mist and the wind, "Gather them in." Neither strength nor understanding had been opposed to her treacherous might. They had been overwhelmed. Was there honour in this triumph? In the wreckage and little bodies that the waves flung against the rocks for a day and a night, lifting them, tossing them? In the choked lungs? In the bruised faces? In the broken spine? In the ripped cheek? In the torn scalp? In the glazed blue eyes? The triumph was cruel as vanity; or, if it were not of the pride of strength, such as is manifest in an infant spit on a lifted spear, but, rather, of greed, it was wanton as gluttony. If there be glory to the Sea, it was glory of hidden mercy; indeed, isolation and toil are things to escape. But if there be no glory, whose is the reproach? Thine, O Sea!

Do Seek their Meat from God

Charles G. D. Roberts

One side of the ravine was in darkness. The darkness was soft
and rich, suggesting thick foliage. Along the crest of the slope
tree-tops came into view — great pines and hemlocks of the
ancient unviolated forest—revealed against the orange disk of a
full moon just rising. The low rays slanting through the moveless
tops lit strangely the upper portion of the opposite steep, — the
western wall of the ravine, barren, unlike its fellow, bossed with
great rocky projections, and harsh with stunted junipers. Out of
the sluggish dark that lay along the ravine as in a trough, rose the
brawl of a swollen, obstructed stream.

Out of a shadowy hollow behind a long white rock, on the
lower edge of that part of the steep which lay in the moonlight,
came softly a great panther. In common daylight his coat would
have shown a warm fulvous hue, but in the elvish decolorizing
rays of that half-hidden moon he seemed to wear a sort of spectral
gray. He lifted his smooth round head to gaze on the increasing
flame, which presently he greeted with a shrill cry. That terrible
cry, at once plaintive and menacing, with an undertone like the
fierce protestations of a saw beneath the file, was a summons to
his mate, telling her that the hour had come when they should
seek their prey. From the lair behind the rock, where the cubs
were being suckled by their dam, came no immediate answer.
Only a pair of crows, that had their nest in a giant fir-tree across
the gulf, woke up and croaked harshly their indignation. These
three summers past they had built in the same spot, and had been
nightly awakened to vent the same rasping complaints.

The panther walked restlessly up and down, half a score of
paces each way, along the edge of the shadow, keeping his
wide-open green eyes upon the rising light. His short, muscular
tail twitched impatiently, but he made no sound. Soon the
breadth of confused brightness had spread itself further down
the steep, disclosing the foot of the white rock, and the bones and

antlers of a deer which had been dragged thither and devoured.

By this time the cubs had made their meal, and their dam was ready for such enterprise as must be accomplished ere her own hunger, now grown savage, could hope to be assuaged. She glided supply forth into the glimmer, raised her head, and screamed at the moon in a voice as terrible as her mate's. Again the crows stirred, croaking harshly; and the two beasts, noiselessly mounting the steep, stole into the shadows of the forest that clothed the high plateau.

The panthers were fierce with hunger. These two days past their hunting had been well nigh fruitless. What scant prey they had slain had for the most part been devoured by the female for had she not those small blind cubs at home to nourish, who soon must suffer at any lack of hers? The settlements of late had been making great inroads on the world of ancient forest, driving before them the deer and smaller game. Hence the sharp hunger of the panther parents, and hence it came that on this night they hunted together. They purposed to steal upon the settlements in their sleep, and take tribute of the enemies' flocks.

Through the dark of the thick woods, here and there pierced by the moonlight, they moved swiftly and silently. Now and again a dry twig would snap beneath the discreet and padded footfalls. Now and again, as they rustled some low tree, a pewee, or a nuthatch would give a startled chirp. For an hour the noiseless journeying continued, and ever and anon the two gray, sinuous shapes would come for a moment into the view of the now well-risen moon. Suddenly there fell upon their ears, far off and faint, but clearly defined against the vast stillness of the Northern forest, a sound which made those stealthy hunters pause and lift their heads. It was the voice of a child crying,—crying long and loud, hopelessly, as if there were no one by to comfort it. The panthers turned aside from their former course and glided toward the sound. They were not yet come to the outskirts of the settlement, but they knew of a solitary cabin lying in the thick of the woods a mile and more from the nearest neighbor. Thither they bent their way, fired with fierce hope. Soon would they break their bitter fast.

Up to the noon of the previous day the lonely cabin had been occupied. Then its owner, a shiftless fellow, who spent his days for the most part at the corner tavern three miles distant, had suddenly grown disgusted with a land wherein one must work to live, and had betaken himself with his seven-year-old boy to seek some more indolent clime. During the long lonely days when his father was away at the tavern the little boy had been wont to visit the house of the next neighbor, to play with a child of some five summers, who had no other playmate. The next neighbor was a prosperous pioneer, being master of a substantial frame house in the midst of a large and well-tilled clearing. At times, though rarely, because it was forbidden, the younger child would make his way by a rough wood road to visit his poor little disreputable playmate. At length it had appeared that the five-year-old was learning unsavory language from the elder boy, who rarely had an opportunity of hearing speech more desirable. To the bitter grief of both children, the companionship had at length been stopped by unalterable decree of the master of the frame house.

Hence it had come to pass that the little boy was unaware of his comrade's departure. Yielding at last to an eager longing for that comrade, he had stolen away late in the afternoon, traversed with endless misgivings the lonely stretch of wood road, and reached the cabin only to find it empty. The door, on its leathern hinges, swung idly open. The one room had been stripped of its few poor furnishings. After looking in the rickety shed, whence darted two wild and hawklike chickens, the child had seated himself on the hacked threshold, and sobbed passionately with a grief that he did not fully comprehend. Then seeing the shadows lengthen across the tiny clearing, he had grown afraid to start for home. As the dusk gathered, he had crept trembling into the cabin, whose door would not stay shut. When it grew quite dark, he crouched in the inmost corner of the room, desperate with fear and loneliness, and lifted up his voice piteously. From time to time his lamentations would be choked by sobs, or he would grow breathless, and in the terrifying silence would listen hard to hear if any one or anything were coming. Then again would the shrill childish wailings arise, startling the unexpectant night, and piercing the forest depths, even to the ears of those great beasts which had set forth to seek their meat from God.

The lonely cabin stood some distance, perhaps a quarter of a mile, back from the highway connecting the settlements. Along this main road a man was plodding wearily. All day he had been walking, and now as he neared home his steps began to quicken with anticipation of rest. Over his shoulder projected a double-barrelled fowling-piece, from which was slung a bundle of such necessities as he had purchased in town that morning. It was the prosperous settler, the master of the frame house. His mare being with foal, he had chosen to make the tedious journey on foot.

The settler passed the mouth of the wood road leading to the cabin. He had gone perhaps a furlong beyond, when his ears were startled by the sound of a child crying in the woods. He stopped, lowered his burden to the road, and stood straining ears and eyes in the direction of the sound. It was just at this time that the two panthers also stopped, and lifted their heads to listen. Their ears were keener than those of the man, and the sound had reached them at a greater distance.

Presently the settler realized whence the cries were coming. He called to mind the cabin; but he did not know the cabin's owner had departed. He cherished a hearty contempt for the drunken squatter; and on the drunken squatter's child he looked with small favor, especially as a playmate for his own boy. Nevertheless he hesitated before resuming his journey.

"Poor little devil!" he muttered, half in wrath. "I reckon his precious father's drunk down at 'the Corners', and him crying for loneliness!" Then he reshouldered his burden and strode on doggedly.

But louder, shriller, more hopeless and more appealing, arose the childish voice, and the settler paused again, irresolute, and with deepening indignation. In his fancy he saw the steaming supper his wife would have awaiting him. He loathed the thought of retracing his steps, and then stumbling a quarter of a mile through the stumps and bog of the wood road. He was foot-sore as well as hungry, and he cursed the vagabond squatter with serious emphasis; but in that wailing was a terror which would not let him go on. He thought of his own little one left in such a position, and straightway his heart melted. He turned, dropped his bundle behind some bushes, grasped his gun, and made speed back for the cabin.

"Who knows," he said to himself, "but that drunken idiot has left his youngster without a bite to eat in the whole miserable shanty? Or maybe he's locked out, and the poor little beggar's half scared to death. *Sounds* as if he was scared"; and at this thought the settler quickened his pace.

As the hungry panthers drew near the cabin, and the cries of the lonely child grew clearer, they hastened their steps, and their eyes opened to a wider circle, flaming with a greener fire. It would be thoughtless superstition to say the beasts were cruel. They were simply keen with hunger, and alive with the eager passion of the chase. They were not ferocious with any anticipation of battle, for they knew the voice was the voice of a child, and something in the voice told them the child was solitary. Theirs was no hideous or unnatural rage, as it is the custom to describe it. They were but seeking with the strength, the cunning, the deadly swiftness given them to that end, the food convenient for them. On their success in accomplishing that for which nature had so exquisitely designed them depended not only their own, but the lives of their blind and helpless young, now whimpering in the cave on the slope of the moon-lit ravine. They crept through a wet alder thicket, bounded lightly over the ragged brush fence, and paused to reconnoitre on the edge of the clearing, in the full glare of the moon. At the same moment the settler emerged from the darkness of the woodroad on the opposite side of the clearing. He saw the two great beasts, heads down and snouts thrust forward, gliding toward the open cabin door.

For a few moments the child had been silent. Now his voice rose again in pitiful appeal, a very ecstasy of loneliness and terror. There was a note in the cry that shook the settler's soul. He had a vision of his own boy, at home with his mother, safe-guarded from even the thought of peril. And here was this little one left to the wild beasts! "Thank God! Thank God I came!" murmured the settler, as he dropped on one knee to take a surer aim. There was a loud report (not like the sharp crack of a rifle), and the female panther, shot through the loins, fell in a heap, snarling furiously and striking with her fore-paws.

The male walked around her in fierce and anxious amazement. Presently, as the smoke lifted, he discerned the settler kneeling for a second shot. With a high screech of fury, the lithe brute sprang upon his enemy, taking a bullet full in his chest without seeming to know he was hit. Ere the man could slip in another cartridge the beast was upon him, bearing him to the ground and fixing keen fangs in his shoulder. Without a word, the man set his strong fingers desperately into the brute's throat, wrenched himself partly free, and was struggling to rise, when the panther's body collapsed upon him all at once, a dead weight which he easily flung aside. The bullet had done its work just in time.

Quivering from the swift and dreadful contest, bleeding profusely from his mangled shoulder, the settler stepped up to the cabin door and peered in. He heard sobs in the darkness.

"Don't be scared, sonny," he said, in a reassuring voice. "I'm going to take you home along with me. Poor little lad, *I'll* look after you if folks that ought to don't."

Out of the dark corner came a shout of delight, in a voice which made the settler's heart stand still. "*Daddy*, daddy," it said, "I *knew* you'd come. I was so frightened when it got dark!" And a little figure launched itself into the settler's arms, and clung to him trembling. The man sat down on the threshold and strained the child to his breast. He remembered how near he had been to disregarding the far-off cries, and great beads of sweat broke out upon his forehead.

Not many weeks afterwards the settler was following the fresh trail of a bear which had killed his sheep. The trail led him at last along the slope of a deep ravine, from whose bottom came the brawl of a swollen and obstructed stream. In the ravine he found a shallow cave, behind a great white rock. The cave was plainly a wild beast's lair, and he entered circumspectly. There were bones scattered about, and on some dry herbage in the deepest corner of the den, he found the dead bodies, now rapidly decaying, of two small panther cubs.

My Stowaway

Robert Barr

> Ye can play yer jokes on Nature,
>   An' play 'em slick;
> She'll grin a grin, but, land sakes, friend,
>   Look out fer the kick!

One night about eleven o'clock I stood at the stern of that fine Atlantic steamship, the *City of Venice*, which was plowing its way through the darkness toward America. I leaned on the rounded bulwark and enjoyed a smoke, as I gazed on the luminous trail the wheel was making in the quiet sea. Someone touched me on the shoulder, saying, "Beg pardon, sir"; and, on straightening up, I saw in the dim light a man whom at first I took to be one of the steerage passengers. I thought he wanted to get past me, for the room was rather restricted in the passage between the aft wheelhouse and the stern, and I moved aside. The man looked hurriedly to one side and then the other and, approaching, said in a whisper, "I'm starving, sir!"

"Why don't you go and get something to eat, then? Don't they give you plenty forward?"

"I suppose they do, sir; but I'm a stowaway. I got on at Liverpool. What little I took with me is gone, and for two days I've had nothing."

"Come with me. I'll take you to the steward, he'll fix you all right."

"Oh, no, no, no," he cried, trembling with excitement. "If you speak to any of the officers or crew I'm lost. I assure you, sir, I'm an honest man, I am indeed, sir. It's the old story—nothing but starvation at home, so my only chance seemed to be to get this way to America. If I'm caught I shall get dreadful usage and will be taken back and put in jail."

"Oh, you're mistaken. The officers are all courteous gentlemen."

"Yes, to you cabin passengers they are. But to a stowaway — that's a different matter. If you can't help me, sir, please don't inform on me."

"How can I help you but by speaking to the captain or purser?"

"Get me a morsel to eat."

"Where were you hid?"

"Right here, sir, in this place," and he put his hand on the square deck edifice beside us. This seemed to be a spare wheelhouse, used if anything went wrong with the one in front. It had a door on each side and there were windows all round it. At present it was piled full of cane folding steamer chairs and other odds and ends.

"I crawl in between the chairs and the wall and get under that piece of tarpaulin."

"Well, you're sure of being caught, for the first fine day all these chairs will be taken out and the deck steward can't miss you."

The man sighed as I said this and admitted the chances were much against him. Then, starting up, he cried, "Poverty is the great crime. If I had stolen someone else's money I would have been able to take cabin passage instead of —"

"If you weren't caught."

"Well, if I were caught, what then? I would be well fed and taken care of."

"Oh, they'd take *care* of you."

"The waste food in this great ship would feed a hundred hungry wretches like me. Does my presence keep the steamer back a moment of time? No. Well, who is harmed by my trying to better myself in a new world? No one. I am begging for a crust from the lavish plenty, all because I am struggling to be honest. It is only when I become a thief that I am out of danger of starvation — caught or free."

"There, there; now, don't speak so loud or you'll have some-one here. You hang round and I'll bring you some provender. What would you like to have? Poached eggs on toast, roast turkey, or —"

The wretch sank down at my feet as I said this, and, recognizing the cruelty of it, I hurried down into the saloon and hunted up a steward who had not yet turned in.

"Steward," I said, "can you get me a few sandwiches or anything to eat at this late hour?"

"Yessir, certainly, sir; beef or 'am, sir?"

"Both, and a cup of coffee, please."

"Well, sir, I'm afraid there's no coffee, sir; but I could make you a pot of tea in a moment, sir."

"All right, and bring them to my room, please?"

"Yessir."

In a very short time there was a faint steward rap at the stateroom door, and a most appetizing tray-load was respectfully placed at my service.

When the waiter had gone I hurried up the companion way with much the air of a man who is stealing fowls, and I found my stowaway just in the position I had left him.

"Now, pitch in," I said. "I'll stand guard forward here, and, if you hear me cough, strike for cover. I'll explain the tray matter if it's found."

He simply said, "Thank you, sir," and I went forward. When I came back the tray had been swept clean and the teapot emptied. My stowaway was making for his den when I said, "How about to-morrow?"

He answered, "This'll do me for a couple of days."

"Nonsense. I'll have a square meal for you here in the corner of this wheel house, so that you can get at it without trouble. I'll leave it about this time to-morrow night."

"You won't tell anyone, anyone at all, sir?"

"No. At least, I'll think over the matter, and if I see a way out I'll let you know."

"God bless you, sir."

I turned the incident over in my mind a good deal that night, and I almost made a resolution to take Cupples into my confidence. Roger Cupples, a lawyer of San Francisco, sat next me at table, and with the freedom of wild Westerners we were already well acquainted, although only a few days out. Then I thought of putting a supposititious case to the captain—he was a thorough gentleman—and if he spoke generously about the supposititious case I would spring the real one on him. The stowaway had impressed me by his language as being a man worth doing something for.

Next day I was glad to see that it was rainy. There would be no demand for ship chairs that day. I felt that real sunshiny weather would certainly unearth, or unchair, my stowaway. I met Cupples on deck, and we walked a few rounds together.

At last, Cupples, who had been telling me some stories of court trial in San Francisco, said, "Let's sit down and wrap up. This deck's too wet to walk on."

"All the seats are damp," I said.

"I'll get out my steamer chair. Steward," he cried to the deck steward, who was shoving a mop back and forth, "get me my chair. There's a tag on it, 'Berth 96'."

"No, no," I cried hastily; "let's go into the cabin. It's raining."

"Only a drizzle. Won't hurt you at sea, you know."

By this time the deck steward was hauling down chairs trying to find No. 96, which I felt sure would be near the bottom. I could not control my anxiety as the steward got nearer and nearer the tarpaulin. At last I cried:

"Steward, never mind that chair; take the first two that come handy."

Cupples looked astonished, and, as we sat down, I said:

"I have something to tell you, and I trust you will say nothing about it to anyone else. There's a man under those chairs."

The look that came into the lawyer's face showed that he thought me demented; but, when I told him the whole story, the judicial expression came on, and he said, shaking his head:

"That's bad business."

"I know it."

"Yes, but it's worse than you have any idea of. I presume that you don't know what section 4738 of the Revised Statutes says?"

"No; I don't."

"Well, it is to the effect that any person or persons who willfully or with malice aforethought or otherwise shall aid, abet, succor, or cherish, either directly or indirectly or by implication, any person who feloniously or secretly conceals himself on any vessel, barge, brig, schooner, bark, clipper, steamship, or other craft touching at or coming within the jurisdiction of these United States, the said person's purpose being the defrauding of the revenue of, or the escaping any or all of the just legal dues exacted by such vessel, barge, etc., the person so aiding or abetting shall in the eye of the law be considered as accomplice before, during, and after the illegal act, and shall in such case be subject to the penalties accruing thereunto, to wit—a fine of not more than five thousand dollars, or imprisonment of not more than two years—or both, at the option of the judge before whom the party so accused is convicted."

"Great Heavens! is that really so?"

"Well, it isn't word for word, but that is the purport. Of course, if I had my books here, I—why, you've doubtless heard of the case of the Pacific Steamship Company *versus* Cumberland. I was retained on behalf of the company. Now, all Cumberland did was to allow the man—he was sent up for two years—to carry his valise on board, but we proved the intent. Like a fool, he boasted of it, but the steamer brought back the man, and Cumberland got off with four thousand dollars and costs. Never got out of that scrape less than ten thousand dollars. Then again, the steamship *Peruvian versus* McNish; that is even more to the—"

"See here, Cupples. Come with me to-night and see the man. If you heard him talk you would see the inhumanity—"

"Tush. I'm not fool enough to mix up in such a matter; and look here, you'll have to work it pretty slick if you get yourself out. The man will be caught as sure as fate; then knowingly, or through fright, he'll incriminate you."

"What would you do if you were in my place?"

"My dear sir, don't put it that way. It's a reflection on both my judgment and my legal knowledge. I *couldn't* be in such a scrape. But, as a lawyer—minus the fee—I'll tell you what *you* should do. You should give the man up before witnesses—before *witnesses*. I'll be one of them myself. Get as many of the cabin passengers as you like out here, to-day, and let the officers search. If he charges you with what the law terms support, deny it, and call attention to the fact that you have given information. By the way, I would give written information and keep a copy."

"I gave the man my word not to inform on him, and so I can't do it to-day, but I'll tell him of it to-night."

"And have him commit suicide, or give himself up first and incriminate you? Nonsense. Just release yourself from your promise. That's all. He'll trust you."

"Yes, poor wretch, I'm afraid he will."

About ten o'clock that night I resolved to make another appeal to Roger Cupples to at least stand off and hear the man talk. Cupples' stateroom, No. 96, was in the forward part of the steamer, down a long passage and off a short side passage. Mine was aft the cabin. The door of 96 was partly open, and inside an astonishing sight met my gaze.

There stood my stowaway.

He was evidently admiring himself in the glass, and with a brush was touching up his face with dark paint there and there. When he put on a woe-begone look he was the stowaway; when he chuckled to himself he was Roger Cupples, Esq.

The moment the thing dawned on me I quietly withdrew and went up the forward companion way. Soon Cupples came cautiously up and, seeing the way clear, scudded along in the darkness and hid in the aft wheelhouse. I saw the whole thing now. It was a scheme to get me to make a fool of myself some fine day before the rest of the passengers and have a standing joke on me. I walked forward. The first officer was on duty.

"I have reason to believe," I said, "that there is a stowaway in the aft wheelhouse."

Quicker than it takes me to tell it a detachment of sailors were sent aft under the guidance of the third mate. I went through the saloon and smoking room, and said to the gentlemen who were playing cards and reading:

"There's a row upstairs of some kind."

We were all on deck before the crew had surrounded the wheelhouse. There was a rattle of folded steamer chairs, a pounce by the third mate, and out came the unfortunate Cupple, dragged by the collar.

"Hold on; let go. This is a mistake."

"You can't both hold on and let go," said Stalker, of Indiana.

"Come out o' this," cried the mate, jerking him forward.

With a wrench the stowaway tore himself free and made a dash for the companion way. A couple of sailors instantly tripped him up.

"Let go of me; I'm a cabin passenger," cried Cupples.

"Bless me!" I cried in astonishment. "This isn't you, Cupples? Why, I acted on your own advice and that of Revised Statutes, No. whatever-they-were."

"Well, act on my advice again," cried the infuriated Cupples, "and go to — the hold."

However, he was better in humor the next day, and stood treat all round. We found, subsequently, that Cupples was a New York actor, and at the entertainment given for the benefit of the sailor's orphans, a few nights after, he recited a piece in costume that just melted the ladies. It was voted a wonderfully touching performance, and he called it "The Stowaway".

Labrie's Wife

D. C. Scott

[Being an excerpt from the manuscript journal of Archibald Muir, Clerk of The Honourable The Hudson's Bay Company at Nipigon House in the year of our Lord, 1815.]

May Twenty-second, 1815

Today something happened which is bound to be of consequence in this outlandish place, and that I will set down here and make of record. Alec, who is getting more gumption now, although as unsteady in all his performances as he was ever, returned from his trip to the Flat Rock, and arrived safe with his two canoes and Ogemah-ga-bow, little Needic and his two sons. It appears that they had, by reason of the rough weather, to lay by at Dry Beaver Islands and had like to have starved if the wind had not gone down, for these fools of Indians will never learn not to devour half their rations in the first day out from the Post. They came in looking like wasps, their belts girt so tightly about their middles.

I could tell the moment I clapped eyes upon Alec that he had some bee in his bonnet, for he can no more control his countenance than an otter can help fishing. His face was all of a jump, and he spoke as if he had no spittle under his tongue. I have a plan to let the youngster speak when he is ready, and by this means I have the enjoyment of witnessing him cast about to get me to question him and assist him out with his story. When we were having a bit of dinner he fairly simmered, but he did not boil until I lit my pipe. Then he could stand my coolness no longer.

"We're to have an opposition!" he blurted out. I did not want to show any astonishment, but I nearly dropped my pipe, such a matter never having been thought of in Nipigon before. "You see," he went on, "I determined when I was at that part of the lake to go over to Keg Island and see if the cache was all right, and on St. Paul's Island, when we went ashore to roast some fish, we found two canoes loaded, and a Frenchman and three Indians.

"He asked me if I was with the English, and I lied to him straight enough, and said No! I was trading alone. Then he wanted to know where our Post was, and I said it was beyond the large island to the west. He said his name was Labrie, and that he was for the North West Company, and was sent in opposition to the English on the lake. So I decided to camp where I was, and not to go to Keg Island, but to come on here. I told him to keep due west, and not to land until he struck the big island, which was Cariboo Island, and not for any reason to camp on a little flat island half way there, which was full of snakes."

The youngster was mighty proud of himself at outwitting the Frenchman, but to take down his pride a bit, I provoked him by saying, "Well, poor Donald used to call you a clavering idiot, but if he had lived to this day he'd have had to invent a new kind of word for you. If your Labrie is anything of a trader he watched you away in the morning, and he will treat us in good Hudson's Bay Company rum when we first meet, having visited your little flat island full of snakes." Off went Alec trying to bite his beard, aping Donald's manner, poor lad; but he had yet a beard no longer than a pinfeather.

May Twenty-third, 1815

I was up before sun this day, as I had a restless night, thinking what I should do now we were to have opposition on the lake, a thing new to me who have scant experience. I determined to be smooth with them and observe them closely, and spoil them if I might with a fair face, and in all events to fight them with what weapons they may choose. I had wakened from a light doze with a sudden thought that I should possess myself of the point of land below the Post where I have always said the buildings should have been placed, which commands and oversees our present position. If it were seized by these pirates of Frenchmen, what then would become of our trade? They would eat it like a bear eats honey-comb. Alec could not see that, and provoked me with much grumbling that it was a useless work and a weary waste of muscle. It is curious how block-headed he is about all matters connected with trade; he has some acuteness belike but of what sort God alone knows. In the end I was mightily satisfied to see a stout staff with the ensign flying, and a small boat-landing, with one of the boats moored. We had the work done before midday, and for the rest of the time I had pleasure in looking down at the point which had an inhabited and secure look, under the Hudson's Bay Company's flag. If the Frenchmen have any idea of the shore about here there will be some *sacré*ing when they find the point taken up, for northwards there is no place for a foothold, and only in a cove, half a mile to the south, can they find level land enough for building upon. So when our Indians come down, and they should be here in a matter of four weeks, they are bound to reach the Post first, and I can keep my eye upon the rascals, who would, if they could, trade with the newcomers and forget old kindnesses and obligations.

May Twenty-fourth, 1815

Ogemah-ga-bow came up to say that one of Needic's boys had died last night, having over-eaten himself after his fast on the Dry Beaver Islands. Rain today.

May Twenty-sixth, 1815

Sundown yesterday on my bench before the door, whereby Needic had made a smudge to keep off the flies, which are now very bad, when I saw a canoe that was none of ours land at the point, and a man step out onto the new boat-landing. He looked all about him as if he was making an inventory of the place, and then he came slowly up the hill. He was a stout-shouldered, low-set fellow, with a black beard and small, bad eyes. Said I to myself as I saw him approach, "There is something mainly dishonest in your make-up, my man, and whatever one may have to do to keep trade from you it won't be very savoury in the doing if your methods are to be used."

"My name's Labrie," he said, running his hand through his hair.

I got upon my legs and said politely, "I heard of your being in the Lake from my man. Will you be seated?"

He said, "No" and looked over his shoulders at the Point.

"You have the Point under your flag," he remarked.

"Aye," I said, as dry as I could.

"The work has marks of newness."

"You are right, it was only finished yesterday."

The blood came into his face in an ugly way.

"Well, there can be no great objection to my trading a little."

"Not there," said I bluntly. "Under my company's flag what we take we claim and keep."

He breathed rather heavily, but held his tongue, and was going to walk away.

"Hold on," said I, "strangers are not treated so here, you must have a dram."

I called Alec, who brought the rum and the glasses. We drank healths courteously, then were ready to cut one another's throats.

"Did you ever taste better than that?" said I.

"I have as good," said he, "though it is the best, I can match it."

"Match it!" said I in a tone of surprise, winking at Alec, who flew as red as a bubble jock. We parted then but just as he was getting away he said over his shoulder, "Your man there has a damned queer idea of direction."

May Twenty-seventh, 1815

Sent Needic and his live boy and Ogemah-ga-bow's brother to Poplar Lodge, to have news of the hunters. The Osnaburgh packs from the north should now be two weeks out, unless the ice is later this year than last. Tomorrow I will put Alec and Ogemah-ga-bow to work clearing out the storehouse and setting things to rights. I am much exercised in mind over my responsibilities. It was bad enough last year, but now I have the whole management, and this opposition to contend with upon the back of it. I begin to be worn with it, what with loss of sleep at night, and thinking about nought else in the day. No sign of Labrie or any of his party.

May Thirtieth, 1815

This morning Labrie came up to borrow an adze, which I lent to him without any question. He seemed to want to be civil enough. When I asked him, however, if Madame Labrie had arrived, he seemed quite put about and mumbled something in his beard, which sounded nearly like "What affair is that of yours?" I paid no attention to him, not wishing to quarrel yet awhile, and without any further parley off he went with the adze, which I am fortunate if I ever see again.

Heat intense today, bring on a great storm of thunder and much rain. Had a great debate with Alec, when we were indoors, as to when the Osnaburgh packs will be in. I calculate in three weeks, as the water is like to be high, they will take the route through Mud Lakes to Negodina, as I wrote Godfrey. The old route to Wabinosh would take them much longer and, what with broken water and two desperate, long carries, there is a great risk of loss by that way. Alec thinks they will be down sooner. There is no doubt they have had a fine winter and if the pack can be safely landed it will be a great matter, and no doubt I shall hear good of it from the partners.

May Thirty-first, 1815

This morning when I was cleaning my pistols I heard a clear sound of laughter. Now laughter is an uncommon thing in this country, visiting us very infrequently. To be sure the Indians laugh, but that to me always has an unmeaning sound, and sometimes a bestial. Moreover, this laughter was different in kind, and one must have listened to it however absorbed he might have been. It was high-pitched and very clear and had something merry and withal innocent about it. It was contagious also and the mere sound of it made my very muscles twitch. There was no one visible, but after I had gazed awhile I saw Alec come up the steps from the warehouse. Not to appear interested before the lad I went back to my work. After a little he came in. I noticed his face was flushed and his manner excited. I paid no attention to him until he had knocked a dish off the table. It broke into three pieces. I was angry with him, good crockery not being by any means very plentiful in this country.

"Good God, man!" I cried. "If you're in such a state that you cannot avoid breaking the dishes, will you lie upon your bed for a while." He glared at me terribly, but had not a word to say. Then I kept quiet for as much as a quarter of an hour, and I could see it was fretting him; he fidgeted about greatly. Then he got up and went to the door.

"It seems to me you take mighty small interest in things."

I said never a word.

"Are you deaf this morning?"

I made no sound. He made no move for a minute, then he said, just as he was going out of the door, in an exasperated way, "That was Labrie's wife."

I could have laughed to myself, but when I had thought upon it for a time I began to perceive something bitter in his tone, and I reflected that of late I had treated him much as poor Donald used unthinkingly to treat me, and that he must be occupying my old position of complaint, and my heart was softened a bit, and I resolved to be more kind to him in the future, who is in much a good boy and canny in a sort about many things.

June First, 1815

I saw Labrie's wife for the first time this morning. An uncommon looking wench, with black hair and eyes and a mouthful of white teeth. I discussed her thoroughly with Alec, who sticks up for it that she is a handsome one. So she is, after her manner, though that I do not acknowledge to Alec. She looked me all over as if I were for sale, and when I coolly turned my back on her, that she might have a good look at that, she went off in a mighty huff.

Alex reports that there are two other women in Labrie's party, rather old and haggish. I have not clapped eyes upon them, not having visited the Cove. Although she went off in a huff, the young wench is a merry one, and it amuses her to hear Alec so aboundingly polite to her with his "Madame Labrie". "Madame Labrie" this and "Madame Labrie" that, whereupon she giggles or breaks out into wild laughter.

June Third, 1815

Needic back from Poplar Lodge, where everything is all right. Had an amusing conversation with the lad Alec anent Labrie's wife. The hussy comes about the house constantly, even when we are not here.

"Now what is she after?" said I.

"You have no understanding of women," he replied. "Of course she will come back when you treat her in that way."

"Now in what way?" said I. "Never do I look at her or pass the time of day with her."

"That is it," he retorts. "You are fairly insulting her, and she comes back."

"Do you try and be sweet to her and mayhap she would stay away."

"It is different with me," he says, biting his whiskers and shrugging up his shoulders, just as the wench does herself. He has taken on a sort of mincing, balancing, half-Frenchified accent, and shrugs his shoulders.

"Are you afraid she would fall into the love weez you, Alec?" I remarked, trying hard to imitate the accent.

"It is not me she will be in love with."

"No, who then? Needic?"

"Needic!" he cried, going off with a great French shrug.

June Fourth, 1815

No word from Godfrey about the packs. I am getting a trifle anxious. Alec says there are more guns than yardsticks in Labrie's quarters, and makes out they are on for a fight. Labrie's wife came up at noon and made us an omelette with gull's eggs and fresh onion-tops. She is a clever wench and sat looking at me as I devoured it. I talked a bit to her. After she left, Alec sat frowning.

"You were very free with her."

"I merely spoke to her, but then she made a good omelette."

"You said too much to her. You nearly told her we expected the packs at Negodina by the Mud Lake route this year instead of Wabinosh."

"Well, and if I did?"

"It is all she wanted to know."

"Well, you seem to be always ready to stand up for the spy, if she be one," said I, turning the French accent upon him. This made him wroth, as it always does.

"You never seem to understand that a woman's not like a man. The best of them you have to watch, and more particularly when one of them is in love with you."

"That does not apply here," I said, "unless you have her assurances yourself."

"I would not make love to a married woman," he said hotly.

"That's why you guard yourself so carefully, is it? You are mighty pious. It is a pity you are not like me. Now for me Mr. Labrie's wife has no attraction whatever, commandments or no commandments."

This set him off again.

"Be careful you, Archibald Muir, that is what I have to say to you."

We could hear the lady herself laughing down at the landing, and it sounded so innocent that I could not refrain from smiling at the boy.

June Fifth, 1815

We had a scene last night with Labrie's wife, for which Alec has to be thanked, and in which I think he had a small revenge for my baiting of him. I will set down the occurrence here although it be against myself, and our national instrument. She had been hardly before the house, and it was in the dusk of the evening, when she asked me to play upon the pipes.

"Will you play upon the bag-pipes, Mr. Muir?" she said in a very civil voice. "I have never heard the bag-pipes."

Now I am always at pains to oblige a lady, if it be possible, so I went in and got the pipes, hearing Alec urge me also, so I had two willing to be pleased.

Well, scarcely had I begun to get the skin filled with wind when Labrie's wife began to laugh. Now I am willing to admit that the foreword to a performance on the pipes may be dispiriting, but I charge that what follows after when the instrument is well controlled, and when the melody pours forth in full cry, would serve to obliterate a greatly more dispiriting prelude. But in this case I did not get beyond that stage, for Labrie's wife laughed with so little judgment that I was put about. I saw something in Alec's face which led me to think that the whole matter was preconceived by him, and with that I laid down my pipes on the bench beside me. Not another note would I play. I am not much versed in women's ways, and what Labrie's wife did puzzled me. But of that I shall give Alec's explanation. At first she kept on laughing, and then she stopped suddenly and came forward looking sober enough, but with the wrinkles of the laughter not yet gone out of her face. There she stood about four feet from me with a bit of her dress in her hand, as I have seen school girls stand abashed having been found at fault.

"You are angry because I laughed?" she said.

I did not answer.

Then she came close to me and made as if to put her hands upon my shoulders, and when I looked straight upon her eyes she dropped her hands, made a sound in her throat, and turned and went away.

Then young Alec began to strut about like a bantam cock.

"I have to thank you for that performance," I said.

"Why would you prevent a woman from laughing?" says he, in a rage. "Don't you know enough of women to let them laugh and let them talk?"

"I can lay no claim to such a knowledge as yourself," said I, in a mighty sneering voice. "In truth I know naught about them."

"You have proved that this night," retorted Alec.

"Expound that, you young oracle," said I.

"Expound? You have sent her away with a sore heart, and she was minded to be playful with you, and that cuts sore on a heart such as hers. Don't you see it, man?" he cried, sort of dashing his hands down.

"I see nothing of the sort. She was angry simply because I wouldn't speak back to her."

"You might have spoken to her or not spoken, and she would never have minded if you hadn't looked at her in the way you did."

I saw it was no use my trying to fathom the young donkey, so I would speak no more to him.

June Sixth, 1815

Labrie's wife was up last night but I would not go out to see her, being tired of the body and her endless chatter. Alec and she talked for an hour; the boy would be contented to go on vapouring forever, I believe. I pretended to be busy with my papers, and in the end she went away. She came to the window just before she went, and I heard her fingers on the sash, but I did not look up, and I heard her low gurgling laugh as she ran away from Alec, who would go down to the landing with her.

He is as polite to her and as formal as if he were living by a code of court etiquette. I twitted him with that.

"Well," he says, mighty stiff, and pulling a solemn face, "she is a woman, and she is another man's wife."

"The last is her great virtue," said I, with a tone of sarcasm, at which he looked scornful and exceeding pious.

June Seventh, 1815

Good news yesterday. Toma came in with a message from Godfrey. The Osnaburgh packs are safe at Cache point on the Mud Lake route. The water is high and they have not had a mishap. In three days they should reach Negodina at the end of the lake. It is, as I have always said, a route more clean and handy than the Wabinosh route, and it will be adopted now from this out.

Woke up with a mighty sore head this morning and had words with Alec. It is inconceivable how domineering that lad has become.

"You were drinking with Madame Labrie last night," he said.

"And my lord is jealous," I replied, sneering at him.

"Ye have made a fool of yourself. What did you tell her?"

"Nothing that I rightly remember. Since when were you ordained my catechist?"

"Now I have told you many times," he said in a parsoning way, "that you did not understand the nature of women, and that you would let slip something that Labrie wanted to know. Now you have done so, I believe, between a glass too much of whisky and a pretty woman."

"Do you call yon a pretty woman?" I said, mocking his accent.

"I pity you!" he said, with great contempt.

He went away swinging his shoulders, much more the master than the man.

To set down the truth, although it be against myself, Labrie's wife came up in the evening of yesterday. I was more decent with the bitch, having had good news, and I treated her to some whisky, and drank with her. Alec was off watching Toma, as he thought Labrie might try to get hold of him. I do not just remember when she went away. God forgive me, I do not rightly remember anything about it.

Hardly had Alec dismissed himself when he came back very greatly excited, but in anger this time.

"They have gone," said he.

"Who?" said I, not thinking for a moment.

"Who! My God! Who? Why Labrie."

"Well what of that?" I said. "It is a good riddance of a vile lot of thieves out of God's country."

"That is all you see to it?" he said.

"Well, what more?" I replied.

"I seem to see that last night you told Madame Labrie the packs were coming by the Mud Lake route to Negodina, and that they have gone to stop them. I have my doubt they will not barter with them. I seem to see that they will capture the furs and that by no very gentle means."

"You have said it before," I cried out, wroth with him and with myself. "So yon slut is what I have always supposed her to be."

A dark look came into his face. "Choose your words!" he cried, taking a step towards me.

"I'll neither pick nor choose my words," I said. "What do you call her then that would take our hospitality and then do us wrong?"

"Madaline would do no such thing," he cried, strutting about in a way that looked comical to me. I laughed at him.

"Madaline! Madaline! We shall see what Madaline will have done when we lose our furs. Why, man, you said out of your own mouth that she had done it."

"You lie," he cried, but it was here not impudence, so I paid no attention to him.

After some parley and conversation, I sent him with three canoes and all the able men, except Needic, to Negodina to see what had fallen out. He is to send me back a letter, as soon as he can, with the word. I am here now quite alone, and in mind very much put about. I have been striving to recall what passed between Labrie's wife and myself, but without any clear recollection. Ah, those women! I well remember my father used to say, "At the bottom of every trouble, there you will find a woman," and my mother used to retort, "And likewise at the bottom of every happiness." Whereupon he would kiss her.

June Tenth, 1815

Last night—waiting for word from Alec. This morning I went down to Labrie's camp with Needic. They had left two tents and some rubbish, and a little green box marked "M.L." Turning the lot over I found two empty kegs marked "H.B. Co.", once full of rum, which they had stolen from the cache on Keg Island. So we heaped all together and set fire to it. It burned merrily, and they are at least by that much poorer.

June Eleventh, 1815

I am in great spirits today. Last night I was awakened by Needic, who had his boy with him. Everything had reached Negodina safely, and there was no sign anywhere of Labrie's party. They will push on at once.

June Twelfth, 1815

This morning Labrie came back. Needic came up and told me, so about noon I took my pistols and went down with him to the cove. They had one tent up and the women were making the fire. The men went off and none of them would speak to us. I stood smiling in a taunting way, and just as I was about to leave, Labrie's wife came over to me. I perceived she had her arm wound in a cloth.

"Well, Madame Labrie, how did you hurt your arm?"

"Why do you call me Madame Labrie?"

"One must call you something. My boy, Alec, calls you Madaline."

Her face grew a darker red.

"You have been away for a while?"

"Yes," she said, "we were at Wabinosh, and I see you burned my box when I was gone."

"Were you ever in love?" she asked suddenly.

"Never," said I, "praise be to God."

"When you are I pray heaven you may be tortured in it."

"I am thankful of your good wishes."

"The other night you told me your packs were coming by Negodina. You understand? It was Labrie who shot me through the arm. He wanted to kill me for taking them to Wabinosh, but the others would not let him."

"The low rascal," I said, "to shoot a woman."

"And *you* have nothing to say about *me*?" She looked at me curiously, and put an odd emphasis on the *you* and the *me*.

"It is fortunate you made a mistake."

"A mistake!" she said. "Your boy Alec is twice the man that you are."

The hussy said that with a fluff of pride.

"Goodbye," said I from my canoe.

"Is that all, Archibald Muir, is that all?"

"Goodbye," said I, "and I hope your husband won't shoot at you again."

I looked back when we had gone a bit, and she still stood there.

She did not make any sign towards me, though I waved to her in courtesy. Then she covered up her face in her hands.

No word of Godfrey and Alec. I sent Needic to Labrie's wife with two gold guineas for the box I had burned, probably the only gold she ever clapped her eyes on, as it is unknown in this trade almost.

June Thirteenth, 1815

The packs came in yesterday evening. Godfrey and the men all well. I mixed a keg of spirits for them and they made a hideous night of it. Too busy to write much now, but can do nothing more tonight. Looking back in the store ledgers I can see no such winter's catch. Great good luck. Labrie's party still hanging around. Alec went down as soon as he got back, and stayed longer than he ought, so I berated him soundly. Tonight at supper he said:

"Labrie shot her through the arm because she had taken them to Wabinosh and had misled them."

I paid no attention to him. By and by he said:

"You will be glad to know that she says you told her nothing about the packs."

"Did she?" said I, puzzled, as she had told me the contrary.

"I don't believe her," he added.

"You're complimentary to the ladies," I remarked.

"Here is something she asked me to give you."

It was the money I had sent her for that box of hers I burnt.

June Fourteenth, 1815

Busy all day between the storehouse and the fur press. Half the Indians are drunk yet. Alec says Labrie and his party have gone. May the devil's luck go with them. I thought Alec looked a trifle white in the face, and as if he was impatient to make me talk, but I had no time to be spending with him.

A wonderfully warm day, and the flies very bad, enough to madden one. Have pressed all the packs and now everything is in order for a move. What a grand night for the partners it will be when they see our canoes full of the finest come to land at Fort William. It should be of profit to me, and I expect to come back here or go somewhere a factor, if I comprehend the rules properly. About an hour ago I had just finished writing the last words when Alec's shadow came over the window. He seemed to stand there over long, and I was just on the point of crying out to him when he moved off. In a moment he came in to me. I did not look up from my writing when he flung a scrap of paper down before me.

"There!" he said, in an odd voice. "I found it under the sash. It fell face down, so I saw printing on the back, I thought it was but a scrap torn off a fur bill."

"Read it," said he.

I turned it over and observed that there were some words in writing on the other side. I made them out to be: "Why do you call me Labrie's wife? She is my aunt. Do you think I would marry an ugly fellow like Labrie? They brought me up here to help their plans. We shall see. If you want to know my name it's Madaline Lesage. I learned to write from the Sister St. Theresa at Wikwemikong. Is it not pretty? M.L."

Then I recalled how she had come to the window, one night not very long ago, when, I opine, she had left the paper there.

"Well!" I said coolly, "and what is it now that you have to say about Madaline Lesage?"

His face had a tortured look upon it. He tried to speak. "She was — she was the bravest, the dearest" — he stopped there and hung down his head. "Oh, my God, you cannot understand. You can never understand!"

He moved away and stood by the door. I thought upon what he had said. No, I did not understand. Then I tried once more to go on with my page. But I was detained by the sound which is as uncommon as that of laughter in these outlandish parts. The sound of sobbing. Just for a moment it brought back to me the sound of my sister's voice as she sobbed for her lover when they brought him back dead and dripping out of the sea. I had a vision of it as if it were snapped upon my eye in a flash of lightning, she leaning her forehead upon her wrists against the wall. I looked up at Alec and there he was leaning at the door-post, his shoulders all moving with his sobs. I understood in a flash. I pray God to forgive me for the sin of blindness, and for always being so dead to others in my own affairs. I went towards him knowing that I could not give him any comfort. So he went out from the house and walked alone through the gloaming. I perceived that a change had come over him. I had always considered him a bit of a boy to be ordered about, but there was a man walking away from me, resolute in his steps, big in his bulk, and weighed down as if he was carrying a load, bearing it as if he was proud of it, with energy and trust in himself.

A, B, and C
The Human Element in Mathematics

Stephen Leacock

The student of arithmetic who has mastered the first four rules of his art, and successfully striven with money sums and fractions, finds himself confronted by an unbroken expanse of questions known as problems. These are short stories of adventure and industry with the end omitted, and though betraying a strong family resemblance, are not without a certain element of romance.

The characters in the plot of a problem are three people called A, B, and C. The form of the question is generally of this sort: —

"A, B, and C do a certain piece of work. A can do as much work in one hour as B in two, or C in four. Find how long they work at it."

Or thus: —

"A, B, and C are employed to dig a ditch. A can dig as much in one hour as B can dig in two, and B can dig twice as fast as C. Find how long, etc., etc."

Or after this wise: —

"A lays a wager that he can walk faster than B or C. A can walk half as fast again as B, and C is only an indifferent walker. Find how far, and so forth."

The occupations of A, B, and C are many and varied. In the older arithmetics they contented themselves with doing "a certain piece of work". This statement of the case, however, was found too sly and mysterious, or possibly lacking in romantic charm. It became the fashion to define the job more clearly and to set them at walking matches, ditch digging, regattas, and piling cord wood. At times, they became commercial and entered into partnership, having with their old mystery, a "certain" capital. Above all they *revel* in motion. When they tire of walking matches, A rides on horseback, or borrows a bicycle and competes with his weaker minded associates on foot. Now they race on locomotives; now they row; or again they become historical and engage stage coaches; or at times they are aquatic and swim. If their occupation is actual work they prefer to pump water into cisterns, two of which leak through holes in the bottom and one of which is water-tight. A, of course, has the good one; he also takes the bicycle, and the best locomotive, and the right of swimming with the current. Whatever they do they put money on it, being all three sports. A always wins.

In the early chapters of the arithmetic, their identity is concealed under the names, John, William, and Henry, and they wrangle over the division of marbles. In algebra they are often called X, Y, Z. But these are only their Christian names, and they are really the same people.

Now to one who has followed the history of these men through countless pages of problems, watched them in their leisure hours dallying with cord wood, and seen their panting sides heave in the full frenzy of filling a cistern with a leak in it, they become something more than mere symbols. They appear as creatures of flesh and blood, living men with their own passions, ambitions, and aspirations like the rest of us. Let us view them in turn. A is a full-blooded blustering fellow, of energetic temperament, hot headed and strong willed. It is he who proposes everything, challenges B to work, makes the bets, and bends the others to his will. He is a man of great physical strength and phenomenal endurance. He has been known to walk forty-eight hours at a stretch, and to pump ninety-six. His life is arduous and full of peril. A mistake in the working of a sum may keep him digging a fortnight without sleep. A repeating decimal in the answer might kill him.

B is a quiet easy going fellow, afraid of A and bullied by him, but very gentle and brotherly to little C, the weakling. He is quite in A's power, having lost all his money in bets.

Poor C is an undersized, frail man with a plaintive face. Constant walking, digging, and pumping has broken his health and ruined his nervous system. His joyless life has driven him to drink and smoke more than is good for him, and his hand often shakes as he digs ditches. He has not the strength to work as the others can, in fact, as Hamlin Smith has said, "A can do more work in one hour than C in four."

The first time that ever I saw these men was one evening after a regatta. They had all been rowing in it, and it had transpired that A could row as much in one hour as B in two, or C in four. B and C had come in dead fagged and C was coughing badly. "Never mind, old fellow," I heard B say, "I'll fix you up on the sofa and get you some hot tea." Just then A came blustering in and shouted, "I say, you fellows, Hamlin Smith has shown me three cisterns in his garden and he says we can pump them until to-morrow night. I bet I can beat you both. Come on. You can pump in your rowing things you know. Your cistern leaks a little I think, C." I heard B growl that it was a dirty shame and that C was used up now, but they went, and presently I could tell from the sound of the water that A was pumping four times as fast as C.

For years after that I used to see them constantly about town and always busy. I never heard of any of them eating or sleeping. Then owing to a long absence from home, I lost sight of them. On my return I was surprised to no longer find A, B, and C at their accustomed tasks; on enquiry I heard that work in this line was now done by N, M, and O, and that some people were employing for algebraical jobs four foreigners called Alpha, Beta, Gamma, and Delta.

Now it chanced one day that I stumbled upon old D, in the little garden in front of his cottage, hoeing in the sun. D is an aged labouring man who used occasionally to be called in to help A, B, and C. "Did I know 'em, Sir?" he answered, "why, I knowed 'em ever since they was little fellows in brackets. Master A, he were a fine lad, Sir, though I always said, give me master B for kind heartedness like. Many's the job as we've been on together, Sir, though I never did no racing nor ought of that, but just the plain labour, as you might say. I'm getting a bit too old and stiff for it now-a-days, Sir, — just scratch about in the garden here and grow a bit of a logarithm, or raise a common denominator or two. But Mr. Euclid he use me still for them propositions, he do."

From the garrulous old man I learned the melancholy end of my former acquaintances. Soon after I left town, he told me, C had been taken ill. It seems that A and B had been rowing on the river for a wager, and C had been running on the bank and then sat in a draft. Of course the bank had refused the draft and C was taken ill. A and B came home and found C lying helpless in bed. A shook him roughly and said, "Get up, C, we're going to pile wood." C looked so worn and pitiful that B said, "Look here, A, I won't stand this, he isn't fit to pile wood to-night." C smiled feebly and said, "Perhaps I might pile a little if I sat up in bed." Then B thoroughly alarmed said, "See here, A, I'm going to fetch a doctor; he's dying." A flared up and answered, "you've no money to fetch a doctor." "I'll reduce him to his lowest terms," B said firmly, "that'll fetch him." C's life might even then have been saved but they made a mistake about the medicine. It stood at the head of the bed on a bracket, and the nurse accidentally removed it from the bracket without changing the sign. After the fatal blunder C seems to have sunk rapidly. On the evening of the next day as the shadows deepened in the little room, it was clear to all that the end was near. I think that even A was affected at the last as he stood with bowed head, aimlessly offering to bet with the doctor on C's laboured breathing. "A," whispered C, "I think I'm going fast." "How fast do you think you'll go, old man," murmured A. "I don't know," said C," but I'm going at any rate."—The end came soon after that. C rallied for a moment and asked for a certain piece of work that he had left downstairs. A put it in his arms and he expired. As his soul sped heavenward A watched its flight with melancholy admiration. B burst into a passionate flood of tears and sobbed, "Put away his little cistern and the rowing clothes he used to wear, I feel as if I could hardly ever dig again." — The funeral was plain and unostentatious. It differed in nothing from the ordinary, except that out of deference to sporting men and mathematicians, A engaged two hearses. Both vehicles started at the same time, B driving the one which bore the sable parallelepiped containing the last remains of his ill-fated friend. A on the box of the empty hearse generously consented to a handicap of a hundred yards, but arrived first at the cemetery by driving four times as fast as B. (Find the distance to the cemetery.) As the sarcophagus was lowered, the grave was surrounded by the broken figures of the first book of Euclid. —It was noticed that after the death of C, A became a changed man. He lost interest in racing with B, and dug but languidly. He finally gave up his work and settled down to live on the interest of his bets. — B never recovered from the shock of C's death; his grief preyed upon his intellect and it became deranged. He grew moody and spoke only in monosyllables. His disease became rapidly aggravated, and he presently spoke only in words whose spelling was regular and which presented no difficulty to the beginner. Realizing his precarious condition he voluntarily submitted to be incarcerated in an asylum, where he abjured mathematics and devoted himself to writing the History of the Swiss Family Robinson in words of one syllable.

Biographical Notes

Robert Barr (1850–1912). Born in Glasgow, Scotland, he was brought to Canada by his parents at the age of five. He taught school in Canada and wrote for the Detroit *Free Press*. He moved to London, England, in 1881, where he edited the weekly edition of the *Free Press* and founded and edited, with Jerome K. Jerome, the humorous magazine *The Idler*. Many of his works were published under the pseudonym "Luke Sharp". Barr was a prolific writer whose works include *In a Steamer Chair*; *The Face and the Mask*; and *In the Midst of Alarms*.

Mrs. Harriet V. Cheney (née Foster) (1824– ?). Born in Brighton, Massachusetts, she was one of three sisters who regularly contributed to the *Literary Garland*. With her sister Mrs. Frederick Cushing, she edited a children's magazine, *The Snowdrop*, in Montreal. As well, she published several novels, among them *The Child of the Tide* and *The Rival Chiefs*.

Norman Duncan (1871–1916). Born in Brantford, Ontario, he worked as a newspaperman in the United States from 1895 to 1900. He was later a professor of English at various American universities. He published a collection of realistic stories, *The Way of the Sea* (1903), and several popular novels, among them *The Cruise of the Shining Night* (1907) and *Dr. Luke of the Labrador* (1904).

Thomas Chandler Haliburton (1796–1865). Born in Windsor, Nova Scotia, he studied law, served in The House of Assembly from 1826 to 1829, and was appointed judge. From 1829 to 1832 he contributed to a series of articles entitled "The Club", which appeared in Joseph Howe's newspaper, the *Nova Scotian*. *The Clockmaker; or, The Sayings and Doings of Sam Slick of Slicksville* appeared serially in the *Nova Scotian* in 1835. It appeared as a book in Halifax in 1836 and later went through a number of English and American editions. Two later series of the Clockmaker books appeared in 1838 and 1840. Haliburton was a prolific writer. His works include *The Old Judge* (1849), *The*

Letter Bag of the Great Western (1840), and *The Bubbles of Canada* (1839).

Stephen Leacock (1869–1944). Born in Hampshire, England, he came to the Lake Simcoe area of Ontario as a child. He taught at Upper Canada College and later was a lecturer in Economics and Political Science at McGill University. He wrote a number of books on politics and economics, but is remembered now for his collections of humorous anecdotes, among them *Literary Lapses* (1910), *Sunshine Sketches of a Little Town* (1912), and *Arcadian Adventures with the Idle Rich* (1914).

Mrs. Rosanna Eleanor Leprohon (née Mullins) (1832–79). Born in Montreal, she began contributing to the *Literary Garland* at the age of fourteen. She published a number of novels, many of which were translated into French. Her best known are *Ida Beresford* and *Antoinette de Mirecourt*. After her death, her poems were collected and published as *The Poetical Works of Mrs. Leprohon*.

Susanna Moodie (née Strickland) (1803–85). Born in Suffolk, England, she was a member of the literary Strickland family and sister to Catherine Parr Traill. She married J. W. D. Moodie, an army officer, and moved with him to Canada in 1832. She became a frequent contributor to the *Literary Garland* and its successors. Many of the sketches that make up *Roughing It in the Bush* (1882) first appeared in the *Literary Garland*. *Life in the Clearings Versus the Bush* (1853) is a similar work. As well, she wrote a number of novels, among them *Mark Hurdlestone* (1853), *The Moncktons* (1856), and *Flora Lyndsay* (1854).

Thomas McCulloch (1776–1843). Born in Renfrewshire, Scotland, he was ordained in the Presbyterian Church in 1799 and was sent to Prince Edward Island in 1803. He moved to Nova Scotia where he founded a theological seminary and later became president of Dalhousie University. *The Stepsure Letters* appeared serially in the *Acadian Recorder* during 1821/22 and was later published as a book in 1862. Another serial, *William* (1824), appeared as *Colonial Gleanings: William and Melville* (1826). He published a number of religious pamphlets as well.

John Richardson (1796–1852). Born in Queenston, Upper Canada, he served in the War of 1812 and was commissioned in the British army. He spent twenty years in England where he worked for various English newspapers. In 1840 he returned to Brockville where he founded a newspaper, the *New Era*. He wrote several poems, of which the best known is the long narrative poem *Tecumseh; or, The Warrior of the West*. As well, he wrote a number of pamphlets on military matters. He is chiefly remembered for his novels: *Wacousta; or, The Prophecy* (1832); *The Canadian Brothers; or, The Prophecy Fulfilled* (1840); *Westbrook, the Outlaw; or, The Avenging Wolf* (1851).

Charles G. D. Roberts (1860–1945). He was born near Fredericton, New Brunswick, and educated at the University of New Brunswick. He edited *The Week* (1883) and taught English literature at King's College (1885–95). Roberts travelled extensively during his life, and lived for several years in New York and in London. He was a prolific and highly regarded poet, novelist, story writer, and editor. His work had a strong effect on the major Canadian poets of his day: his cousin Bliss Carman, Archibald Lampman, and Duncan Campbell Scott. Among his collections of animal stories are *Earth's Engimas* (1896), *The Kindred of the Wild* (1902), and *The Watchers of the Trails* (1904).

Duncan Campbell Scott (1862–1947). Born and educated in Ottawa, Scott began his career in 1879 as a clerk in the Indian Affairs Department of the federal government and in 1923 was appointed Deputy Superintendent of Indian Affairs. He is known chiefly for his poetry. *The Magic House and Other Poems* (1893), *New World Lyrics and Ballads* (1905), and *The Green Cloister: Later Poems* (1935) are among his volumes of poetry. As well, he published two collections of short stories: *In the Village of Viger* (1896) and *The Witching of Elspie* (1923).

Edward William Thompson (1849–1924). Born in Toronto and educated in Ontario, he served with the Pennsylvania cavalry during the American Civil War and in the Queen's Own Rifles during the Fenian raids on Canada in 1866. He was editor of the Toronto *Globe* from 1879 to 1891 and literary editor of the

Boston *Youth's Companion* from 1891 to 1901. He then became Ottawa correspondent for the *Boston Transcript*. He was a close friend and critic of the poet Archibald Lampman. Thompson wrote chiefly short stories. Among his collections are *Old Man Savarin and Other Stories* (1895) and *Walter Gibbs, The Young Boss and Other Stories* (1896).